All Over a Bead

"This is ridiculous. I didn't take anything," I told Lynn.

"Oh, really? And what about the bead you're holding in your hand?"

I held both hands out, palms up. "What bead?"

"A thief and a magician. Do you cheat at poker, too?"

I decided that retreating would be the best way to respond.

"Now, if you'll excuse me . . ." I started for the door but Lynn stepped in front of me. She was about the most obnoxious person I'd ever met, but even so, I drew the line at pushing her out of my way.

"I'd like you to move," I said. "If you don't mind . . ."

"Oh, but I do mind. I mind a lot." Lynn wasn't just sneering now; she was genuinely furious. She stepped closer, and I could smell her musky perfume and her heavy breath. I could hear some women coming up the pathway below us and recognized Sande's laugh.

"I'm leaving now," I said, stepping around Lynn, "unless you'd like to keep me here by force?"

Lynn turned to face me, and the sneer was back. "By all means, go right ahead. I'll talk to Officer Peterson in the morning. Oh, and say hi to all the girls as you pass them on the path. They'll be my witnesses that you were here."

Praise for the mysteries of
Barbara Burnett Smith:

Bead on Trouble

Barbara Burnett Smith

BERKLEY PRIME CRIME, NEW YORK

THE BERKLEY PUBLISHING GROUP
Published by the Penguin Group
Penguin Group (USA) Inc.
375 Hudson Street, New York, New York 10014, USA
Penguin Group (Canada), 10 Alcorn Avenue, Toronto, Ontario M4V 3B2, Canada
(a division of Pearson Penguin Canada Inc.)
Penguin Books Ltd., 80 Strand, London WC2R 0RL, England
Penguin Group Ireland, 25 St. Stephen's Green, Dublin 2, Ireland (a division of Penguin Books Ltd.)
Penguin Group (Australia), 250 Camberwell Road, Camberwell, Victoria 3124, Australia
(a division of Pearson Australia Group Pty. Ltd.)
Penguin Books India Pvt. Ltd., 11 Community Centre, Panchsheel Park, New Delhi—110 017, India
Penguin Group (NZ), Cnr. Airborne and Rosedale Roads, Albany, Auckland 1310, New Zealand
(a division of Pearson New Zealand Ltd.)
Penguin Books (South Africa) (Pty.) Ltd., 24 Sturdee Avenue, Rosebank, Johannesburg 2196, South
Africa

Penguin Books Ltd., Registered Offices: 80 Strand, London WC2R 0RL, England

This is a work of fiction. Names, characters, places, and incidents either are the product of the author's imagination or are used fictitiously, and any resemblance to actual persons, living or dead, business establishments, events, or locales is entirely coincidental.

BEAD ON TROUBLE

A Berkley Prime Crime Book / published by arrangement with the author

PRINTING HISTORY
Berkley Prime Crime edition / January 2005

Copyright © 2005 by Barbara Burnett Smith.
Cover art by One by Two.
Interior text design by Stacy Irwin.

ISBN: 0-425-19999-1

BERKLEY PRIME CRIME®
Berkley Prime Crime Books are published by The Berkley Publishing Group,
a division of Penguin Group (USA) Inc.,
375 Hudson Street, New York, New York 10014.
BERKLEY PRIME CRIME is a registered trademark of Penguin Group (USA) Inc.
The Berkley Prime Crime design is a trademark belonging to Penguin Group (USA) Inc.

PRINTED IN THE UNITED STATES OF AMERICA

10 9 8 7 6 5 4 3 2 1

*This one is for Margaret who took me in as family,
and who supports everyone's dreams and aspirations.
With much love.*

Acknowledgments

It is most important to thank Caroline Young Petrequin, who is my final reader, and who always helps me bring the book together, even when I have questionable scenes! Her time, effort, and friendship have made me a better writer.

I would also like to thank the talented artisans of the Austin Bead Society. I can only stand back and marvel at the amazing things they do with beads, and how willing they are to share their knowledge. Mary Newton has been especially helpful, both with beading and reading!

I am also very appreciative of my agent, Nancy Love—when I needed a champion, she was there. Every writer deserves her kind of support.

Without my editor, Gail Fortune, this series would not exist. I'm thrilled that it does, and that she wanted me to bring it to life. Thank you.

Many people support me on a regular basis so I can write: Linda Bartholomew, Relda Ivey, Gregg Jacques, and Alyssa Reid. It's lucky for me that I have them.

And, of course, Gary is the one who always supports me, loves me, and thinks I'm an amazing writer. What woman could ask for a better husband?

To one and all, thank you.

You can visit me at www.BarbaraBurnettSmith.com

One

"Boom boom,
Ain't it great to be crazy?
Boom boom,
Ain't it great to be nuts like us,
Silly and foolish all day long.
Boom boom
Ain't it great to be crazy?"

Camp song
—origin unknown

i feel the need—" I held up my hand to do a high five with Beth. "The need to bead!"

Our hands missed as she bent to grab a blur of gray and white fur. "Sinatra!" The kitten streaked for the open front door behind me. "Catch him!" she said.

In a move that had to be left over from when my children were young, I caught him with one hand, while I swung Beth's front door closed with the other. Rather proud of myself, and grateful for stretch jeans, I straightened up. "I've got him," I said.

Beth was glaring in our direction. "That cat . . ." she said.

He was five months old and part Lilac Siamese and part

whatever wandered through the neighborhood and took his mama's fancy. Whatever his breed, he was pure trouble. "Mr. Sinatra, are you causing Beth grief again?"

"Yes, he is," she said.

To contradict her, he started nuzzling my neck, purring happily as if that had been the plan all along. I trained my blue eyes on his even lighter ones. "Don't you try to sweeten me up," I said.

"Are you sure you won't take him?" Beth asked. "He's just not right for us. He and Ron really don't get along."

"Alpha males," I muttered. Of course, they didn't get along; alpha males don't, even when one is a cat and the other is a supposedly mature man.

"Regardless, it's causing a problem. I'll pay you," she went on. "Sinatra even likes you best."

"I'm thinking about it," I said, looking at her for the first time. We had both gotten perms a few days earlier and now my hair, which once upon a time was just blonde without the silver "highlights," looped in big, soft curls. Suave, I called it, not to be confused with the shampoo name. Unfortunately, Beth's light brown hair was frizzy and sticking out wildly. That was just typical, and one of the reasons I worry about her—Beth can never seem to catch a break.

Today she appeared even more off-kilter than usual. It was nearly two in the afternoon, and she was still in her pajamas with her reading glasses askew on the end of her nose. "You said you'd be ready," I reminded her.

"I'm sorry, Kitzi. The way this day has gone, we're lucky I'm not running down the street naked, brandishing knives."

I love Beth dearly, but it wasn't a visual I chose to dwell on.

To my left I could see into her bedroom where her suitcase was open with a few things hanging out of it. Two bedrolls stood near the door, but her bead boxes were missing, a sure sign she wasn't finished packing.

"So, tell me what's wrong," I said, putting the kitten on

the floor. He immediately attacked a large-leaved plant. "Sic 'em, Tiger," I said.

"Don't encourage him, and nothing's wrong, just insane," Beth said. "I had planned to be ready, in fact, I was right on schedule, but there are mitigating circumstances." She moved toward her antique coffee table and picked up a piece of paper.

"It was you who insisted we get there early," I reminded her.

We were headed to Camp Green Clover, a kid's camp that had been our place for R & R since we were children. To be more exact, I was eight years old the first time I rolled over in my camp bunk to see Beth watching me; I'd been crying because I was homesick. The counselor had advised me to "stop it right now" and had marched out the door. Beth made a joke of that, commiserating in her own inimitable style, and after a few minutes she had me laughing.

I had thought Beth was the smartest, funniest, and bravest person in the world. That was almost fifty years ago, and those years have proved me right. Beyond that, Beth is the most loyal friend I've ever had. She knows things about me that I wish had never happened, and she's been gracious enough to pretend she's forgotten.

These days we attend Green Clover during the twice-yearly Craft Retreats, where rubber stampers and bead-a-holics can find fellowship without the distraction of twelve-step meetings.

I looked at my watch. We'd planned to arrive early enough to get bunks in our favorite cabin, the Lazy L. The camp was only about a twenty-minute drive south of town, so if Beth hurried we could still make it. "How long is it going to take you—"

"Read, before you say another word." She handed me the paper she'd picked up.

It was an e-mail from GRNCloverGAL, our friend Cordy Wright who now owned the camp.

I read. *Tivolini buyer is coming for the weekend. She's looking for new beaded jewelry designs. Bring something fantastic. Cordy.*

"Tivolini?" I said with reverence. "Really? Tivolini as in the Tivolini catalog?"

"Genuflect when you say that."

Not quite Horchow or Nieman Marcus, but close. "What an incredible opportunity."

Beads have been popular since caveman days. Back then they used seashells strung together for money, like a prehistoric Club Med. After that almost every culture in every location around the world used beads for jewelry and ornamentation. Tutankhamen's tomb held thousands of beads, and so did Mayan temples. Beaded jewelry is so in vogue right now that even Dr. Laura is making necklaces, and that woman surely has other ways to spend her time.

Beth has worked with beads for years, making everything from tiny amulet bags that are to die for, to jewelry, and once, even a beaded top for her daughter.

She doesn't make her own beads, instead she has the unerring eye of an artist for all things beautiful, and she puts beads together in such a way that her jewelry is outstanding. She sells her one-of-a-kind pieces to specialty shops and artsy boutiques, but she's always resisted submitting work to the likes of Tivolini. They would purchase her designs and have them mass-produced. I don't think she's held back because of any artistic principle, but more because she lacks self-confidence. Tivolini is considered the very top of the line. If Cellini were producing work today, it would be for Tivolini.

To me their catalog is a dream book, or do I mean drool book?

"I spent all day," she said, "creating some new pieces to show them."

"You did? Beth, this could mean the big time!" Finally, this could be Beth's turn to shine. "So you really want this contract?"

Beth removed her reading glasses to look at me squarely. "I want this more than I wanted sex with Clifford Balzo in twelfth grade."

"No kidding." I was delighted. "It's time for people to take notice of your work."

I meant all people, not just buyers. Since their wedding day, her husband, Ron, has acted as if he had married beneath his station. He treats Beth's design work like a little hobby that's harmless, but borders on useless. Even when Beth started getting contracts, he was more annoyed than pleased and refused to say she was an artisan or a bead designer. He called her "crafty." In return, I call him Mo-Ron, but only to myself.

"One thing is for sure," she said, "If I lose out, it won't be because I didn't try." There was a desperation to her expression that I'd rarely seen before. "I'm good, right?"

"You're way beyond good—you're unbelievable. Beth, you are the best designer I've ever seen—"

"Thank you. Don't get carried away."

"Okay. Then tell me about young Mr. Balzo," I said. Between summer camps Beth lived in Tulsa while I had lived in Texas, which meant we missed some significant events in each other's lives. Clifford Balzo was obviously one of them. "And did you?" I went on.

"Did I what?"

"Don't be coy."

"Clifford Balzo could have sex with any girl in school plus half the teachers, and I mean anytime, anyplace. Why would he bother with me?"

I studied her very casual expression. "Apparently he did. How was it? Where was it?"

"In the backseat of my father's Buick. It was awkward but interesting."

"I'd like to hear about it some time."

"I'm sure the details have slipped my mind," she lied.

"Maybe they'll come back to you at camp. After a few margaritas."

"I doubt it."

"So, what did you make?" Clifford Balzo might have been a fun interlude, but this was serious business. Bidness as we say in Texas. "Not that it matters, because everything you make is wonderful. Do you know the buyer?" I frowned. "It can't be anyone who's come to camp before, can it? I mean, we'd have heard long before this, wouldn't we?"

"All I know is what's in the e-mail. I tried to talk to Cordy, but she hasn't called me back. I do know that with Tivolini there's going to be some very stiff competition."

"TonyCraft will be in there," I said. Tony Campanelli does design work and puts out kits under the name Tony-Craft. He's a fortyish and good-looking male in an arena where most of the participants are slightly-past-middle-aged women, which makes him the darling of the clan. He's also talented, but his designs are more predictable than Beth's. Beth's flair is what puts her above the others. "He's no competition unless the Tivolini buyer is a woman who can be swayed by a good-looking man in tight jeans."

"The buyer could be a male," Beth said. "Who could still be swayed by a good-looking man in tight jeans."

"Don't dwell on it." I had moved on to the next competitor in the line. "We can count on May Feather to be flaunting her wares." That sounded tacky, and I didn't mean for it to. I like May, except now that she was suddenly in competition with Beth.

May was a semi–Native American who works primarily in turquoise and silver. Many of the silver beads she uses come from the craftsmen in her tribe, which is why her work is so expensive. She is also beautiful, as are her designs. "You think Cordy told May?"

"I would imagine."

"Even the Tivolini Company has to make a profit, and May's things are pretty, but they can't be duplicated."

"I come not to praise Caesar, but to bury him," Beth said. "I can only control my own work."

"You're right. Besides, your designs will win the buyer over."

She let out a long breath. "I wish I had your confidence."

"You should have." Before she could argue against herself, I had another idea. "You know, we could do some things to tip the scales in your favor—like a dinner party at my house."

"I don't know . . ."

"We could really make a splash. We'll invite the governor."

"Just the governor? Not the president?"

"The president isn't in town," I said. "And this is serious—it's how business is done today, with lots of schmoozing. I'll tell you what, we could create an event to go along with the dinner; something like a trunk show, but lots more elegant." The more I thought about it, the better I liked it. "I think the governor would do the trick. People are very impressed by him." He's a cutie who can hold up his end of a conversation. And a soup spoon, for that matter.

The governor and I aren't close, but we're "family friends." I am a Camden, daughter and granddaughter of governors and the niece of a U.S. senator. I was also a Texas senator for four years before I quit for two very good reasons: first, any jackass can get elected, and I realized that way too many of them had been. Second, I don't take well to compromise.

Most of the time being a Camden is the same as being a Smith or a Jones, but there are perks. Knowing people in high places is one of them, and when I can use those connections, I do. I particularly like using them for the good of the deserving, and Beth was deserving.

Beth said, "That's an awful lot of trouble, and I don't want that kind of fuss."

"You're worth it."

"And, I'd rather not."

"Okay, we'll make it smaller. How about just a luncheon with the governor's wife? It can still be special." Ideas started popping. "Here's my plan, we'll get a limo to pick up the buyer—everyone loves some pampering. Oh! And as a parting gift we'll give everyone a bracelet. One of your pieces, of course. Or, earrings, since those would be cheaper. I can help you make them, if you come up with the design."

"Kitzi, you're doing it again."

"I am not; I'm just talking about a luncheon."

"Yes, you are."

I looked at the expression on her face and felt myself shift from drive to neutral in one deflating instant. I'd been leaping ahead with my plans, disregarding Beth's reluctance. "Damn. I'm sorry; I *am* doing it, aren't I?"

"It's okay," she said. "It's what I expect from you. And admire."

I'm told I take after my grandfather, the wildcatter robber baron, who served sixteen years as governor of Texas. In some ways he was larger than life, building a magnificent mansion to reflect his personal exuberance. He also made sweeping changes in government policies, as well as shifting the type of people who served the state. He was big on equality and giving everyone a chance. When it came to wielding power, the man had all the moves down pat, but he was also the biggest teddy bear in the state and had a hard time saying no to anyone in real need. Those traits garnered him as many detractors as supporters.

I adored my grandfather and grew up believing that there wasn't a problem in the world my granddaddy couldn't fix. As I've learned the hard way, that's a terrific trait for a grandfather, but it can be overdone in a friend.

I sighed. "I'm fixing you," I said.

Beth patted my arm. "Not me, just the situation. Even though I love it when you pull rank, let's not, okay? 'Just stop it now.' "

I smiled at the old phrase from camp. "Okay, I won't send out the invitations, yet. Although it is a very good idea—"

"You're right, but I'd prefer to see if they like what I made. Do you want a preview?" she asked.

"Absolutely."

She breathed heavily. "Okay, come on."

She led me through her carefully decorated living room and on toward her dining room with its big double doors. They were closed, as always. In a house that was ruled by her husband and her seventeen-year-old daughter, Shannan, the dining room was the one place where Beth could spread her wings, and beads, and create havoc.

Beth designs like an impressionist paints—fast, messy, and beautifully, sometimes working on several designs at once, stringing one while moving around selecting beads for the next. I would love to have her kind of talent, but I don't. I'm a novice, with very little patience for the intricate work. I can and do, however, copy from the very best, which is why they put instructions in beading magazines.

She opened the doors; the sunlight sparkled off the dining room table and its contents. In the center were four design boards, gray fuzzy boards with numerous channels and pockets for beads. Every one was filled. I could see the start of several pieces, one in turquoise strung with black beads carved like cinnabar. Another had freshwater pearls and deep indigo crystal cubes.

Every spare inch of tabletop held boxes and bowls, all with beads or findings, the metal pieces that hold a necklace or bracelet together. There were crystals in at least a dozen colors all shining like diamonds. There were lampwork beads, Bali silver, fire-polished bi-cones, as well as nuggets of rose quartz, citrine, a pale aquamarine, and dozens more. Strands of freshwater pearls spilled out of a plastic case, and clear tubes of tiny Delicas in a dozen colors filled another.

I tried not to gasp, but the room always took me like this—all the sparkling treasures of Aladdin's cave heaped in one place.

I was still entranced when I heard a sound behind me. I

turned and there was Sinatra; he is not allowed in the dining room for good reason and some inner sense had alerted him to the opportunity. He was racing through the doors.

He leaped upward. "No!" I said, grabbing for him.

I missed.

He sailed above the littered landing field, all four legs stretched out straight. He hit with a *whoomp*. Then he slid.

As if in slow motion a good fourth of the boxes, beads, and bowls skimmed to the end of the table, and showered over the edge like a waterfall.

Then, silently, the beads all but disappeared in the thick shag carpet.

Two

i stared at Beth. She looked at the floor, then at Sinatra, who was sitting proudly in the middle of the table, purring loudly.

I couldn't even talk. It was Beth, her face pale, who finally broke the silence.

"You know my black coat?" she asked. "I think it's going to have a fur collar this winter." She reached for Sinatra, but I grabbed him first.

"I'll take him," I said, holding the kitten. "Right after camp, I'll take him home with me." The Camden Manse has survived lots of pets, from firebellied frogs to dogs and ferrets, so surely it could handle one small cat.

Sinatra snuggled against me as if he knew he'd just been adopted, and that his new "parent" was going to be a cinch to train.

I held him away from my body. "Don't you start with me." More gently than he deserved, I placed him in the other room and closed the doors quickly. When I turned back around and took in the chaos again, the enormity of what had happened sunk in. "Oh, my God."

"Prayer helps, but I think this mess needs human intervention."

"I'll help." I lowered myself to the floor, remembering why I rarely wear jeans anymore. But I made it and began raking my fingers through the carpet. I came up with a handful of beads and bits of fuzz. They went into a bowl, and then I plunged my hands into the carpet for more. As I separated the long strands of rug I saw that below the first layer of visible beads were many more—tiny seed beads and minute crimp beads in silver and gold. Again I looked at Beth; I'm rarely out of words, but this had done it.

"We'll get a vacuum cleaner," she said. "It takes awhile, but it works."

I assumed she knew what she was talking about but the task seemed monumental. There had to be several thousand dollars worth of beads buried in the carpet. And what about the new designs? Were they complete, or had they still been on the boards, waiting the final stringing and tying off?

"Your pieces for the Tivolini buyer? . . . They aren't? . . ." I gestured around us. It was unthinkable, and I couldn't bring myself to say it.

"No, I was finished with those."

The tightness in my chest eased. It wasn't an irreparable disaster.

As I pawed the carpet for more beads, I heard Beth's daughter, Shannan, come in the back door. Beth has two children, Brian, who is in college and Shannan, age seventeen, who is my goddaughter.

Shannan was little and cuddly when my two kids were busy gaining independence and making the simple title *mom* a four letter word. When she was three I took her to see the musical *Annie* and from then on, she was my partner for the theatre. She loved plays, and she could belt out "Tomorrow" with the best of them. By second grade she quoted Shakespeare like other kids said their ABCs.

She called me her "other mother." That was also the role Beth played for my children, nurturing them when I was too busy, listening when I was too emotionally involved to be silent. I've always said that loving each other's kids is the best thing friends can do for each other; Beth and I have done that. It has given the term *extended family* a new twist. It has also added new dimensions to the lives of our children.

Beth grew up in what she described as a normal suburban home, but she is imaginative and artistic, both traits she's shared with my children. Meanwhile, I took Shannan and Brian to some of the events I'm expected to attend. Shannan has conversed with George and Laura Bush, and sat in on a legislative hearing when she needed information for a school paper.

She calls me Tante Kitzi. The *tante* is an honorary title, and Kitzi is what almost everyone calls me. It comes from the days when I was little. My cousin claims he couldn't say Missy Katherine, which was my grandfather's pet name for me. My mother says she made up the name. Katherine Zoe Camden. Kit Z. I believe my mom.

"There is a vehicle blocking the driveway," Shannan announced as she swept into the room and surveyed us. "I couldn't get into my place."

At the pronouncement, Beth's expression of annoyance mirrored my own. It wasn't Shannan's independence—we knew that was coming. But in the last few months the distance between us had become charged with something akin to hostility. I know teenagers go through this phase, and I'm sure my own did, although I can no longer remember specifics—which just shows that a failing memory can be a good thing.

Still, Shannan's general level of annoyed anxiety tends toward the extreme. At first I'd thought it was her boyfriend, but a month ago she dumped him saying that his "humor was lame, and his taste in movies puerile."

There was something wrong in Shannan's life, and all my best efforts at talking and listening had produced no results in finding out what it was.

Shannan's gaze took in the table, then came back to me; I was still down on all fours. "I parked on the street so you can get out," she said.

"You had to park on the street?" I asked, straightening my back. "Now there's a hardship."

She looked puzzled, not sure if I was teasing.

"Actually," I went on. "That isn't a bit important. We are running late, you included, and Sinatra just cleaned the table. There are beads all over the floor." Some were hidden and the carpet glittered between the design boards and bowls.

Shannan looked at the rug. "That's Sinatra, for you." She turned to go, and for the second time that day I was out of words.

Luckily Beth wasn't. "Not so fast," Beth said. "I need your help. Put a new bag in the vacuum cleaner and then start—"

"Mo-ther," Shannan said. "I have other things to do. I promised Christie that I would meet her at the mall. She needs help picking an outfit for the French Banquet. I need something new, too. And that's before I drive to that camp."

That camp. Not even the name, although she knew it perfectly well. Shannan had begged to go with us when she was little, but children aren't allowed during the Craft Retreats. At seventeen she is old enough and had condescended to attend. I was still wondering why. For Beth, it was plain to see she was trying to reconnect with her daughter.

Beth said, "I'll make a deal with you, Shannan. You vacuum, and I'll pay for the dress."

"You're kidding, right?"

"No."

"Daddy says that as long as I live at home, I never have to buy my own clothes."

Beth carefully knelt down on the floor and began picking up bowls and bead boards. "You aren't paying—I am. You are merely earning the pay. Now get the vacuum cleaner and don't forget to put in a fresh bag. Otherwise, you'll be picking beads out of the dust until well past the time when you should have gone to the banquet. Then you won't need a new outfit."

"But, you always say that a commitment—"

"Except that you shouldn't have made the commitment because you already had plans to go to camp. I know your life is busy, and I'm sorry about that, but the banquet is two weeks away; you can shop next weekend and ride to camp with me." Beth sat a little straighter. "I assume you want new jewelry to go with the outfit?"

Shannan thought about it during what seemed to me like an ominously long time. "Look," she finally said. "This just isn't going to work. I'm not going to camp—"

"No!" Beth's response was primal; I'd heard it from other friends when they'd been told things like, "I'm going to live with Dad." Or "You can't see your grandchildren." That *no* fought off a threat to motherhood and anyone in their right mind heeded it.

"It's not a choice, Mother," Shannan was saying. "I have too much—"

"No," Beth said again, now struggling to her feet. "I've already paid for the weekend and arranged for you to take off school tomorrow."

"But I don't want to go—"

"You cannot stay at home alone."

"I'm not. Dad is going to be here—"

"No." No arguments allowed. "You will help me vacuum, and then we'll ride to camp together." She turned to me. "Kitzi, leave this mess. Shannan and I can do it."

"I don't mind—"

"I know, but it's better if we divide and conquer. We'll get the beads, and you can go stake out our bunks."

Shannan shot me one pleading glance, as if I should recognize the undercurrents and take her side. I didn't, and I couldn't. When she realized that, she turned with disgust and left the room. Something was going on here that I didn't understand.

"Is she going to be okay?" I asked Beth.

Beth let out a long breath. "I think getting away for a few days is the best thing for her. Really," she said, surely seeing my doubtful expression. "We'll only be an hour behind you; I'm not going to separate everything today." She started fanning her rapidly flushing skin.

"Are you okay?"

"Fine."

"A hot flash?"

"I prefer to think of them as personal summers," she said. "You've stalled long enough—let us do this and you go."

"Okay, if you're sure." Despite my guilt at leaving her, she was right; I needed to reserve our bunks, and she needed to talk with Shannan. "Do you want me to take your new pieces with me?" I asked.

"No. I don't think I'll even show them to you now. Maybe later at camp."

I nodded. "Okay, I'm off." I turned and headed for the door picking up Beth's and Shannan's bedrolls on the way. "I'm going to take these."

I could only hope that whatever was going on would smooth out during our time at camp—like Green Clover could work some magic. It had in the past.

Three

"We welcome you to Camp Green Clover
Mighty glad you're here
We welcome you to Camp Green Clover
Give a mighty cheer.

We'll sing you in
We'll sing you out
To you we'll give a mighty shout—
Hail, Hail the gang's all here,
Now that you're at Camp Green Clover."

Camp song
—origin unknown

My first good breath of camp air was a combination of cedar, dust, and some scent that took me back to tetherball on a hot summer afternoon.

Amazing how little the place had changed, and how many years I'd been coming here. Beth, too. We started as campers back when we were wearing bell-bottoms the first time.

As the years progressed, so had we, first becoming junior counselors and then real counselors. Eventually, of course, we had grown up and moved on from such frivolity, replacing it with the very serious business of marriage and raising children. There had been no camp during those times, but Beth and I were both living in Austin by then, so at least we saw each other.

It was about twenty years ago that another camp friend of ours, Cordelia Wright, bought Green Clover and decided that it should make money throughout the year, rather than just during the summer.

First she tried corporate retreats, but executives expected *cordon bleu* food and amenities. Green Clover is rustic, even a little cutesy with a saloon and a general store that look like they came from an old movie set. The cabins are simple, and many kids have slept in the bunks, some without complete nighttime bladder control.

Not considered an amenity.

When the corporate events failed, Cordy began a series of holistic health retreats. Unfortunately, during the very first one a skunk got trapped in a cabin, spraying several participants; then mounds of fire ants invaded the campfire area where morning meditations were being held. Those creatures of nature weren't considered amenities, either, and the holistic folks were no more forgiving than the executives.

Things shifted when Beth and I, visiting parents at the time, started reminiscing about all the fun we'd had at Green Clover. Our reveries had turned into complaints that we couldn't come back, which is when Cordy's eyes lit up and the idea of the Craft Retreat was born.

Now the twice-yearly events start on Thursday at dinnertime and continue through Sunday at five. We'd like them to be longer, say four weeks instead of four days, but most women are married and can't leave home for that long. I no longer have a husband and my children are grown, so I'd come, but I suspect I'd be pretty much alone.

During the Craft Retreats we are still given full run of

the camp, meaning that we can take the canoes out on the river, sit around the campfire munching s'mores, and go horseback riding, although crafting is the big draw. Particularly beading and rubber stamping. It's like dude ranching with a productive outcome.

"Kitzi! Kitzi!"

"Hey, Miss Kitzi!"

I slowed my Land Rover and looked to my left. Two women were waving from the steps of a trailer parked among the scrub pines and old live oaks. Jane and Angie, the Eastern Contingent, as we called them.

I waved, feeling a bubble of excitement rising in my stomach. "Hi! How are y'all doing?"

"Great!" They were vendors as well as crafters, and they brought some of the wonderful things we spent our money on. Jane sold bead supplies, while Angie carried rubber stamps, embossing powders, stamp pads, and special papers. The trailer was both for sleeping and schlepping, as Angie liked to say.

Behind it I recognized the small trailer of May Feather. It was hard to miss, since it had an Indian feather design and her name in brilliant turquoise.

Parked ten feet away was a Fifth Wheel, also well identified with the words TonyCraft. Tony was the only man who stayed on the grounds during the Craft Retreats.

The narrow, dusty road took a turn, and I caught my first sight of the cabins. I drove on past and arrived at the main area of the camp with the dining hall below me on the right, and the "town" of Green Clover on my left. I drew in a breath and grinned. I was like a kid at Disneyland. What came first? Cabin? Town?

Through the open doors of the Old Tyme General Store I could see frenzied activity as more vendors unloaded boxes in readiness for our arrival. Attached to the store was the Saloon. Big and high ceilinged, it had a fireplace, small library section, and a bar where we piled the snacks we'd brought for late-night sessions of creating and talking. It was also in the Saloon that we set up the demonstrations and classes. Beside it was the small Assayer's Office, where I needed to check in.

I parked, looking in every direction at once, not wanting to miss a thing. A tall, rangy woman with short, silver-streaked dark hair was loping out of the office.

"Cordy!" I called. "Cordelia."

She swung around, and took two long steps to reach me. "Kitzi Camden. How are you?" She slapped me on the back, a Cordy version of a hug.

"I'm great," I said. In her jeans and checked shirt she looked every bit the camp owner. The look and the lingo weren't bad for a girl who'd graduated cum laude from Rice University. "How are you?" I asked.

"Going crazy. Plumbing problems at the Bar B, and a new cook who just doesn't get it. She seems to think that I should know exactly how many people will be here, and what time they'll be arriving. I keep telling her—we've got seventy registered, and despite my best efforts to get accurate schedules, they show up when they do. I know that about twenty will be here tonight, but most can't get here 'til tomorrow." She shook her head in disgust. "Did you drive in alone?"

"Beth and I were coming together, but she had a disaster involving her cat and several hundred beads."

"That sounds ugly. Unless she glued them on the cat for artistic effect."

"It wasn't quite that way." I looked around. Others were going in and out of the buildings, but no one seemed to be paying attention to us. "So what's the story with the Tivolini buyer? How did you find out? And what kind of contract are they talking about?"

"I don't have any idea what kind of contract. Just that she's looking for new jewelry designs and—"

"Cordy!" someone shouted from the dining hall below us. "Cordy!"

"Oh, brother," Cordy said. "It's got to be about the cook

or the plumbing, and that tone doesn't sound like good news." She turned in the direction of the caller.

"Wait," I said. "So, who is the Tivolini buyer?"

"Cordelia!" the call came again.

"I've been sworn to secrecy," she said. "Which seems pretty darn silly. Drama queen stuff. But you might bribe me with a couple of glasses of wine. You did bring some didn't you?"

"You must be kidding. I'd never break the no-alcohol rule," I said. It was a lie, and we both knew it. We all brought liquor.

"That rule was my first mistake," she said, and then rolled her eyes. "Oh, wait, you brought that terrible wine. What's it called?"

"Muscovito, and it's not terrible. I happen to like it a lot, which is why I brought three bottles."

"For a woman who's hobnobbed with the rich and famous, you sometimes have the worst taste in the world."

"I prefer to think of my taste as eclectic," I said. "Oh, but I did bring some beer, too. Beth's bringing some margarita mix and a blender."

"Cordy!" The shout was even more exasperated than before.

"Save me a beer, then. Or several. Gotta run." And she did exactly that, disappearing downward on her long legs toward the dining hall.

I went inside the Assayer's Office and checked in, and then peeked into the Old Tyme General Store where the booths were already set up. I found myself being drawn toward the beads the way a crow is drawn to shiny objects; I had to remind myself that I could gaze to my heart's content later, but now I had things to do. I got back in the Land Rover, and with a feeling of homecoming, drove up the hill to the Lazy L.

Tucked there in the trees, the cabin looked just about the way it had the first time I'd seen it almost fifty years before. Like most of the cabins, the Lazy L has waist-high walls and screens to the ceiling. Actually, there was no ceiling, just the interior of the roof, with the scribbled names of some of the braver campers who had slept there over the years.

The floor was concrete on the lower level, and wood on the second. I took all three bedrolls and carried them into the sleeping porch. It was the smallest of all the rooms, containing only three metal bunks, each with two tiers. The metal had once been painted silver, but that was during the senior Bush's administration so now there's only a rusty brown color left.

There were two new mattresses, which I immediately switched onto my bunk and Beth's, and then I made up our beds. As soon as I was done, I moved my Land Rover to the parking area near the front entrance and trotted back across the camp. I counted that as my exercise for the day and decided to take a rest at one of my favorite spots, a rock above the Lazy L that overlooks most of the camp.

I sat down and sighed. During my very nasty, not to mention very public, divorce many years back, Green Clover was a place I could hide out; rumors and newspaper stories couldn't seem to penetrate the trees around the camp. My dad always said I was a trooper during his political campaigns, but when I was the one in the spotlight and it became too much, I hid here. At Green Clover no one cared who your family was, or what you did for a living, or what your soon-to-be-ex-husband had been up to.

Contentment oozed through me as I watched the activity below. I spotted Tony Campanelli's dark hair and slim body as he carried boxes into the store. He was stopped every few feet by women who wanted to pat and pet him, and even from up here he looked pretty darn charming.

I saw May Feather taking the steps three at a time as she came up from the dining hall toward the road and the store. Most Native Americans I know are short and strongly built, but May was the Disney version of a beautiful Indian maiden. Her body was long and lean, and her hair was dark brown and heavy. She wore jeans and a white shirt with a denim vest. She also wore beads. I couldn't tell exactly what they were, but at her throat was turquoise with something coral, and of course, silver. Her designs are good, no doubt about it.

May isn't pure Native American. She's part Arapahoe, but when I pressed her on the subject once, I discovered that she was three-fourths something else, and she knew as much about being Arapahoe as I did about being Scottish, German, English, Greek, Swedish, and French, which are all part of my genetic makeup. May had never lived on a reservation, although she had a cousin who did.

Her ancestors, whatever their race, passed down some outstanding genes. May is absolutely stunning, and when she wears a piece of jewelry, other women want it, but I think, mostly they want to look like May. She's not shy about her appearance, either. She usually has on low-cut blouses or has her shirt undone more than the usual one or two buttons, although it may be to show off the necklaces she makes. Whatever the reason, with May, cleavage is a bonus for the men around her. I'm always in awe of women with that kind of self-confidence, if that's what it is.

As I watched, a man came up the path behind her. He must have said something because her body stiffened as she swung around.

He was tall, slender, and fit his jeans and T-shirt quite nicely, although his age was hard to judge. Not too young, since there was gray glinting in his dark hair. Or was that just brown? Late forties? Fifties? I was too far away to tell. His back was to me, but I could see that he was nodding. Was he the new cook? No, he didn't look like a cook. Maybe a new handyman.

May jerked her head up, and she looked angry. He half-turned, and I caught my breath—it wasn't . . . it couldn't be . . . or was it?

I was craning forward now. "Turn your head, you sumbitch," I said under my breath. I was almost sure that it was him—Jeb Wright. Cordy's older brother. But what the hell would he be doing here? Last I'd heard, which was quite a while back since no one mentions his name to me anymore, he'd gotten married to an investment banker in New York. Nice move for a CEO of some financial company. He'd been planning to build an empire, and I was going to help. I thought.

It had started when I was coaching him on his public speaking skills. In those years, right after my messy divorce, I was just getting started training again, and Cordy had been pleased to recommend me to Jeb. My credentials were exactly what he was looking for; besides my degree and several years of training for an international conglomerate, I was a Camden. Camdens know about politicking—it's in our blood.

And so I'd helped Jeb. I'd taught him to organize his thoughts and speak them with passion. How to sell his dream to others. At some point the relationship went from professional to personal. We dated, we made love, and one of us, the not-so-smart one, fell *in* love. That was me.

Just hearing his voice on the phone was enough to make me stammer. When we worked together, with his eyes staring into mine, and his beautiful voice filled with the fervor that I taught him, I let all my defenses down.

Back then he was in his late thirties, three years older than I'd been, and he had big plans for the rest of his career. He kissed me good-bye with deep regret and went back to New York. It tore my heart in two, even though he said he'd call often and I'd be flying up to join him soon.

Right. Unfortunately, the calls tapered off and I never even visited. Instead, I got the bad news from Beth one day: Jeb was engaged and would never be coming back to Austin.

Watching him now, I could feel my stomach doing the roller coaster thing just like it had when we'd dated. And I wasn't even sure it was him.

I stared down at the two of them. The sun was lowering

to that golden time when the world shimmers, and even women my age, fifty-seven, can look really beautiful. Or at least, we remember the days when we were young and thought we were beautiful. The final sunlight made his dark hair glisten. But was it Jeb? Or was I just hoping? And why in the world would he be here . . . in jeans, arguing with May Feather?

I let out a breath. Beth would call this another "Jeb sighting." She likened them to UFO sightings, since they were just about as dependable. Right after his engagement I'd seen him everywhere, calling Cordy to find out if he was in town. It never was Jeb, and finally I stopped mentioning when I thought I saw him—I couldn't take the pity.

This was probably May's new assistant. I seemed to recall that her assistant had been a young female, but that could have changed. The man could be her husband— just because she used to be divorced didn't mean she couldn't have gotten married again.

He reached out holding something in his hand, and she swung around and raced down the hill toward the dining hall. For a moment he watched her go, his body taut, then he went farther along the path and disappeared among the trees.

May was scheduled for one of the premier demonstrations that night, which meant that soon enough I'd know who and what that man was. And he'd better not be Jeb Wright, because if he was, I had a few choice words for him.

I was debating my next move when a vehicle pulled in front of me, the tires skidding on the gravel.

"Excuse me—" I started to complain but I was facing the steel of a Hummer 2. The door opened and a woman's arched foot with pale metallic-lavender toenails appeared. The foot was wearing high-heeled platform sandals that would never do for trotting up and down the dirt trails of Green Clover. It was attached to a leg clad in tight jeans. Eventually the entire woman appeared. While her body was slim and youthful, the skin on her face was leathery and sagged. She had to be my age, but she hadn't weathered well. She looked, as we say in Texas, as if she'd been rode hard and put away wet.

She was holding something in her arms that was covered by half a sheet. It appeared to be a human head.

She pointed a lavender acrylic nail at the cabin. "Is that the Lazy L?"

"That's it," I said.

"And are there empty bunks?"

"Should be some in almost any room."

"But, I can't park here, right?"

"Well, you can unload here, but then you have to move that hunker to the area near the front gate."

She rolled her eyes. "How come there're so many damn rules around here? No cell phones, no alcohol, you have to park by the gate—what kind of a Nazi camp is this?"

I wanted to tell her that she was welcome to leave at any time, but I remembered my upbringing. "Some of the rules we don't take very seriously. You know, it's like Camus said, 'Every man has a moral code of his own likes and dislikes.' Only we have rules that we follow or not, depending on *our* likes and dislikes."

She raised one eyebrow. "Camus and I aren't that well acquainted." She glanced around. "I'm meeting my cousin, and she wants to be in the main cabin of Lazy L."

"Go right through that door and pick any bunk you want." I was too curious to let her go. "Who's your cousin?"

"Sandra Borders. She's flying in from L.A. tomorrow."

"Oh. I see." Sande is little, cute, and vibrant with life— just about as opposite of this woman as anyone could get. "I haven't introduced myself. I'm Katherine Camden. Kitzi." I held my hand out, which she ignored.

She looked me over, a tiny smile twitching at her mouth, or maybe it was a sneer; it was hard to tell. "I'm Lynn Donaldson." She looked at the bracelets on my wrist. "Did you make those?" I thought I heard amusement in her voice.

The bracelets are very basic, just beads on elastic cording, but I think they're quite gorgeous. Most are black glass, intermixed with some delicate gold carved beads, and then a variety of different green ones to add color. They were made by my mother, who can't handle latches and such, with the help of my granddaughter, Shelby. Shelby, who is five, picked out the beads because she has unlimited funds—when she's with my mother.

"A gift," I said, putting my hand back on the rock. In my opinion, it's not the hours that go into a project, but the final look that counts. I thought these had turned out exceptionally well, and I've received many compliments on them. Not only that, they have great sentimental value. "What kind of bead work do you do?" I asked.

"All kinds." She touched the intricate necklace at her throat which probably took a week to make, and looked like a shiny, thin rattlesnake coiled around her neck. "I put beads on mannequins and heads, too."

"You do?" I looked at what she was carrying and understood.

Artists decorate almost everything from baskets to birdcages with beads. All are pretty much a feast for the eye, but the work I've seen on mannequins, or to create figures, are most fascinating to me. Many would be right at home in museums, and they take months to create with an amazing mix of textures and colors.

And the woman in front of me beaded mannequins. It would follow that the shape under the sheet was that of a Styrofoam wig stand, covered with beads and whatever else came to her lilac-nailed hand.

"Have I seen your work in *Beadwork* magazine or *Bead and Button*?" I asked, trying not to look at the sheet. "There were some articles—"

"Those weren't about me. My pieces are noir." She held out her arms as if to tempt me with the hidden piece. "Would you like to see?"

"Sure. I'd love to."

I stood up and helped her lift the sheet straight up, try-ing not to pull any tiny pieces loose, but a black seed bead still hit the ground. Then I stepped back and did my best not to choke.

It was a woman's head, the top covered in deep garnet glass beads, like a tight fitting cloche. The face was beaded as well, the olive green eyes ringed in lashes of tiny black crystals. The lips glistened lusciously, but it was the neck and its accoutrements that stunned me. A beaded dagger with a black hilt had been stabbed in it, and maroon beads had been strung to form droplets of blood. It was beautiful and downright disturbing at the same time.

"Well," she said, her tiny smile challenging me. "What do you think? Is this your kind of thing?"

I stared at the brilliant, but garish, head. "It's amazing," I said, at my most diplomatic. I hoped the enthusiasm in my voice made up for the lack of compliment in my words. "Absolutely incredible. It must have taken you forever."

She dismissed my answer. "Just one divorce." She threw the sheet back over the head. "One really ugly divorce."

I stared at the woman, wondering if my bitterness had ever showed so clearly on my face. I sincerely hoped not, but it wasn't something I would have recognized. I said, "I'm sorry. I've had one of those myself."

She looked at me for a very long time before the half-smile came back. "Yeah?"

"Yes. Unfortunately. In fact, I read somewhere that one in four of us will go through a very tough divorce."

Again she took her time; finally she said, "You know something?" She studied my face. "That's no fucking consolation."

She turned, and with her head under her arm, swept into the Lazy L.

Four

"We're the crafty campers
We're beadin' buddies all day long
We like to bead, and that's our creed,
And this here is our song."

[repeat faster, four times]

"We're the big beaders, at Camp Green Clover."

Camp Green Clover retreat song

"We call this the gourd knot," May was saying. Everyone crowded around as her beautiful hands wove bright aqua beads into a bracelet. We'd had dinner, sung the first of our camp songs, and then adjourned to the saloon where the demonstrations were taking place.

"It looks just like the peyote stitch," Beth said.

May brought up her lovely face and said, "Native Americans only call it the peyote stitch if you are actually making a peyote."

Whatever the hell a peyote was.

I wasn't planning on sitting through all of May's presentation, but I wanted to get into the *bead of things*. I was really waiting for Beth's demonstration because she always has some trick or twist that gives even the really good beaders a new idea. Beth is very popular. When you schedule her for an hour beading demonstration, you may get her for half a day if that's what it takes to make sure everyone understands what she's teaching. She answers every question and helps anyone who needs it. And her humor, which admittedly can be used with scalpel-like precision, is usually directed at herself, rather than at the bead klutzes like me.

Beth stepped closer to me, and I said to her, "May's hands move like a Balinese dancer's."

May smiled at the group in general. "As I'm sure you all know, Native Americans have been doing beadwork for hundreds of years, so the skills and knowledge have been passed down from generation to generation."

Beth put her hand over mouth and whispered to me, "I'll bet my great grandmother and her great grandmother swapped techniques. And beads."

I could see the women on the plains, working away together, using beads to bridge the language barrier.

"Beads have long been a Native American tradition," May continued. She bent over and gave us a view of her lacy black bra. "But despite what you may have heard, Manhattan was not purchased for twenty-four dollars' worth of beads. In fact, on the bill of sale, no beads were mentioned. Manhattan Island was purchased for approximately sixty guilders.

"The tribes in that area did use wampum. The actual word is *wampumpeake*, and it's not money. It is small, tubular beads made of white or violet seashells." She looked up from the array of materials in front of her. "Jennifer? Jennifer." Her assistant appeared, a curly haired blonde with short, bright red nails. I had met her briefly at dinner. Being the youngest two at camp, she and Shannan had chosen to sit at a far table by themselves and to slip out as soon as the meal was finished.

The man who'd looked so much like Jeb, might be Jeb, was definitely not May's assistant.

"Did you need something?" Jennifer asked, from the edge of the crowd.

"I'm almost out of the aqua beads." May looked up. "I thought I told you I needed several tubes."

"You did? I'll run to the trailer and get—"

"Never mind. We don't have time for that now."

Jennifer's young face flushed a bright pink, and she dropped her eyes. "I'm sorry." After a deep breath her head came up, and her composure was back. She looked more at the crowd of women than at May. "With all the rush of trying to get here and set up, I'm afraid that just got past me. It was all my fault."

There were nods of understanding.

May conceded, looking with purpose at her watch. "It doesn't matter; I won't have time to finish the bracelet anyway."

Beth was scheduled at eight o'clock, and that was only about fifteen minutes away.

As May continued to work, she went on with her talk, "Now, as I was saying about wampum . . ."

I'd heard the story before, and I would never make the bracelet she was teaching us to create. It took many little beads, way too many for me to deal with, and too much time. I admire the women who do such beautiful work with seed beads, just as I am in awe of women who quilt and needlepoint and manage all those other wonderful handicrafts. I am, unfortunately, type A to the plus level. Microwaves were made for me, as were quickie crafts. I once hook latched a rug and after the third day of watching it progress slowly, row by row, I paid my daughter to finish it. Not only that, I think I paid her some exorbitant fee to have it done in a week or get it out of my sight. She and her brother took turns, and when it was complete we gave it to my mother so none of us had to look at it.

I slipped backward toward the door and realized that Beth wasn't far behind me.

Once outside, I said, "Everyone seems interested." I

gestured toward the window where we could see May.

Beth glanced inside but dismissed the demonstration. "Did you see who else is here?"

Jeb's name was almost out of my mouth before I stopped myself. If I was wrong again after so many years, Beth would start worrying about me. "Who?" I asked.

"Lynn Donaldson."

"Who?"

"She's in our cabin. About this tall—"

"Oh, the noir beader. Miss Hummer Two. How do you know her?"

"Her husband was one of the partners in Ron's law firm. Carl Donaldson. I'm sure I've told you about her. She's the one who announced loudly that her husband preferred brunettes. You have to remember the story." When I still looked blank, Beth explained, "It was at the firm's Christmas party two years ago, and several of us were talking about the new female anchor on one of the TV stations. Lynn announced loudly that Carl wouldn't notice because he preferred brunettes. And then she said something like, 'maybe because they look better against his silver-haired belly.' The conversation went downhill from there."

"I'll bet. Nice way to embarrass the whole room."

"Everyone except Lynn. She made a few more juicy remarks, and Carl took her home. It was the last time I saw her . . ."

"She told me she was divorced," I said. "A really bad divorce."

"That's an understatement."

"Did you know her very well? Was she always so catty?"

Beth dropped her voice. "Always catty, but in a funny way. You know the kind. You'd be talking at a party and as soon as someone left the group, she'd make an insightful, and very nasty, remark. Made me afraid to leave the room."

"Have you seen her beadwork?"

"No. I'm surprised she still works with beads." Beth glanced inside the saloon, looking thoughtful.

"There's something on your mind," I said.

"I don't know how much of this is true, it could be pure D gossip—"

"I'll settle for gossip."

"According to one of the other wives, Lynn's husband was having an affair with a woman he met through Lynn."

"Beth, there you are," Cordy said, appearing in the saloon door. "I've been looking for you. Fifteen minutes 'til showtime."

"I'm ready, except I've got to get some pliers from the Lazy L." She glanced at her watch. "Be right back."

I waved and started to say something, but she was gone, moving up the hill toward the cabin.

"Are you coming in?" Cordy asked me.

"Not yet; I think I'll get reacquainted with the camp. Is Cheech still here?" Cheech is my favorite horse.

"Of course. And I left some carrots in a bucket outside the stable."

Now there's a service you won't get at the Hilton.

"Thanks," I said, but she was gone, too, leaving me on my own for that walk.

The night was perfect for a quick ramble around the camp, meaning it wasn't too hot or too cold, and the humidity was low enough that you didn't have to drink your air through a straw. I took in a big breath and glanced at my watch. I had time to wander before Beth's demonstrations. When it was over, we'd all get down to some serious fun.

First thing I did was head down past the dining hall and over to the campfire area. I've spent a lot of time here in my life, participating in silly skits and watching lots of others. It makes me smile just to see the wooden stage. I went down and tromped across it for old time's sake, before I moved on toward the river.

There's a path through some trees, and then you have to climb down rocky steps until you reach the water. The river is shallow and rocky there, the perfect place to stay cool while you sunbathe—back in the days when we did sunbathe. In more recent years, most of us slather ourselves with SPF 45 and sit in the shade reading a book, only using the river as a place to briefly cool off before we duck for cover again.

A quarter mile or so farther on the river gets deep and swift just before it passes the public campground. It's there we used to swim and have canoe races.

I didn't walk down the bank, but I did get close enough to dangle my hand in the water.

I don't know why, but I kept expecting to meet other people. Not just Jeb, although I suppose he had crossed my mind, but I thought that someone ought to be out and about. Finally I decided that everyone else was attending the demonstrations, leaving the rest of the camp for me.

Since I didn't have to share, I visited the horses at the barn, taking inside a few of the carrots Cordy had left in a bucket. Cheech got one, along with a small palomino mare named Goldy.

By that time I smelled, rather happily, I have to admit, of horse, so I headed up the hill to the Lazy L, where I washed my hands and grabbed my car keys. I'd been in such a hurry to see the camp earlier I hadn't locked the Land Rover, and while locking vehicles isn't something we used to do at Green Clover, the world has changed.

I was almost at the front entrance when I heard my name being called.

"Tante Kitzi!" The voice was Shannan's, jerky and upset. She was running.

"What's wrong?" I asked. On the dark path I couldn't see her face. "Are you okay?"

"I, I'm fine. Can I borrow your car? I won't be gone long."

"My car? Why?"

"I just need to use it, that's all. Can I?"

Shannan's not covered on my insurance, plus, she'd been in an accident that was entirely her fault a month before. "I'm sorry, honey, but you know I can't."

"Oh, please. I'll be very careful."

"I can't. Because of my insurance. What about your mom's—"

"She won't let me. That stupid wreck." She was breathing heavily, in part from the hurry, but there was something more. "I have to leave *now*."

I held up my keys. "Then I'll drive you."

"Really?" She grabbed my arm and pulled me forward. "But we have to go right now."

"Okay," I said as we ran to the Land Rover.

This could be a breakthrough in my relationship with Shannan. I might actually find out what had been troubling her, and I was willing to drive her to Waco or Tucumcari if it would help.

Once inside the Rover, I started the engine. "Now tell me what this is about. And which way?"

"That way," she said, pointing toward the old road that would take us to the highway. "I just can't believe it. I knew I was right—I just knew it!"

I turned left onto the dark country road. "Knew what?"

She took several breaths, sorting through her words. "I was out by the front gate, and I saw my dad. He was here. At Green Clover."

I chewed on that for a moment before I nodded. "Okay." I couldn't imagine why he'd be here. "Is he okay?"

"I don't know. I just saw his car." Her anxiety was back, and she seemed to debate what to say next. Finally she blurted out, "He picked someone up. Out front. Just now." She was fighting tears, and the tight voice reminded me of the little girl I had so adored. "Don't you see? He came and got someone."

"Honey, did he pick up your mother?"

"No! She's doing her demonstration. Someone else. He didn't see me." She swallowed a few times, then took a shuddery breath. "It's a long story."

"I'll take you wherever you want to go, but you have to explain." And then I waited in silence while we bounced over the bumpy road and around a pothole. Up ahead I could just make out a red glow that might have been tail lights or a jackrabbit carrying a flashlight.

Shannan took several breaths. "My dad has been acting weird lately. He goes out at night, and he always says he's going to some off-the-wall place. Like Golfsmith or the woodworking shop. Places Mom and I would never go. And he always leaves around seven-thirty, but he doesn't get home until late. Sometimes after eleven."

"Okay." That wasn't great dad behavior, but we were talking about Mo-Ron, so I didn't see any reason to panic. Although there was something odd, since most stores close at nine or ten. "Tell me why that upsets you?"

"I followed him a couple of times, and he didn't go where he said he was going." Dear God. "At first I always lost him, but then I realized that he wasn't paying any attention to the cars behind him. Only one night I was so busy staring at him that I had that accident."

She had rear-ended another vehicle. Luckily, the damage had been minor, and the other driver understanding.

"Can't you hurry?" she asked.

I swerved, narrowly missing a pothole. "Not on this road," I said. "Go on; you followed him." And we were following him again. Except I hadn't heard another car at camp and the lights ahead of us could be anyone's. I sincerely hoped they belonged to some innocent passerby and we were on a futile mission.

"He went to Weldon and Company," Shannan said. "You know that big fancy hardware store south of town?"

"Did you talk to him? Did he know you were there?"

"No." She was straining forward against the seat belt as if the extra effort would make us go faster. "I got scared. I was afraid he'd be mad at me, so when he pulled into the parking lot, I just drove past. Finally, I went home. Well, it was a school night, and I knew that mom would start yelling if I stayed out late . . ."

"It was the right thing to do; you needed to go home." We

came to the stoplight at the highway. "Which way now?"

"Turn right. We're going back to Weldon and Company."

I had serious misgivings about this little venture, but I turned as she directed. "Maybe he's just planning some home repair project," I said.

Now that was lame. I could not imagine Ron Fairfield contentedly browsing through an aisle of bolts. His hobbies were watching football, playing golf, and running. He wasn't handy with his hands, and even he admitted he could make a major project out of changing a lightbulb. "Maybe the night you saw him he was getting something for the office. An extra key, maybe." That wasn't any better. Ron is a partner with a law firm. He doesn't do office maintenance, he has people for that. Lots of people.

Shannan was calmer now and getting quieter, but her focus was still on the road and cars we were passing. If she expected to see her dad's black Lexus, she was disappointed. "But he didn't go out just one night, remember? He does it all the time."

I drove in silence for a few minutes, moving in and out of the late evening traffic with more alacrity than usual, but the haste was for Shannan's sake. I didn't really think the few extra minutes mattered; Ron was either going to be there or not. I kept trying to convince myself he was not.

"Honey, I know you're worried about your dad, but you haven't said why. What do you think he's doing?"

"I don't know. I just want to go and find out if he's really there."

Which meant she had a good idea and wasn't ready to tell me. I had a suspicion, too, but I hoped I was wrong.

"Are you positive that was your dad's car at the camp? A lot of cars look alike these days and it's black, so in the dark—"

"I know his license number. It was him, and he did pick someone up. I'm not crazy, honest."

"A woman?"

She hesitated. "I, I don't know."

So that settled it in my mind—Shannan suspected her father was having an affair. It was the only answer I could think of for his behavior, if Shannan was reporting it accurately. I couldn't see him as part of the Mafia, and he didn't have the balls to be a terrorist. Running drugs was strictly out of his reality, since he once chastised Beth for taking a Vicodin after a root canal.

I took a breath, my eyes on the road. Ron Fairfield might not be one of my favorite people; however, Beth was, and if he was doing something that would hurt her, he needed to be stopped. But was Shannan was the one to do it? Or me?

"You know," I said, as I exited the highway just down from Weldon's. "He might not be there. And if he is, what are you going to say to him? I think we ought to skip this and—"

"No!" She shook her head. "I have to see. Don't you understand? I'm not a child, and I need to know what's going on. I love my dad, and I'm the one person he'll listen to if he's doing something . . . I don't know. Something." When I didn't say anything she added. "It's for my mom, too."

I wanted to put my head on the dashboard and cover it with my arms, but that was out of the question since I was driving.

I certainly didn't want to find Shannan's dad; luckily, the chances of him being at the same place were slim. And why in the world would he be at a hardware store? The whole thing made no sense to me.

"All right," I said, as I spotted the bright lights of Weldon and Company's parking lot up ahead. "We'll check for his car, and if it's there we'll decide on our next move. If not, well, we'll have to go back to camp."

She took in a breath. "Okay, but he's going to be there. You'll see."

"I'm sorry," I said to Shannan as the exit doors slid open in front of us. We stepped out into the dark night that was turning muggy.

Ron Fairfield was not at Weldon and Company. We had checked the parking lot for his car first, and then we'd gone up and down every aisle of the store, just in case. There was nowhere else to look; I slid an arm around Shannan. "Honey, maybe he's already gone home."

She didn't look convinced, but she pulled out her cell phone. "I'll call the house and see." She dialed the number, listening to the ringing as we walked to the Land Rover. After a moment she hung it up. "He's not there," she said. "I know, I'll try *his* cell phone."

I thought it was a bad idea, but I didn't discourage her. She dialed a second time, and I heaved a sigh of relief when she still didn't get an answer. By then we were at the Land Rover, climbing in. "I'm sorry," I said again, putting the key in the ignition. "At least we tried." I couldn't imagine confronting him and a possible girlfriend in the middle of a hardware store. And why here? That still puzzled me, but there had to be a logical explanation for all of this, and to be fair, which I didn't really want to be, there was still the chance that it was an innocent explanation.

I swung the car to the left to avoid an oversized pickup that was coming toward us, then turned again. We were at the far corner of the lot.

"Tante Kitzi! Look!" Shannan said. "There's another parking area back there."

Behind the loading dock and down a sloping ramp was a small area for cars. It was dark, inconvenient, and when a truck was unloading as had been happening earlier, completely inaccessible. Now I could see that a half a dozen vehicles were parked there looking like dead bugs on a black rug.

"Probably for employees," I said.

"No! Wait. Slow down." I did as instructed and she

stared down, her nose all but pressed against the window. "He could be there—just let me look a minute."

I stopped completely. "Take your time." A few more minutes and we'd be headed back to Green Clover. I'd be having a well-deserved glass of wine. Despite what Cordy said, I liked that wine—

"He's there! That's my dad's car, I'm sure of it. On the right. See it? Under the trees, almost all the way down."

There were cars parked along the building on the left, and some on the right under huge trees where there wasn't much light. It was difficult to tell if Shannan had really spotted her dad, but there were cars. One was something like Ron's Lexus. At that distance and at night a lot of cars look alike.

"We can't be positive."

"I'll go see—" She was about to the open the door, but I stopped her.

"Hold on. We need to think about this. If it is your dad, what in the world is he doing, and what are you going to say to him?"

"I don't know." She took her hand off the door handle. "Maybe we should just drive down there so we can see for sure. I mean, I could be wrong." Suddenly she was worried again.

The bad ideas were piling up, but since we'd come this far . . .

"Okay," I said. "I will."

"But turn off your lights. Please."

I nodded and switched them off. "Here we go, Double O Seven." She didn't smile, and I didn't either.

I drove slowly down the ramp, then into the lot, keeping as far to the left as I could. I went past the Lexus in question almost coasting, then backed into a space across from it so we could observe it more easily.

Shannan gasped. "It *is* daddy's car." Only this time she didn't attempt to leave the Rover. I think she was as surprised as I was. "He's in there."

I stared at the car—he certainly was. At least someone was. There was just enough light to see someone very large inside and then the dark form separated into two.

Damn. Ron Fairfield was making out with someone in the parking lot of a hardware store. Worse, the two shapes moved together again for more kissing.

"We have to get out of here," I said, reaching for the gearshift.

Shannan grabbed my hand. "Don't hit them—"

"I'm not going to."

"Let's wait until she gets out of the car, and then we'll hit her hard!"

"Wrong." I wanted out of there so badly I forgot that I was in reverse, and when I pushed on the gas pedal the Rover shot backward. "Damn." I slammed the brake just before we hit the wall behind us. "Sorry. Are you okay?" I took a breath.

Shannan nodded, her face pale, her eyes still intent on the Lexus. "Fine."

"Good. Then we're getting out—"

"We can't go! He's cheating!" Shannan said. "Can't you see?"

"He's cheating on your mother. It doesn't have any thing to do with you." I reached again for the gearshift.

Shannan tore her glare away from her father's car and whirled to face me. "Yes, it does. He'll leave and marry her, and I'll hardly ever see him. He'll spend all his time taking her places, and, I won't even get a good-night call! Don't you understand? This affects my whole life. Everything. Nothing will ever be the same again."

Shannan had lost her father to another woman.

She wasn't the first young girl to be in that situation, and she was right—this other woman, if Ron loved her and married her, would take away from Shannan's time. It would make a difference in the relationship she had with her dad, too, because divorces always did.

What Shannan wasn't thinking about was that within a

year she'd be leaving for college and things would change anyway.

I reached out to touch her arm, but she jerked away. "Honey," I said, "what this doesn't do is take away any of your father's love for you. Do you understand that? There isn't a woman in the world who could take your place in his heart."

"It's happened to my friends. Their dads walks out and don't even look back! Christie hasn't seen her dad in months." She glared at the darkened car. "Whoever she is, I hate her! She's trying to ruin our lives. We have to find out who she is."

Just then the dark forms slipped down out of sight. My anger shot up like a rattlesnake's tail. How could he hurt Beth this way? And what about Shannan? If that car started rocking there was no way I could stop her from physical violence, and I wasn't sure I'd want to.

I clicked the button locking all the doors on the Land Rover. "We have to leave."

"No!" Shannan started jerking at the door. "Let me out of here; I have to know who that is."

"Okay, okay. Calm down. We'll find out." I took a breath and put the car in drive. For better or worse, I had an idea. "Put on your seat belt. Now."

Shannan, confused and still in shock, did as she was told.

"Hang on," I said, "and no matter what happens you are not to open that door. Do you understand? Now, promise me."

"Okay." She nodded, but looked more puzzled than ever.

"Okay. What good is it having this monster SUV if I don't put it to use once in awhile?" With that I put my foot on the gas and gently eased it forward. I intended to get right up behind Ron's car and bump it. Then I'd turn on my lights. The Rover was high enough that the lights would stop them from seeing us, but they'd know they'd been caught.

Shannan saw what I was going to do. "You're going to—"

"Yes, I am," I said.

When we were within ten feet of the Lexus, Shannan changed the plan—she rammed her foot down on top of mine.

"Shannan, no!"

Too late. We shot forward and slammed Ron's car hard. On impact, Shannan and I jerked forward. As soon as I recovered, I hit my headlights and the high beams. Two heads popped up from the backseat of the Lexus.

I reversed the Rover, cut my lights and whipped out of the lot, tires squealing on the ramp.

He had to have been blinded; they couldn't have recognized us.

But I recognized them. Both of them.

I turned the Land Rover around and as we were pulling out of the parking lot, Shannan said, "It was my dad all right." She took a shaky breath. "And May Feather."

My own breathing was hardly calm. I was heading toward the highway, trying to think of the appropriate thing to say or do. I still couldn't believe that we'd rammed them. Or that we'd even found them. "Shannan," I said. "We shouldn't have done that. I should have refused to take you there—"

"I'm glad you did. I needed to know."

"Except," I paused to add emphasis to my words. "You can't say one word of this to anyone tonight. No one. You *can't* tell your mom, and you *can't* call your dad."

Shannan was pale in the lights of the oncoming cars. "Why? Mom deserves to know, and I have several things to say to my father."

"I'll bet you do, but now is not the time. This is the kind of thing you have to sleep on. We'll both do a lot of thinking, and then tomorrow we'll make some decisions. As they say in the military, we want as little collateral damage as possible. We don't want your mother to be hurt."

Shannan said, "But why May, of all people? And do you think this has been going on a long time? I mean, I know she's beautiful, but she can also be a bitch—that's what

Jennifer says. My dad and May Feather. I can't even imagine them together!"

"Then don't. This might be the first time they've ever met like this."

"That's bullshit; I told you, he's been here before. I'll bet he met her those other times, too. She must have finished her stupid demonstration and run to his car. I'll bet Jennifer had to put everything away—"

"That's Jennifer's job."

"Why doesn't May live on some reservation with the rest of her tribe? And when I do talk to her, I'm going to say a few things that she won't forget. And she's too old to dress the way she does, like a slut. And she is a slut . . ."

I let her vent until she wound down and we were almost at Green Clover. She eventually became silent, breathing heavily, thinking hard. I felt sorry for her, but sorrier for Beth, and furious with Ron.

Damn him and May and the horse they rode in on. What were they thinking? And what was going to happen now?

When we pulled under the Green Clover archway I slowed the Land Rover and said, "I'm serious, Shannan, you have to promise not to say or do anything until we can talk about this tomorrow."

"Why?"

"I told you, because neither one of us is thinking clearly right now and whatever we do, we're liable to be *very* sorry about it afterward. I'm already very sorry."

"Don't be." She turned to me. "It wasn't your fault. It was mine."

"I don't think that part much matters." I parked and almost jumped out of the Land Rover, so we were out of there in case Ron came driving up to drop off May. I locked the SUV and steered Shannan toward the main part of camp. "Come on, we'll get a soda." I made sure that she stayed beside me. The one thing I couldn't let happen was a confrontation between Shannan and her dad. Or May. I'd already done enough damage.

"Dining hall or Saloon?" I asked. I felt as if I were walking through rubble, like the aftermath of a tornado, only it was the rubble of Beth's marriage and I was responsible.

The fact that I hadn't caused the problem should have been a consolation, but I had unearthed it. It was that bearer of bad news syndrome.

"Either one, I guess," Shannan said.

"You know what I want?" I said, turning toward the Lazy L. "I want a glass of wine. Let's go up to the cabin."

"Whatever," she said with a shrug.

"And I'm dead serious, you can't say a thing."

She stopped to look at me. "I promise I won't, not tonight. But, Tante Kitzi, I want you to know one thing—when I do get to face my dad, there is going to be one huge explosion."

I didn't doubt it a bit.

Five

The cabin wasn't empty. Beth was there, mixing margaritas in a whirring blender. Shannan went straight to her mother's side.

"Mom, hi," she said. When she gave Beth a hug, it seemed both protective and as if she was seeking comfort.

Considering the way Shannan had been acting of late it wasn't surprising that Beth was suspicious. "Where have you two been?" she asked.

I wished my headache would go away along with the memory of the previous hour. "Just off walking," I said. "You know, around the camp."

"Really? You both look like hell."

"It's hot out there," I said, climbing into my bunk. "I think I'd look a lot better if I had one of whatever you're concocting." I was trying not to make eye contact because I was afraid Beth could read my guilt.

"I'm going to the john," Shannan said, heading out the door.

I sat up. "Shannan—" But she was gone, leaving me alone with Beth and worried about what to say.

Beth watched me. "Are you sure you're okay?"

"Fine, really. I just overdid."

"You want your margarita here or at the Saloon? I was just going back up."

"Here. I'm staying here." There would be big-time partying this evening; the Saloon would be like a mosh pit for beaders with everyone working on the things they didn't have time for at home. It's also where we catch up on each other's lives and families.

Tonight wasn't the night for me to make idle conversation.

In fact, I wasn't even sure I could walk back to the Saloon now that my knees had gone rubbery. Beth poured me a plastic cup of margarita, and I took a sip. The tingle made me squirm.

"What do you think?" she asked. "It's low carb and low sugar."

"It's good," I said, not caring a whit about carbs or sugar—my own interest was in the alcohol.

Beth raised the pitcher as if to toast. "I've now lost two pounds, and these may become my routine dinner. Or lunch."

The screen door opened and a thirtyish young woman stumbled in dragging what appeared to be a brand-new sleeping bag, a designer duffel, and a huge, black leather purse. The door slammed behind her. "Please tell me this isn't the Lazy L."

The diversion took Beth's attention off of me.

Beth said, "Okay. This isn't the Lazy L."

"Thank God." The young woman was tan and sleek with the casual, but expensive sophistication I see in the high-tech computer firms; it's not the look most of the women at the bead retreats cultivate. In fact, she wasn't wearing any beads at all. Her jewelry was all silver, large and, unless I missed my guess, pricey.

"But it really is the Lazy L," Beth added.

"And this is the sleeping porch?"

"Yes." Beth pointed toward an interior door. "That way is the party room, beyond that is the downstairs main cabin. If you want the second floor, take the stairs on the other side. They are a little more enclosed than this."

The duffel made a huge racket as it plopped on the

floor, and I stopped myself from rubbing my head. Next, the young woman dragged her sleeping bag and purse across the room toward the far bunk before she turned her attention to the cabin and its lack of amenities. "I keep remembering an article that my aunt sent me about Green Clover."

"What article?" Beth asked.

"It was from an old *Texas Monthly*. It said that some of the kids' camps in Texas were, well, instrumental in forming a child's adult life. Like, I think Camp Stewart was supposed to be the place you sent boys if you wanted them to be in politics. And, you know, there was one that favored banking—"

"That old article?" Beth asked, putting the blender pitcher into the ice chest while she stowed the rest of the ingredients. "I think I was going to camp when that came out. Come to think of it, I'm still going to camp."

The young women continued her visual inspection of the cabin, although she seemed careful not to actually touch anything.

Beth said, "It's not the Hilton, but the price is right. I've always found it warm and comforting, like old flannel pajamas."

"I used to come here, but I didn't remember that it was quite so . . . uh, rustic." The upscale look of her tight black pants and sleeveless white blouse made me think this might be our Tivolini buyer.

I paid closer attention to the conversation.

"Do you like rustic?" Beth asked. When the young woman merely swallowed, Beth continued. "Say something, or I'll have Kitzi do the Heimlich maneuver on you."

"Oh, well, it's, uh, okay. But, my aunt's always bragging about the place, and I thought it had changed."

"Not much," Beth said, stretching out on her bunk.

Aunt? But, of course, she would have a connection with Green Clover since very few people heard about the craft retreats any other way.

"I guess any empty bed will do." Beth and I were on lower bunks across from each other, leaving a third set at angles to us on the far wall. The woman selected the top bed of that set. "I'll sleep here." She moved closer to it, tossed her sleeping bag up on the mattress, then moved back. "Euuww. It's stained! Like maybe some kid . . . you know."

"Pee-stained mattresses," Beth said. "All part of the authentic camping experience. If you get here first, you get your pick of the best mattresses. However, I did bring a bottle of Febreeze, in case your stain is of recent vintage." She gestured to the bottle on the window board. "I always bring it for newcomers."

The young woman reached for it. "If you're sure." She sprayed her mattress relentlessly, jangling the silver bracelets on her thin, tanned arm as it moved back and forth along the length of the bed.

Beth glanced at me and winked. As former counselors we knew that the mattresses never smelled, thanks to the junior members of the staff who were forced to haul them out into the sun, rinse them thoroughly with some magical concoction, then drag them back inside when everything was dry. The young counselors were told it built character, but primarily it built muscles.

Beth and I had hauled mattresses one summer until we swore we were going to hitchhike to some distant land. Then, as if by magic, every mattress that had to be cleaned suddenly showed up on top of one of the senior counselor's beds. When accused of putting the mattresses there, Beth and I said that we were tired of lifting mattresses and putting them anywhere. No one ever saw who was doing it. Good news was that after about a week of that, the senior counselors gave the mattress cleaning job to some others, and Beth and I were switched to latrine duty, which wasn't much better.

We'd had a lot of good times over the years maybe because Beth was one of those special people. When I

thought of Ron choosing May over her, I couldn't believe
it. Of course, Beth wasn't as beautiful as May, but then,
who was? And who cared about that?

Ron cared. Shallow, self-absorbed Mo-Ron.

Beth covered her nose to fend off the amount of spray
the young woman was pumping. "That's probably enough,"
she said.

"Oh, sorry." The young woman gave a selected spot one
last squirt then handed the bottle back to Beth. "Thank you."

"You're welcome. By the way, I'm Beth. Graduated
from Camp Green Clover year of . . ." she cleared her
throat. "Well, some year. I'm not giving away all my secrets this early on. And this is Kitzi—another camper from
eons ago."

The margarita was taking effect, so I moved closer to
the edge of the bunk to appear more sociable. "Hi," I said.
"Welcome to the Lazy L."

"Hi. I'm Leesa. With two *es*." The young woman sat
carefully on the empty bottom bunk. "Kitzi is an unusual
name. Is it Russian or something?"

"No, nothing so exotic."

Beth explained, "Her real name is Katherine Zoe, and
she used to be called Kit. Kit Z, so the whole explanation is
pedestrian rather than Russian."

"I've heard the name Kitzi before," Leesa said. "In the
society column in the Austin paper. You know, *Kitzi Camden graciously opened her home for the ballet's Spring Fi-
nale last night—or former Texas senator, Kitzi Camden, cut
the ribbon on last night's gala to benefit some stupid charity or other*." She rolled her eyes. "Like we care where
Kitzi Camden was last night."

Beth put her margarita on the floor with enough force
that I was glad it was in plastic. "Maybe we should have
used last names." She sat up straight, again. "I'm Beth
Fairfield, and this is Kitzi Camden."

It was a bad night. First I'd rammed Ron's car, and now
I was being insulted about being a Camden. I've had plenty

of opportunities throughout my lifetime to develop a hard shell on the subject of my family name, but none of them took. Somehow I always think that people will see the very ordinary me, rather than the Camden name.

What an optimist—instead of Katherine, my parents should have named me Pollyanna.

"*The* Kitzi Camden?" Leesa asked.

"I never quite thought of myself that way, but I'm the only one I know of," I said.

Being a Camden isn't the norm, but I didn't realize it until I turned six. It was my birthday party, and the memory still makes me think of gardenias and ponies.

My grandfather had been alive then, and when he wasn't busy being governor, he grew gardenias in his conservatory. For my birthday he'd had a florist make me a wrist corsage of them, which I wore during my party. The party was at his house—the Camden Manse as it's known to the public, all eight thousand square feet of it, surrounded by four acres of grounds. Back then I thought that if heaven was all it was reported to be, it would be like my grandfather's house.

That was long before the extravagant parties that kids have these days, but my mother had gone to a lot of trouble to get some Shetland ponies for us to ride. With the corsage and the ponies, I was one happy little girl, and I wasn't a bit interested in opening presents or playing Pin the Tail on the Donkey. I only wanted to stay in the saddle and look over the party from my vantage point, which was several feet higher than usual.

That was fine for awhile, but then someone complained that I was taking more than my turn.

Another of my guests, Susie Lynn Dornan, responded, and while the exact words have slipped away over the years, I do remember that she called me a spoiled brat. The all-knowing Susie Lynn also said that all Camdens were spoiled and that Camden Manse was "ugly and stupid."

I was so mad I literally saw red. It wasn't that she'd said terrible things about me—she'd said them about my whole family and, even worse, about my grandfather's house. I would have run over and pounded her a couple of times, but I couldn't get off the pony, probably because, if I know my mother the perfectionist, I was strapped on.

I do, however, clearly remember the showdown with Susie Lynn that came later. I was saying good-bye to my guests, and she thanked me for inviting her, no doubt at the coaching of a parent.

Instead of the standard reply, I said, "You're not welcome." That might have gone unnoticed, but I was young and I pushed my luck. I proceeded to tell her that I wasn't a brat, and that *she* was one. Things escalated with her saying something about how the Camdens were nasty rich people who showed off their money. Since I'd never seen anyone in my family waving dollar bills in the air, it was obvious Susie Lynn was not only a brat, but a liar, too.

I pushed her to the ground and told her she would never come back to this house again, and after that I bit her nose.

She screamed bloody murder, which worried me, but I was still quite pleased that I had defended my family and myself.

As one would expect, when my mother arrived on the scene she didn't see it that way. I was instructed to apologize, and Mrs. Dornan gave me a dirty look, although as I recall she was overly nice to my mother.

I refused to apologize because even at six I had my principles. My mother apologized in my stead and marched me off to exile in the green guest room.

I liked the room so that didn't much bother me. My worry was that my grandfather would be mad at me. I stewed a good while before he got home and heard about my little row with Susie Lynn. I was listening through the door when my mother told him to go upstairs and give me a good talking-to.

He did come upstairs, and he slipped into his favorite spot on the old rocker, but I don't think his words were what my mother had in mind.

"Honey, I hear you been wildcattin'." I burst out crying, and he held me while I told him my side of the story.

As the family legend goes, my granddaddy was so proud that I'd defended the family homestead he made a promise that someday I would live there in the Camden Manse. Much to my cousins' consternation, while I don't own the entire house, I own the majority of it, and our branch of the family has lived there since my grandmother passed away.

And Susie Lynn Dornan has never been invited back. The Camdens might be spoiled, but we are at least consistent.

Lucky for Leesa that when people make unkind comments these days, I don't bite. Hadn't in years, at least without more provocation than that.

I straightened my worn camp T-shirt, with its faded green clover. "What former senators are wearing these days," I said, trying to smooth over the gaff.

Instead of apologizing, Leesa glared at Beth as if the rudeness were her fault. "Right."

Now, I am a kinder, gentler Kitzi Camden than I used to be, but her glare caused my old responses to rise up. I added, "I've also wondered who reads that stupid society column in the first place." Tacky, tacky. "So, what is your last name?"

The young woman blinked, and in her favor, she said, "That was mean of me, and I'm sorry. I'm Leesa Jansen. My aunt is Cordelia Wright."

"Oh. You're Cordy's—" I froze and my heart slammed to a stop. If Cordy was her aunt . . . then her father was . . . no, no, she was too old.

"Who's your father?" I asked.

"Zeke."

Zeke. "Ezekiel Wright." The oldest brother, not Jeb.

I heard Beth say my name, but I was concentrating on breathing again. I'd known Leesa couldn't be Jeb's daughter, but there was just that moment . . .

"My grandmother loved long biblical names," Leesa

said. "Ezekiel, Nathaniel, Jebediah. The family joke is that we're lucky she didn't have a—"

"Deuteronomy," I said without thought. I'd heard that before, from Jeb.

Beth shot me a worried glance before she said to Leesa, "So, why are you at camp? Do you live in Austin?"

"No. But we're having a family reunion, and Aunt Cordy said I should sleep up here."

My chest felt like it was going to cave in. It was really happening, after all these years. Her entire family would be here at Green Clover. Taking their meals with the rest of us, sitting around the campfire at night, walking the trails to the river. At fifty-seven years old, my fantasy had turned into a nightmare. Jeb and I were coming face to face.

Beth said, "But the camp is full with the craft retreat. This doesn't seem like a good time . . . I mean, there are a lot of women here . . ." She finished lamely, probably realizing the family reunion wouldn't be canceled on her say-so.

Leesa rolled out her sleeping bag and climbed up to her top bunk, seemingly oblivious of the effect her words had on us. "Oh, it's Uncle Jeb's fault. He's always so busy, and Aunt Cordy was determined that he was going to be here for this get-together. He said this was the only time he could leave New York, so we're all staying until Tuesday—" Leesa leaned over from her aerie. "Excuse me, could one of you hand up my pillow? It's in that bag down there."

I sat up and smacked my head on the iron bed above me.

"Are you okay?" Beth asked.

"Oh, fine," I said. "Fine. Really fine." Except Jeb was here; I *had* seen him talking to May Feather. And I would have to face him, too, which in the long run had to be a good thing. I needed to lay his ghost to rest. After all, I was fifty-seven years old and not getting any younger.

As I rubbed my forehead, I saw a second option. I could pack up and go home. All the signs were pointing in that direction, and I was betting that I could take Shannan with me, and maybe Beth, too. We'd get a villa somewhere in Spain. Beth would never have to know about Ron and May Feather. Who could find us in Spain?

The problem with being fifty-seven is that you know when your thinking is off the mark. I had wasted a lot of years without a real relationship because somewhere in the far reaches of my mind I had still believed that Jeb was coming back. It was past time that I saw him again, and it wasn't going to be traumatic. Yes, I had been surprised when I'd noticed him with May, but I'd put it aside and gone on with the day. I hadn't prowled around looking for him, and I hadn't even asked Cordy about his presence.

Our relationship had been years ago. He might not even recognize me—maybe I wouldn't feel a thing.

And maybe an arctic cold front would pass through hell.

Sure as the world, he would recognize me, even with the years and a little extra weight. However, I could pretend I didn't remember who he was . . .

As for feeling something, yes, I was pretty sure I would, but with a little luck what I felt would be annoyance at myself.

"Excuse me, is someone getting my bag?" Leesa asked.

Beth rolled out of her bunk and moved across the floor to Leesa's things. "Which bag?" she asked.

"Oh, you can just hand them both up, I guess."

Beth did so with fervor, causing Leesa to flinch.

"Kitz, how about another margarita?" Beth asked, reaching in the cooler for the pitcher. She held it out to me.

"No, thanks. I'm fine," I said, aware that Leesa was watching us. "Fine. Just fine."

But, I wasn't. I felt like a tsunami was headed for Central Texas, and it had rolled over me on the way. "Well, maybe another one. A half."

She filled my cup.

A high-pitched cell phone began to ring. I remembered Ron and May. What if he'd recognized me? What if he was calling to accuse me—or maybe it was the police calling—

Then I realized with relief that my phone was turned off.

"Excuse me," Leesa said, pulling a tiny flip-phone from a pocket of her DKNY purse. The phone rapidly increased in volume before she opened it and said, "Hello? Oh, hi. Where are you?"

A woman came racing through the inner door. "Tell me that wasn't a cell phone." She spotted Leesa chatting and raised her voice to call out, "Cell phone!"

A responding shout came from the upstairs. "Cell phone!"

Another woman appeared in the doorway. "Cell phone!" she sang out loudly.

Leesa looked puzzled but held up a finger, as if to hold the women off, then said into the receiver. "It's a little noisy here. I'm already at Green Clover—"

"Cell phone!" The words resounded around our part of the camp. "Cell phone! Cell phone!"

The women came from every direction. They packed the sleeping porch and when it was full, crowded outside the doors. I even saw Lynn, the noir beader, slide inside, looking very pleased, maybe at Leesa's discomfort.

"Cell phone! Cell phone!"

Leesa had broken a camp taboo, and everyone joined in to sing.

Six

"Cell phone, cell phone, cell phone!
We don't allow the cell phone.
It means you broke a rule . . .
And while we won't be cruel,
Forget those calls
Or it's back to the malls,
Or cleaning horse stalls!
Cause . . .
No cell phones. NO-OO-OO cell phones
At Camp Green Clover!!"

Green Clover camp song

Leesa looked like someone being attacked by fluffy bunnies, and there was no way she could fight back. Wide-eyed and confused, she said very quickly into the phone, "I'll have to call you later." A punch of the button ended her conversation.

There was cheering and laughter as the women started back to the Saloon.

"I remember my first year at the Craft Retreat," one said, waiting her turn to get out of the tiny sleeping porch. "Back then we actually put up with cell phones."

A woman close to the door added, "I hate the damn things, and I'm glad they're not allowed. Wish we could sing on the highway when some jerk is weaving lane to lane, busy yakking."

"Me, too!" another said.

As the room emptied, someone slapped Leesa on the back. "Don't worry, you'll catch on."

"And, I'd turn that thing off, if I were you," Lynn said, as if she were the keeper of the rules instead of a newcomer to Green Clover. "You don't want to shovel horse shit."

Beth turned. "Lynn? How are you? I saw you from a distance earlier, but I couldn't catch up with you to talk."

Lynn's expression went from surprise at seeing Beth to a snide half-smile. "I'm wonderful. Happy as a clam," she said. "Haven't I always been? If you'll excuse me, I'm working on a head upstairs. The glue is drying even as we speak." She looked at me. "No knives in this one, but the eyeball is twisted and . . . well, you'll have to see it when I'm done."

When she was gone Beth said, "She's working on a head?"

"She covers mannequins with beads," I explained. "The one I saw was unique, to say the least."

Leesa said, "Knives in heads? I guess that's unique, not to say completely bizarre. This whole day is bizarre." She snapped her cell closed, running her fingers over the outside of the case like a little toy. "And I can't talk on my cell phone?"

"That's correct," Beth said. "If you have to make a call, go to the road outside camp. If you take another call inside Green Clover, there's real trouble."

"That wasn't trouble? Talk about primitive! Does this mean no cell phones, as in *none at all* for the entire weekend?"

"Welcome to Green Clover," I said, taking a large gulp of my margarita. My throat almost closed from the frozen drink, and I couldn't say another word.

Beth rose from her bunk, "and now it's time for some serious beading." She turned to me. "Ready?"

"I'm ready to get out of here," Leesa said, picking up her leather purse. "I'm going for a walk. I'll see you all later." And with that, she swung down from the bed and waltzed out the door passing Shannan in the process.

"Mom?" Shannan said, stepping inside. "Are there any diet drinks? To take up to the Saloon? Aren't you coming?"

"Sure. Look in the ice chest outside. Kitz, what about you?"

I was staying. "I'm going to get some sleep. Lots of sleep."

Beth gave me a long look, as if she suspected that I was going to be doing something else. Maybe prowling the camp looking for Jeb, but that wasn't on my agenda. I needed to do some serious thinking on how I was going to handle the Ron and May affair. Short of murder, I couldn't think of a thing that would be effective.

"Are you all right?" she asked.

"Sure, I just have a headache," I said. "I'll finish off my margarita and take a nighttime pain reliever; that ought to cure what ails me."

"I don't think the manufacturer of either product recommends the combination," Beth said, picking up the blender.

"Well, my personal physician, Dr. Katherine Camden, thinks it's just the thing."

"Okay, then. Good night."

Everyone on the small porch was still asleep when I crept out of my bed. Beth was sprawled across her bunk, the sheets flung down, one arm hanging over the side. On the bed above her Shannan was burrowed under her covers like an animal in a protective pose, and I looked at her sorrowfully. I hoped she'd had a good time the night before, because I was afraid today wasn't going to be a happy one for her or her mother.

I had slept like the dead, but then I always do when I'm stressed. I'd heard people coming in during the night and opened my eyes enough to see rays of flashlights, but basically I had slept. It's what I do when there's too much to think about and no ready answers. I still had no idea whether I should tell Beth what we'd seen, and if I was going to say something, I certainly didn't know *how* to tell her.

I was even stewing over when to tell her. Would it be better to let her have her meeting with the Tivolini people first so she could be at her best with them?

If I did that, and she got the contract, then I would ruin her moment of glory by saying something about Ron and May. But, telling her if she didn't get the contract would be like kicking her when she was down.

I could feel the headache lurking inside my head just waiting to come back.

A shower helped, and so did clean clothes. I even put on some eye makeup, which is important when your coloring is as light as mine. It's also important when an ex-heartthrob is lurking somewhere on the same patch of earth.

I looked closely at myself in the old speckled mirror, wondering what Jeb would see when we met up. When I was young, people used to tell me I looked like Marilyn Monroe, and I suppose I did if you took away some of her flash. But she only lived to thirty-six, so there's no telling how she'd look at my age. As for me, I wasn't as slender as I'd been or as blonde, although there was still more blonde than silver.

The perm was soft, and everything fell into place like I'd planned it that way. I put on some lipstick so I was a little less pale in the morning light, although I still didn't look young, or even forty.

Well, that was life, and today was just another part of it. Maybe a more difficult part since today I had to face everything I'd avoided last night. My car was first on the list. No telling what the insurance company would say or what it could cost me to get the front end fixed.

I made my way across Green Closer saying hello to the few campers who were already out and about. At the road I turned toward the front gate, the dread building with every step. When I came to the parking area, there sat the Rover, blue and tall in the morning sunshine. First off I noticed that it was a little dustier than yesterday, but all I was seeing was the back end. Then I started around it.

The side panels were fine, which I'd expected. Then I stepped up to the front end. The paint was unsullied. I stared. There were no scratches and no dents.

In disbelief I circled the Land Rover again and still found no sign of our misadventure at Weldon's. Apparently the winch on the front, added at my brother's insistence, had taken the brunt of our collision.

I could hardly believe it, but I wasn't going to question my good fortune; at least it did away with one worry. Unfortunately, I was pretty sure the Lexus hadn't gotten off so easily. Ron must have been furious that something big and dark had careened out of the night to plow into his beloved car. And his beloved May? Now, that didn't bear thinking about.

For the first time I wondered what Ron was doing today. How was he feeling? I hoped I hadn't hurt him or May. At least, I hoped I hadn't caused any permanent damage to them, but a little worry would do them good.

I have an uncle with a roving eye, along with other wayward body parts, and as a child I remember family talk about him and how he'd hurt my aunt. I also remember my grandmother slapping him once, even though he was a grown man. What she'd said to him stayed with me. "If you're going to break someone's heart, you do it quickly and move on. You don't tear them to pieces bit by bit."

As I'd gotten older, I realized how smart my grandmother had been. Was Ron planning a clean break? Or no break at all?

Poor Beth. What could I say to her?

The only thing I knew for sure was that I was still

thinking about that, and I intended to keep on thinking for a while longer. It might be wise to have a talk with May Feather. She might listen to reason; after all, Mo-Ron wouldn't be that much of a catch.

Except May wasn't the whole problem. It was Ron who needed the confrontation and I didn't think he'd respond well to advice, a threat, or even my grandmother's wisdom. Especially if he realized *how* I knew what he was doing.

I started for the dining hall.

My head was down, and my thoughts inward when someone grabbed me from behind. I jumped and whirled to find Tony Campanelli.

"Tony! Damn. You scared me."

"I'm sorry," he said, releasing my arm. "Have you heard? I'm still in shock—I can't believe it," he said. "This is just so beyond reality."

"What is?" My voice was snappy; I wasn't in the mood for anyone else's histrionics.

"You haven't heard." Tony has never had a deep tan, but in the morning light he looked waxy.

"Are you all right?" I asked.

"I'm fine." He looked around, and even though we were alone on a side trail, he dropped his voice. "Kitzi, the police were here. When I woke up, I heard them talking to Jennifer, May's assistant, and then they came and talked to me." He paused and swallowed hard. Finally he said, "It was about May Feather."

My heart stuttered. Had she and Ron been caught in that dark parking lot? Maybe they were in the hospital.

Tony ran his fingers through his curly hair, taking his time. Was that excitement or dread on his face?

"What about May?" I asked a tad sharply.

Tony said, "I'm sorry to tell you this, Kitzi, but . . . she's dead."

"Dead?" My body went cold. Had I killed her last night when I rammed them? Oh, please God, no. "How did she die? Was it a wreck?"

"I don't think they know—"

"Then where?" I demanded, grabbing his arm.

He looked surprised. "Some people downstream at the public campground found her body; it was half in the river, right at their campsite this morning."

I let out my breath. I hadn't killed her. And then, with some horrible relief, I realized May's affair with Ron was over.

I shuddered and must have made a noise because Tony grabbed me. "Are you okay?" he asked.

"Fine." He didn't let go. "Really," I said. "I imagine I'm in shock. But, I don't understand. Why was May in the river? She hated water." Once I had invited her to go canoeing with me, and she had declined saying, "Wrong tribe—I don't swim."

He shook his head. "I don't know."

Had I caused a fight between May and Ron? Was she so devastated that she'd killed herself by jumping in the river? Was that even a possibility?

I didn't know, but the guilt was all but drowning me, and I put my hand to my head, wishing my brain would shut down, or at least slow down. "It was some kind of accident, right? Is that what they think?"

"I guess so." He didn't look positive. "The sheriff said there'd been a mishap; I'm pretty sure that's the word. I remember thinking, no one really says 'mishap.' Do they?"

"I don't know, Tony."

We heard someone coming toward us and turned to find Cordy hurrying up the path. "Kitzi!" she said. "I was looking for you." When she reached us she was breathing hard.

Tony said, "I've already told her about May."

"It's just tragic!" Cordy's face was flushed rather than white like Tony's. "I still can't believe it."

"Neither can I," Tony said. "Did you talk to the police? Did they tell you anything?"

"Mostly, they just asked questions and slowed the process of getting ready for breakfast." Cordy was taking deep breaths as if to calm herself. "But, they did say maybe she was out hiking last night and fell off the cliff into the river. They're searching all around right now to figure out what happened—the deputies, I mean. Sheriff Gonzales asked me for permission to be on camp property, but I don't think he had to. That was just courtesy on his part."

"He seemed like a nice guy," Tony said.

"I hope, since we've got so many people here."

This was going to affect the retreat and Green Clover, too. I touched her arm. "Oh, Cordy, I'm sorry."

"Thanks. I think I'll feel real bad about May later on, but right now, I'm just, I don't know. Something."

"Do you think people will leave?" Tony asked.

"Most of them can't. They flew in, and the airlines won't let them change tickets like that—not without paying an arm and a leg. I suppose most of the women could go to hotels, but that's going to be expensive, what with meals and all." She took a breath. "And we've got more arriving today. It's too late to tell them to stay home—those damn airlines would just keep their money."

But this wasn't really about airlines, this was about Green Clover. And Cordy, and May. Then I remembered that it might also be about all of us. Beth, Shannan, and Ron. And me.

"I'm going for coffee," Tony said. "Maybe my brain will kick in. Cordy, if you hear any more, let me know. Oh, and if it's any consolation, I won't be leaving. I'll do my demonstrations as usual."

"Thanks, Tony," she said, giving him a quick pat on the arm. "And don't say anything to anyone just yet. Everyone can at least have a good breakfast."

"No problem." He turned and went carefully down the path to the dining hall. His walk was missing its usual bounce.

I found my breath and my manners at the same time. "Is there anything I can I do?" I asked. "You know I'll support you however I can."

"Don't leave, either, okay? Stay here, and somehow we'll keep the retreat going." Cordy bit her lip. "And, Kitz, would you make the announcement at breakfast? Nothing flowery, but something about May for those who didn't know her. Oh, and tell everyone how sorry I am that May got hurt . . ."

It was hard for her to admit the truth, that May Feather wasn't just hurt, but dead. I was having difficulty accepting it myself.

I thought of May's surprised look in the glare of my headlights. Would that come out? What if May had gotten a whiplash, and it made her dizzy? Maybe it threw her balance off so when she got back to camp and went for a walk . . .

"Yes," I said, talking to squash my thoughts. "I'll say something. Don't you have a bio on May? There was something in the newsletter you sent out. I could use some of that, or anything else you have. And I'll tell everyone that the retreat is going on. Is that what you had in mind?"

"Something like that; I just don't know what else to do."

"You're doing fine," I assured her. The Camden portion of my brain, the part that had faced the world in good times and in bad, was kicking in, clearing my thinking. "I have an idea," I said. "What if we have a memorial campfire this evening—our own sort of service? It would be a way to honor May." I didn't say it, but it might help make Saturday and Sunday more normal, too.

Cordy saw that and nodded. "That's perfect. We'll do the campfire at eight."

"I don't give eulogies; can you get a minister for tonight?"

"I'm sure I can. That retired minister from the Unity Church was going to do Sunday morning for us. I think she'd come down."

Green Clover has a small outdoor chapel where nondenominational services are held every Sunday during the camping season. As a kid, I always griped about having to get up early for chapel on Sunday, but the services were nice, and sometimes my parents came. I was glad the tradition continued.

"I'm going to be very brief this morning," I said. I'd agreed to do this because of sorrow for May, and some of my own guilt, but it still left me wondering what I was going to say. "I'd better go make some notes. Oh, and if there are questions, I'd like you to handle those."

She nodded. "Damn, I just feel so bad that this happened."

"I know you do." I turned to go but had another thought. "Cordy," I said, stopping her. "People could find out about this before I make the announcement. They might ask about May. And her assistant already knows. Wasn't she staying in May's trailer? Where is she now?"

"Jennifer? I don't know, but I'd better go find her." She shook her head. "May and I were never close, but she was a nice person and she didn't deserve to die so young. She was talented, too."

"A very talented designer," I agreed.

That's when I remembered Tivolini and the proposed contract. "The Tivolini buyer," I said. "Is she here? Will she stay?"

"Yes, she'll stay. Look, I'll get to Jennifer and ask her not to say anything just yet." She still looked overwhelmed. "Thanks, Kitzi. I knew you'd help."

"You're welcome." I was thinking about May, and what to tell people about her. I remembered her hands, stringing the beads with such fluid beauty as she worked. That's what I wanted to focus on.

Cordy was still talking to me.

". . . I hate to tell you . . ." She closed her eyes, as if sorting through her thoughts.

"I'm sorry," I said. "What were you saying?"

"Never mind. It can wait."

"Are you sure?"

"It wasn't important. I'll see you in a few."

"Okay." I had moved on to think about Shannan and how this was going to affect her. Would she feel guilt? Or relief?

I had to break the news to her before breakfast so she'd be prepared; I couldn't let this come at her out of the blue—

And then I realized—she could already be talking about May to her mother.

In her innocence, she could be talking about May to anyone.

Seven

swerved up onto the main path and crashed into another person. The poor man almost had to pick himself out of a tree I'd hit him so hard.

"I'm so sorry. It was my fault," I said. He was in his early fifties with thinning brown hair. I helped him brush off his jacket. "Are you okay? I didn't realize I was such a powerhouse."

"You know the math problem about two trains coming toward each other at sixty miles an hour? I think that was us." He stood up straight, and I realized that we were about the same height. "I'm fine," he said. "How about you?"

"I'm okay. I was just in such a hurry—if you're sure you're all right, I'd better get going." I turned, but at a more seemly pace.

"Uh, ma'am. If you have a minute, I sure could use some help."

I looked at him more carefully. He wasn't a camper, and he wasn't someone from Dripping Springs or Wimberley. His shirt and pants were khaki colored and his work boots had seen a lot of use. The jacket I'd brushed leaves off of was olive green and only partially zipped. The shine of metal peeked out from the left side, and that could only be a badge. I was talking to someone official, probably one of the officers investigating May's death.

"Sure," I said. "It's just, you know, if I could . . . I mean, I don't—"

"That'd be just fine." He added a smile to the ambiguous phrase, but he didn't move. "You heard about the misfortune down at the river?"

We'd gone from mishaps to misfortunes.

"Yes. I was just going to—" I stopped and straightened. "Here's the thing: Cordelia, the owner of the camp, asked me to make an announcement at breakfast about May Feather; I was on my way to write something up. I sure don't want to put my foot in my mouth."

He nodded. "Yes, ma'am."

So did that mean I could go or I should stay?

I just couldn't be as obtuse as he was. "I don't have a whole lot of time."

"I guess breakfast isn't too far off?"

I looked at my watch. "About twenty minutes, but people will be gathering for coffee."

"Did you know May Feather well? You must have if you're going to make the announcement." He was drifting toward me so that we were face to face on the path. "Old friends?"

I had to talk to this man, and I figured it would be best to do it in his own language. Good ol' boy. Some say it's the language of Texas politics, and you have to speak it if you want to be understood. I'm not nearly as good at it as our esteemed former governor, Ann Richards, but I can hold my own.

"I wouldn't say May and I were old friends," I said adding a little more Texas accent. "I've known her for . . ." When I realized how long I'd known her, it almost jolted me out of my drawl. "I met her about ten years ago, but I don't remember where. I saw her mostly at bead functions, and I'm not a regular attendee. I just show up a couple of times a year. There are lots of others who are more involved—" Like Beth, and if I didn't keep my mouth shut, I was going to get her in trouble.

"And what would those 'bead functions' be?" he asked.

"Bead Society meetings. Bead Shows. Exhibits."

"Did you two socialize outside of those events?"

"No, we never did."

He nodded. "I see. I seem to be holding you up. I didn't get your name."

"Katharine Camden. Kitzi Camden."

One of his eyebrows went up, and I waited. Either he had loved my politics, my father, and my grandfather or he hadn't, and he might even want to tell me about it.

"I'm Sheriff Ben Gonzales," he said, holding out his hand. We shook and he added, "I can see now why you were picked to say a few words." His hand was rough from weather and use. "I just have one more question for you, Ms. Camden." For the first time, I noticed the rumpled notebook sticking out of his pocket. "You know anyone who was a good friend of May Feather?"

I took a breath, exhaled, and counted to three before I spoke. That's what I train people to do when they're thrown by a question from the media, but it was the first time I'd ever used it with a cop, since normally I'm on their side. "No, I'm afraid I don't know who her close friends were." What about enemies? Competitors? Lovers? Like Ron Fairfield? The sheriff didn't ask, and I didn't offer. "I assume May's assistant, Jennifer . . . uh, Jennifer . . ."

"Webster," he said.

"Thank you—I just went blank. Silver moment," I said. "Wasn't she close to May?"

"Yes, ma'am. Anyone else you can think of?"

He was watching me carefully.

"May used to be married, but she divorced years ago. She didn't have children. I don't know of anyone else." *Liar, liar, pants on fire.* "I'm sorry I can't help you—we just weren't, well, we didn't talk much at all, and when we did it was about beadwork."

He nodded politely. "Thank you for your time. I'm just trying to find out who she was with last night after her demonstration." He looked inquisitively at me, and even though I could envision May's face in the glare of my lights, I kept my mouth clamped shut. My silence felt like a lie.

"Well, then, Ms. Camden," he said, "I'll look forward to hearing what you have to say at breakfast."

He moved a lot quicker now, and I was looking at his back in the olive jacket before I realized that he had information I needed. "Wait, Sheriff. Do you have just a minute more?"

He turned. "Yes, ma'am?"

"Uh, could you tell me a few things? Everyone will want to know how May died. And when. Can I get that from you?"

"I wish you could, but I don't know how she died just yet. The medical team will make that judgment. As for the time of death, they're going to have to tell me that, too."

He wasn't being any more helpful than I had been, which I suppose was all right, since turnabout is fair play. "Do you know if she drowned, or if she was killed by the fall?"

"No, ma'am," he shook his head sadly. "I just can't say."

"But she was found this morning? At what time?"

"Around six-thirty." He looked at his watch and said, "I'm sorry I can't be of more help. I'd best be off. Oh, and Ms. Camden, if you ever need a job, you'd make a fine reporter."

"A job?" He assumed that I was useless, just like some people assume all Camdens are useless unless we're in political office. There are those who think the time we spend in office is a big waste, too. Mostly our political opponents.

However, I do work. I train people how to speak in public. Besides straightforward presenting, I share with them a whole bag of tricks that can be used on reporters and the brand of politician who thinks he and his ideas are better than everybody else's.

The temptation was to use a few on a sheriff.

I didn't. I showed him—I gave him what I teach, which

is straightforward communication. "I have a job," I said, the drawl disappearing. In its place my diction was crisp and my words concise. I was standing up taller, too. "I'm a corporate trainer. I also coach people in public speaking and working with the media."

"Well, isn't that something. I'll bet you're real good, too. Did you teach the president how to speak? He sure has gotten better recently."

"No," I said. "I've worked with the former Texas attorney general. Isn't he the highest-ranking law enforcement officer in the state?"

Sheriff Gonzales started to smile. I should have remembered that to officers in the field, the attorney general is nothing more than a politician. So much for my attempt at one-upmanship. "Yes, ma'am, he certainly is," the sheriff said. "You've done a real fine job with him—I've heard him speak a time or two, and he's quite articulate."

"Thank you."

"Well, I'll let you get to your speech writing."

I turned and went.

Here it was only Friday and I was wishing that the retreat were over. It was hard to be enthused when May was dead.

On an entirely separate track, I was not excited about running into Jeb. And what would happen if the sheriff found out I'd lied to him. Or if Ron found out I'd spied on him and rammed his car.

I had certainly made the most of my short time at Green Clover. Whatever else went on this weekend, I could only hope that no one, absolutely no one, ever found out about May's affair with Ron.

Unfortunately, that secret was in the hands of a seventeen year old, who could be spilling it at that very moment. That got me moving, and I was almost at the cabin when I spotted Beth coming out the door.

"You must have really crashed last night," she said. "Are you all right?" She looked tired, and her hair wasn't improving.

"Sure. Fine. Why wouldn't I be?"

"When we went to bed, you were out cold."

"Must be the fresh air or the sleep of the just," I said. "Where's Shannan?"

"Sleeping." She shook her head. "My dear daughter was hanging out with Jennifer last night and for some reason, don't ask me why, she got into our liquor supply. You'll find that you're short a lot of beer and some rum."

Another sin tacked onto my account. But had she said anything? "That's a disgusting combination. And the rum wasn't mine."

"It's no one's now, because Shannan drank it. I found her sitting on the rock a little after midnight. She could barely walk."

"Damn." Swearing was added to my growing list of sins. "I'm sorry. Is she all right? Did she say why she drank so much?"

The worried expression I had seen way too often lately on Beth's face was back. "No, but you know how she's been. There's no point in trying to talk to her now. She's dead to the world."

I shuddered at the choice of words. "Okay."

"I'm going for coffee. You want to come along?"

"Actually, I have something to do. And, Beth, I have some bad news," I said. "Brace yourself."

"There's more? Green Clover is supposed to be our happy place."

"This isn't happy. I just talked to Cordy and Tony. This morning, early . . ." I couldn't find the words.

"Yes?"

"This morning, May was found in the river downstream by some campers. She's dead."

Beth turned a sickly shade. "How? How did she die?"

"Nobody knows. I met the sheriff just now, and he says the medical examiner will have to tell them. She could have drowned, or, I guess, died from the fall."

At this, Beth flushed a bright pink.

"Are you okay?" I asked.

"Fine. Personal summer." She put her hand to her throat, maybe to cool her neck. Then she shook her head. "I just, I just . . . I'm speechless."

I thought I saw worry in her pale eyes. And then I realized the obvious—if Shannan had noticed her father's prolonged absences, Beth must have, too. The question was, did she know Ron was having an affair? And did she know it was with May? So, was this news a relief, or additional concern to Beth? And what was she thinking now?

We stood there, looking at each other, neither of us willing to say what was on our minds. What I really wanted to do was hug her and offer that old line about how everything was going to be fine, but that would be admitting things were wrong.

"I have to write up an announcement," I finally said. "You know, to tell everyone."

"Oh, sure. That's a good idea." She was pale again. "I was going to the dining hall . . ."

"I'll meet up with you there. Save me a place. Maybe near the door."

She turned to carefully climb down the trail. I didn't even hurry this time. Shannan had gotten drunk and, in part, it was my fault because I had ducked my worries through sleep.

And May Feather was dead. I kept coming back to that like it was brand new—seeing her surprised look, seeing her beautiful hands moving the beads.

The other thing that kept weaving through my mind was all the convoluted connections people had with her. Shannan, who might be glad May was dead, and Beth who might be if she knew of the affair. And how was May's assistant, Jennifer, taking all this?

Only thing I could do was take the next right step, and I was pretty sure what that was.

I slipped inside the Lazy L where it was dim and cool. It took me a minute to see that Shannan was alone on the sleeping porch, still curled in a defensive posture, with only her streaky brown hair poking out of the covers. She looked like Beth in her teen years, pretty, a little plump, and so vulnerable beneath that quirky humor, I was sometimes afraid she'd break.

And now things were going to get worse for Shannan.

"Shannan. Shannan, honey." I pulled back the covers enough to reveal her face, then stroked her T-shirt covered shoulder.

"What?" She turned her head so I got a whiff of breath that smelled like vomit. "Tante Kitzi?" It was a soft, sad, little voice.

"I need you to wake up," I said. "Something happened while you were asleep."

Her eyes widened, and she raised her head. "Oh. That hurts."

"I'm sorry, but I understand you deserve it. Are you awake?"

This time she rolled over completely. "Yes. Why?"

"Honey, I have some news, and it might be a shocker. Are you ready?"

"Uh-huh." She still looked half-asleep.

"Okay, here goes—May Feather died last night. She either fell off a cliff or went into the water some other way, but she's dead."

Shannan blinked and shook her head, fighting off my words. "Where?"

"Downriver."

Shannan's face turned paler, and her red-rimmed eyes widened. "Could it be a mistake? Is there any way—"

"None," I said. "There's a sheriff here, and he's talking to people, trying to learn who was close to May. He asked me about the last time I saw her."

"Oh, no!" She jerked upright, but kept her voice down. "Did you tell him what we did last night? Hitting my dad's car?"

"No. And that has to stay a secret between us."

If anyone found out, then the affair would be public knowledge. Very public. I didn't care what that did to Ron, but I cared a lot about Beth and Shannan.

Besides that, my little adventure would be spread around fast.

The Camdens are hardly the Kennedys, but in Texas we're always good for news. A Camden using a car as a battering ram would interest a lot of reporters. *Texas Monthly* and the *Austin American-Statesman* would be all over it. Even the wire services might pick it up. My mother would have a stroke, and my cousin Houston Webber would use it to cause grief for my entire family. He doesn't much like me as it is, since I have the house and changed my last name back to Camden after the divorce. He'd use this as reason to start another legal fight for the house.

I could just imagine him claiming that I wasn't capable of caring for the Camden Manse, which he considers some kind of national trust. He has no clue how many doors don't close properly, and how much paint has to be replaced yearly, and how the tiles chip or fall off the walls, and how we've dealt with mold and a sinking foundation just because the place is old.

Even as the thoughts of my family went through my mind, I knew they were nothing compared to how awful this could be for Beth and Shannan.

"Tante Kitzi, I'm so sorry," Shannan said. "It was all my fault. And if someone finds out . . ."

"I think we need some kind of story," I said, pretending it didn't bother me to tell her to lie. Problem was, I couldn't see any other way. "I'll bet somebody saw us leave the camp or looked for us while we were gone. We have to tell the truth about that." She nodded agreement with me. "We can say that you talked to your father on the phone, and he sounded funny, so we went to find him—"

"No. We can't mention my dad at all," she said. "If we do, then the police might want to talk to him, and they could find out about May and him."

As a five-year-old Shannan used to beat me at chess. She has the kind of mind that sees opportunities and repercussions with every move. If I ever go back into politics, I'm bringing her on staff.

"You're right," I agreed. "But at some point, we'll have to explain why we left camp and where we went. Maybe if we have an answer, no one will ask." I thought about the problem, but it was Shannan who came up with something.

She said, "My birthday is coming up, and I would like some beading tools. Needle-nose pliers, some wire cutters, maybe some copper wire; the kind of things we might find at a hardware store. Weldon and Company was the closest one to camp that was open."

"We didn't buy anything."

"No," she agreed. "But that's like you. You wanted to shop and see what they had, just to make me happy, but you'd buy from one of the vendors here. You always do that."

I was surprised that she'd noticed. My grandfather is the one who taught me that you only have one vote on the ballot, but you also vote with every penny you spend. If you shop a national chain, you're saying *no* to a local merchant. If you spend your money on candy, then someone will make more of it.

Shannan was right that I wouldn't take a sale away from the women who came all the way to camp to sell us supplies.

I nodded. "We went to look at things for your birthday. We didn't see your father. Or May."

"That's right. And I don't think they even knew each other."

"They've met," I said. I remembered a night when we'd all had dinner together after an exhibit at the Austin Club. "But just barely."

"Oh. Okay."

I slid my arm around her shoulder. She was shaking, and it couldn't be from the temperature. "Honey, don't worry, okay? You probably won't have to talk to anyone."

I hated that I was putting Shannan in such a bad position.

"That's not a problem," she said.

And suddenly I saw scenarios that Shannan had recognized all along. The possibility that her father not only picked May up here, but that he had come back with her and been inside the camp. That perhaps he was with May right before she went into the river. And what if, God forbid, he had something to do with May's death?

In which case, Shannan had a great deal more to worry about than a lie or two.

Eight

" . . . some consolation in knowing that her designs will be enjoyed by generations to come."

Someone once told me that we teach what we need to learn; maybe that's why I'm still training people to speak—because I don't have it mastered completely yet. No matter how many techniques I use, I sometimes feel like I miss the magic mark, just a little. I felt especially inadequate as I faced the women of Green Clover. My words needed to give information, and at the same time heal the hurt that information caused.

Judging by the faces staring back at me, I wasn't succeeding. Maybe the words weren't in me, but more likely it was going to take time for people to be okay with what had happened. Some people had moist eyes, others were white with shock.

Up to that point, breakfast had been near normal, but now the joy of Green Clover had evaporated into the air. I noticed a woman at a nearby table wiping a tear off her cheek. I'd heard at a recent meeting that she was just finishing radiation treatment for breast cancer, so being at camp was, for her, like a declaration of life. At least until she got the final test results. Now, I had told her about another tragedy.

Beth and Cordy, who were sitting near the back door,

looked pale. Like everyone else, Cordy used the Craft Retreats to renew her spirits; her dad had passed on just a few
months back, and she was still grieving. One more grief.

I've always heard the term "heavy heart." Lyndon Johnson said it a lot during the Vietnam War, and now I felt it
clear through my body. I hadn't been a great friend of May,
and I had hated that she'd been having an affair with Beth's
husband, but none of those things were punishable by
death. May was still one of our community, a piece of us
that made the whole. Whatever her flaws, we all had them,
and she shouldn't have died.

Fighting the heaviness inside me, I lifted my chin and
went on, "May will be missed by all of us—those who
knew and loved her as a friend, and by those of us who
learned so much from her as a teacher. Naturally, the
demonstration she had scheduled for this afternoon will
be canceled—"

"No, that's wrong." Jennifer, May's assistant jumped
up. Her eyes were wide and a little too bright, her lips so
pale they were almost white. Her red nail polish was
chipped, as if she'd been peeling it off. She looked around
at the women, then at me and seemed to shrivel inside her
skin. "I'm sorry, I didn't mean to interrupt, it's just that you
all know how proud May was of the beautiful work she
did." Nods from the women encouraged Jennifer, and she
stood a little straighter. "I'd like to do the demonstration for
her. As a tribute to May, so people carry on the designs."
She faltered, her eyes on me. "If you don't mind . . ." the
young voice trailed off. She looked so unhappy.

I didn't doubt that May was hard on Jennifer at times,
but still they knew each other well, and I was betting this
was the first time Jennifer had been faced with a death so
close to home. It used to be that we learned about the cy-
cle of life and death by watching our grandparents age
and pass away, but grandparents are young nowadays. I'm
a grandparent, and I'm certainly not ready to die. That

first death we experience is always a shock, and I guessed that Jennifer wouldn't get over May's death easily.

I glanced at Cordy in the back of the room, and she was nodding vigorously.

"Of course, you should do the demonstration, Jennifer," I said. "The demonstration will be held as planned, and this evening at eight, we'll have a special campfire to honor May Feather. Everyone is invited to attend."

I took a breath before I finished. "And I'm sorry I had to give you all this terrible news. Cordy and the staff of Green Clover offer their condolences as well."

Not a cup clattered, and not a fork touched a plate. I stepped from the center of the room. I couldn't look at the sad faces as I walked between the tables, then out the door, careful to close the screen quietly.

Cordy was right behind me when I reached the path. "Thanks, Kitzi. I just couldn't have done it myself, and you said it just right. I appreciate it," she said.

"You're welcome." I felt a hundred years older and fifty pounds heavier than I had yesterday at this time. Then I'd been buoyant as I got ready for camp.

I guess I want every meal at Green Clover to end with songs and awards instead of the slumped shoulders I'd seen this morning. The news I'd delivered made everyone look old and worn. I tried to console myself with the fact that at least the retreat would continue and maybe there would be some time to heal.

"What did you think of Jennifer volunteering to do May's demo?" Cordy asked. "I feel so sorry for that kid. I hope I did the right thing by letting her go ahead with it."

Beth joined us in time to hear Cordy's remark. Together we started up the path, our steps deliberate and slow.

"Maybe it will be good therapy for Jennifer," Beth said. I nodded agreement.

Cordy said, "I just hope she does okay. Not that anyone else cares, but Jennifer needs a win."

She sure looked like she needed one. I nodded, saying, "I hope Jennifer doesn't judge herself by May's standards; May's technique always seemed flawless in the front of the room."

"It did, didn't it?" Cordy said. "I also think a lot of her popularity came from her way of weaving in legend and stories while she was beading. And she never made a mistake or missed a step."

There was a moment of silence before Beth said, "May's designs were very good, too."

Beth didn't like to talk about other people's designs, but she was honest to a fault.

I come not to praise Caesar, but to bury him.

Did Beth know she and May were in competition for the attentions of her husband, as well as the Tivolini contract?

I couldn't shake the pale image of May's face in my headlights. And Ron's, too.

I stopped abruptly.

"What's up?" Cordy asked. She and Beth were both staring at me.

"Oh, I just, I just keep thinking . . ." my words trailed off. "I just want to do some thinking. I need to get away for a few minutes. Would you excuse me? I'll be back in a little bit."

They nodded in silence, respecting my need for solitude. Except I wasn't going to be alone. Someone had to tell Ron that May was dead, and I seemed to be the one to do it. If not, that chore might fall to Beth, and I couldn't let that happen.

There was road construction on the highway, so the drive to Beth's took me almost thirty minutes. I put the extra time to good use, trying to convince myself that this was some noble effort on my part. A gesture that people like Nelson Mandela or Mother Teresa might make.

It's like trying to convince yourself that eating a pound

of See's candy won't make you gain weight, and I can't lie to myself like that for very long.

The flaw in the self-talk was that I was going to tell Ron for my own reasons and it wasn't about Ron at all. I was protecting Beth. Austin is too large for May's death to be on a newscast, and Ron wasn't likely to get a paper from the little communities near the camp that would cover the story. Which meant Beth might be the one to break the news to him, and there was no telling how he'd react. I couldn't imagine him in tears, but there was no reason to chance it.

If I was really honest, I was also protecting myself. If Ron knew who caught him last night, then we needed to get that handled now, before it became an issue with repercussions that neither of us wanted. It had to be talked over in private.

My third reason was the least noble of all. I wanted to see his face when he heard about May. It wasn't quite as mean-spirited as it sounded. Mostly I hoped seeing him would help me understand their relationship.

Reasons aside, when I pulled up in their driveway, I was half-hoping he wasn't home.

I didn't even get out of the car at first. I just sat there, looking at Beth's house, realizing that I wasn't sure I liked it. It was a two-story, dark redbrick home with a neat circular drive, one tree, and a few straight-arrow boxwood hedges. Nothing was allowed to shed or sprawl, and nothing much flowered, either. I guess flowers could make a mess.

The place was too antiseptic and stuffy to be Beth's house. When we were in college, we'd talked about where we'd like to live, and Beth had wanted a snow-covered A-frame, or a geodesic dome, or an overgrown English cottage with vines and flowers. This was Ron's idea of a house—a little stately, exceptionally tidy, and boring as hell. It didn't have the curb appeal of a fire hydrant.

A knock on my window startled me.

"Are you all right in there?" It was Mrs. Martin, Beth's

next-door neighbor—the one who saw all and knew all. Ron particularly disliked her because sometimes in the evenings, she and her male friend, Ernie, sat in her driveway on plastic lawn chairs watching the world go by. I don't think Ron objected to the watching so much as he did to the cheap chairs.

"Ms. Martin, how are you?" I said, cracking the door so she'd move and I could get out of the car.

"I'm fine, but I'm not the one sitting in a hot car," she said, swinging the door open with vigor.

"Don't mind me, I was just thinking about something," I said and stepped out. "You know how that happens sometimes."

"Can't say as I do, but then I'm pretty much on top of things, unlike some people I know." I had no idea which people she was referring to, but I didn't ask, because she went right on. "What are you doing here? Beth is away for the weekend. She's at some bead thing at a kid's camp outside of town. Green Clover, that's it. Won't be back 'til Sunday."

It appeared Ms. Martin's reputation for knowing all and seeing all was well earned. "As a matter of fact, I'm staying at the camp with her."

"So, what are you doing here? Only Ron is home."

She looked at me suspiciously, as if I might be having a tryst with Ron—I shuddered to even consider it.

"Well, I'm glad he's home," I said. "Beth's doing a demonstration today, and she forgot some beads that I need to pick up." I looked at my watch. "Oh, and I need to hurry if I'm going to get back on time. Nice seeing you."

"And you." She went back to her house, while I hurried up the brick steps to the front door and rang the bell. God was going to punish me for all my lies.

There were long narrow windows on either side of the door, and through the glass I heard Sinatra yowl loudly. Then the door opened and Ron Fairfield was in front of me.

He looked tired, but other than that he seemed the same as always.

A little under six feet, he had fine, light brown hair and a thin, slightly pear-shaped body. He did have a nice smile with straight white teeth. Even counting those, I didn't get what May saw in him. I didn't get what anyone saw in him, but then men who think they know it all have never been my type.

"Kitzi. Hello."

"Ron, good morning," I said in response. At least we knew each other's names.

He stared at me for several seconds before he said, "Is everything all right at camp?"

I nodded automatically. "Oh, sure. Fine."

"That's good. Come in. Come in."

On the floor was a cage and inside was Sinatra looking lost. He meowed hopefully at me.

"Wait a minute, Ron," I said, stopping a few feet inside the door. "Everything isn't okay. I have some bad news, and I thought someone should tell you in person."

His expression flashed to concern. "Is Shannan—"

"She's fine," I said quickly. "Sorry, I didn't mean to worry you. Beth's okay, too," I added. "I don't know if you need to sit down or what. This could be upsetting."

"Upsetting?" His concern switched to amusement. "Certainly we can sit down if you'd be more comfortable."

He gave a sweeping gesture in the direction of the living room, and his expression made it pretty clear that he was humoring me.

I stood my ground. "Never mind. This will do." He turned back around to face me, then I said, "I'm sorry to tell you this but it's about May Feather."

"May?" He looked wary as hell.

"Yes. I thought someone should let you know. She—" I couldn't do it, not like that. Not even to Ron.

"Whatever you have to say," he snapped, "just say it."

I nodded. "All right. Ron, I'm sorry, but this morning May was found in the river by some campers. She's dead."

At first the anger stayed on his face, like he'd forgotten it was there. Then he swallowed and his expression went completely blank. No words came from him and he didn't move.

I felt bad about spouting off like that. No matter what he'd done, he was a human being, and I'd just hurt him. "I'm sorry," I said. "Are you okay? I'm sure this isn't easy to hear."

He began to breathe carefully, like he was relearning the technique and might get it wrong. "No, no, that's fine." He looked at the floor, then back up to me. "I'm sorry to hear it."

He took his time before he spoke again. His face was back under control, but his voice was tighter than usual. "This must be hard on all of you."

"It is."

"How is Shannan?"

"She's just fine." I wanted to say more about her, but what? I didn't want to tell him she'd gotten drunk, because to Ron that was a sin requiring punishment. "She's made a new friend at camp," I said. Then I remembered that Jennifer was May's assistant, so there wasn't much more to add.

"Good. That's good," he said, but he didn't look like he was really listening. "And how is Beth taking, uh, it?"

"Just fine," I said. "We're having a memorial campfire for May tonight."

He nodded his head in a small gesture of understanding. "I'm sure people will like that."

I waited, but he didn't add anything. He didn't even ask why I'd driven to town to deliver the news, and since I couldn't bring it up, it felt like there was something big and smelly between us. It didn't leave us anything to say.

Ron shifted leg to leg, looking out the window.

"I'd better go," I said, turning and hitting the wire cage

with my leg. For something to fill the silence I asked, "Why is Sinatra in there? Has he been bad again?"

"What?" Ron's gaze returned to the room, then down to the cage. "Oh, Sinatra. He's going to the animal shelter. He isn't suited for our house." Sinatra yowled and Ron frowned.

"The shelter?" I said. "You can't just take him like that! He might be put to—"

"He can't stay here." Ron was firm and angry. It was misplaced anger, I was sure, but that didn't matter a whit to me, and it certainly wouldn't matter to Sinatra. Ron added, "I can't have him here."

"Fine, but he's *my* cat. Beth gave him to me yesterday, and I was going to pick him up when camp was over."

Ron nudged the cage with his toe. "He needs to go now. He's too much to deal with. Especially with . . . everything."

I could understand that managing Sinatra on top of May's death might be a bit much, but Ron had decided to get rid of Sinatra before he knew about May. What kind of a person takes a family pet to the pound without even consulting his wife and daughter?

I looked closer at Ron, but there was nothing to see except a plain old face, and not one that I found particularly attractive. His expression was perfectly blank.

I'd forgotten that Ron was a lawyer and a good one who made a lot of money with his high-profile real estate cases. If this control was something he'd learned in law school, then he'd been trained well. Too bad it made him even less appealing.

"Fine," I said. "I'll take Sinatra with me now." I snatched up the heavy cage and almost fell over with the weight.

"If that's what you want," he said as I struggled.

The wood-and-wire box was huge, but after some adjustment I was able to open the door. Since Ron hadn't offered to help, I had to wrangle the cage outside and across to the driveway by myself while it slammed against my hip

the whole way. I didn't say good-bye, and neither did Ron.
I did hear him close the door behind me.

"Mo-Ron," I muttered.

When I rescued Sinatra, I wasn't thinking ahead. I hadn't
thought about having to take him back to camp. My house
was another fifteen minutes away in the wrong direction,
and I had a demonstration to give that morning. It was my
first demonstration, and I didn't want to be late for it; under
the circumstances that would be very hard on Cordy. Another thing, I wasn't willing to part with Sinatra just now.
He'd been too close to being given away, or worse, and I
wanted him where I could keep an eye on him.

He must have felt the same way, because as soon as we
were in the car and I opened the cage door, he climbed up
on my shoulder and started purring. It made me think of
the song about having a bluebird on your shoulder.

"Are you my bluebird?" I asked him. "Because I could
really use a bluebird, what with everything else that's
happening."

He purred even louder, so I reached up to pet his tiny
body. "You know," I said as we started off, "you could be
just what everyone needs at Green Clover." He jumped
from my shoulder to my lap, where I could pet him more
conveniently. "See what I mean? The perfect little sweetheart. You just need to stay this way."

I was almost to the highway when he stood up and
poked his head through the steering wheel. "Not a smart
move," I said. "Get out of there."

He looked at me, then around the front seat and down to
the floorboard. He was poised on the edge of the seat. "No,
you don't!" But he did. He jumped down to the floor and
went right under the brake pedal.

I nearly had a wreck hauling him out, but I managed it.
Then I pulled off to the side of the road, much to the annoyance of an eighteen-wheeler behind me.

To Sinatra I said, "You may *not* get on the floorboard."
He purred. "You've just been grounded. Or you can call it a
time-out. Whatever you call it, you're back in the cage." I
leaned over the seat and popped him inside which caused a
few pitiful yowls. "Vent all you want, but you're staying in
there while I'm driving."

I went a few more blocks to a strip mall with a pet store,
and sucker that I am, I took Sinatra out and carried him
around while I got all of the things he'd need at camp.
Three people offered to take him off my hands because
he's so darn cute. Fine for them to say, but they didn't
know that Trouble really was his middle name.

That I could deal with. Unfortunately, *my* middle name
was going to be mud if I had to face Beth before I could
figure out a good explanation for why I had him.

Nine

"Run, run
little deer, now run.
The hunter
has a gun.
He's a mean old man
from a wicked old clan.
So run
little deer,
now run."

Camp Green Clover song

We arrived at the Lazy L battered but unbloodied. I like to think that meant I had won, but the truth is, Sinatra had spent the rest of the ride on his first-class perch on my shoulder. I did make him wear a collar and a leash, which I had kept clamped in my hand.

"What are you doing with Sinatra?" Beth asked as I came in carrying the cat and his newly purchased belongings. I'd been hoping she wouldn't notice, which just shows my state of mind.

Beth was alone on the sleeping porch, sitting in an old straight-back chair with a TV tray in front of her. On it were beading materials and a flat bracelet of deep olive greens and blacks, which was taking shape. It was almost two inches wide, and Beth had added a few bright turquoise beads that made the design pop.

"And do me a favor," she added. "Please don't let him loose just yet." On the tray was an old towel so the beads wouldn't scatter, but that wasn't going to help a whit if Sinatra decided to leap up there.

I placed him on my bed along with all of his new accoutrements.

"I'll control him," I promised, holding the end of the leash.

"Kitzi, you are a woman of amazing talents, but I seriously doubt that even you can do that. He is an infant and a wild animal, neither of which can be controlled."

"Not such a wild guy—besides he's also adorable."

"No argument from me." She was working away, only glancing up periodically. "But you haven't said why you went to get him."

"Oh, you know," I said, depositing his new litter box in the corner and filling it with a layer of gravel. I turned my attention to the things that went in the cage. Sinatra loved the crinkling of the sack and crawled into it as soon as there was room.

I took my bath towel, folded it half a dozen times, and laid it down in the bottom of the cage; it covered about two-thirds of the space and was almost three inches thick. Talk about a soft, fluffy bed; Sinatra was going to love it. And I was going to have to dry off with a hand towel after my showers, but Sinatra was worth it.

Beth had dropped all conversation for the moment, and I decided I'd made it through without any third degree from her. That was a good thing. Next I filled Sinatra's food and water bowls and put them in the other part of the cage. It was going to be a happy little home—

"Ron was at the house?" she asked.

I'd been a tad premature in my relief. "Yes," I said. "I

didn't break in, if that's what you're concerned about." Actually, I have a key, but I hadn't remembered it until that minute.

"Well, then I don't have to worry about the silver being missing."

I smiled. To an observer this might look like a casual conversation, especially since Beth hardly looked up from her work. I wasn't feeling a bit casual, and I doubted Beth was, either. Her fingers work separately from her mind, and beading is how she gets her thinking done. She was thinking hard.

When all my preparations were complete I climbed onto the bunk beside Sinatra. He immediately moved close to me, his blue eyes watchful as I stroked his fragile body with its soft fur. I adored the little guy. "I hope Cordy doesn't get upset," I said, "but I wanted some comfort. You know."

"No, actually, I don't." That woman knows me way too well. "Why didn't you tell me you were going to go get him?" she went on.

"Why I went for Sinatra?"

"I hate when you do that."

"Answer a question with a question?"

"Not funny."

"Sorry," I said. "Actually, it's simple. I was walking around the camp feeling lonely, and I thought of Sinatra." I leaned forward so I finally met her gaze. "And you know me. I just got in the Rover and left."

I could see on her face that she knew there was more to the story, but she let it drop. Why? Because she was aware of Ron and May's affair?

"What was Ron doing?" She asked.

"I don't know what he was doing."

I didn't want to tell Beth what a jerk her husband was. Of course, she lived with him, so she must have known.

"Okay," she said, glancing at me again. "Then why did you look steamed when I asked about him?"

"Oh. That."

"Yes, that."

"If you must know, Ron did upset me. When I got to your house, he had Sinatra in a cage and he was going to take him to the animal shelter. I know—you're going to say that wasn't all Ron's fault, since we didn't tell him you'd given Sinatra to me—"

"No, I wasn't going to say that."

"Well, it is in his favor, but still he was getting rid of Sinatra without telling anyone." I rolled over on my back so I wasn't looking directly at her. "And that's why Mr. Sinatra is at Green Clover."

"I wondered where you'd gone."

"What did I miss?" I asked, snuggling with the kitten.

"Right now there's a demonstration on making lamp-work beads, but I decided not to attend. If I did, I'd have to start making my own beads, and you know how addicted I get to things. I'd never get my house clean or a book read."

"You could always hire someone to clean." I sat back up. "Oh, I almost forgot; my demonstration's in a little bit. Don't let me be late." She nodded and I added, "Any more word on May's death?"

"Not that I've heard. Everyone is so upset." Beth let out a sigh and finally focused on me, not her work. "Maybe we should all go home."

"I can't," I said. "I promised Cordy I'd stay for the weekend, and that's a promise I intend to keep."

"But there are mitigating circumstances. Jeb is here, re-member?" When I shrugged, she looked me over. "You can pretend it doesn't matter, but, I'm not sure I'll believe you."

"It's been a long time—"

"I know that, and I also saw your face when Leesa said his name."

"It's a big camp, and there are plenty of other things to hold my attention. My demonstration, for one. The Tivolini buyer. May's memorial tonight." All true, but thoughts of that darned Jeb weren't far from my frontal lobe. I'd have cut and run, but I couldn't think of a way to do it and still maintain any dignity. I'm big on dignity.

"How's it going?" Leesa said by way of a greeting as she came in. She looked like all the cool had gone out of her, and I doubted the effect had been caused by heat and humidity, although there were plenty of both.

"Fine," I said.

She climbed up to her bunk and laid down, her head over the edge so she could watch us. "Nice bracelet," she said to Beth.

"Thanks. It's the technique I showed how to do last night."

Obviously, Leesa hadn't attended the demonstration, either.

The kitten observed from his spot beside me, but as soon as he was over his intimidation I knew he'd be clawing his way to the ceiling. Or up a tree, or worse. I picked him up and cuddled him for a moment, stroking his fuzzy head.

"Do you do any beading?" I asked Leesa.

"Actually—"

The door opened and Jennifer, May's assistant stepped inside. She was holding sheets, blankets, and a pillow and her head moved side to side taking in the sleeping porch. "Hi. Is Shannan here? Isn't this where she sleeps?"

Beth said, "No and yes. Her bunk is above mine, but right now she's on a trail ride with the Eastern contingent. She'll be back in a little bit."

"Oh." Jennifer's shoulders sank. "She said there's an empty bunk in here and if you don't mind, I'd like to move in. I was staying in the trailer, but I don't, like, you know, feel, uh . . ."

"You don't need an invitation; you just pick a spot and move in. Up there," I said, pointing to the bed over mine, "or down there." I indicated the space beneath Leesa. "Your choice; we'd be pleased to have you."

I thought I spotted tears in her eyes as she heaved her bedding onto the mattress above me. "Thanks." She swallowed a couple of times. "I just don't want to stay alone right now, especially in the trailer. You know . . ."

She wasn't much older than Shannan, and here she was facing May's death alone. Poor kid. I stood up and put an arm around her shoulders, leaving Sinatra on my bunk. "Make yourself at home. I can't imagine anything worse than being off by yourself with everything that's happened. Do you need any help making up your bed?"

"Oh, no. I can do it. But thanks."

"We're glad you're here," Beth said, looking up. "Shannan will be glad, too. She could use a friend at camp who's near her own age."

Sinatra didn't like being alone, so he stretched out his long pink tongue in a yawn, looking for a little attention. Then he meowed and jumped up, clinging to the waistband of my sweatpants with his sharp little claws. I let out a yelp.

"Oh, how darling," Jennifer said, reaching out to help me extricate him. "Is he yours?" When we got him loose, she cupped him in her hands and he began to purr. It was all the encouragement she needed. "He's so cute! Is it okay if I hold him?"

"Go ahead," I said. "In fact, I could use someone to pet-sit for the next hour or so—"

"Really? Could I do that?"

"Absolutely. If I leave him alone I'm afraid someone will accidentally let him out. He's so darn little, and he moves so quick."

"And if you tie his leash to a bunk," Beth added, "he'll either hang himself or manage to take the cabin down."

Jennifer was appalled. "How can you say that? He's so precious. I'll stay here with him. I'm going to practice for my demonstration, and he can watch me."

I shook my head. "Not a good idea. He doesn't watch," I said. "He likes to play with beads and get in the way, but he's not a watcher. If you're going to work on something, maybe I'd better put him in his cage—"

"No, don't do that," Jennifer said, pulling him back.

"I need some company. Please let him stay with me." Her big blue eyes reminded me of Sinatra's.

Beth said, "I'll hang out for a while, too. Just in case." In case Jennifer found herself with a kitten from Planet Destruction.

Jennifer placed Sinatra on her bunk and while she tried to make her bed, he attacked the sheets. It was the first time I heard her laugh.

"I haven't met you," Leesa said to Jennifer. I'd almost forgotten Leesa was there, and she made no effort to get down from her perch. "I'm Leesa. With two *es*."

"I'm Jennifer." She turned around, once again holding Sinatra. "I'm May's . . . I was May's assistant. You know . . . May is—"

"I know," Leesa said. "I'm sorry."

"Thanks."

"How are you doing?" she asked Jennifer. "Cordy said you talked to the sheriff. Are you all right?"

Jennifer was holding onto Sinatra like a child might snuggle a stuffed animal, only he didn't look like he was going to put up with it for long. "I'm fine. I just need to be around people and not spend too much time thinking about what happened to May . . ." Sinatra leaped to the bed and she let him go.

"Was that terrible? Your interview with the sheriff?" Leesa asked.

"Well, I guess it wasn't too bad. I don't know. There was something . . ."

"What 'something'? What's the problem?" Leesa pushed.

"From the questions, I'm pretty sure the sheriff thinks someone was with May . . . you know . . . when, when she went over that cliff." She closed her eyes and shuddered.

Someone was out walking with May, and they didn't report the fall?

"Wait," Leesa said, sitting up straight. "You mean someone saw it happen, and they didn't tell anyone? Or someone pushed her? There's a big difference."

The remains of my breakfast rumbled in my stomach. May's death had to be an accident that no one could have predicted or prevented.

Jennifer looked puzzled. "I don't know."

Beth turned white.

Without a particle of doubt, I knew that Beth would never have physically lashed out at May, even if she'd caught her in the act with Ron. Beth's shock was sympathy for May. Or Jennifer.

But—what if Beth thought Shannan had seen something? Shannan might have witnessed a confrontation, and then gotten drunk to wipe away the memory.

"You're saying she was murdered?" Lynn was standing in the doorway. Apparently, she'd been eavesdropping, and now she invited herself into the conversation.

"Murder?" The word jumped out of my mouth. "No one said anything about murder. Why would you even think that?"

"Well, if someone else was there." Lynn looked at Jennifer. "Well, is that possible?"

"I don't know," Jennifer said, swallowing hard.

Beth sat forward, "Lynn, leave her alone. She's been through enough without a third degree from us."

"Well, we have to find out what happened," Leesa said.

Lynn agreed. "If there's someone around who could choose any one of us for his next victim, then we need to know about it. We need to take precautions, too. It could be time to head home."

Jennifer flushed. "Oh, God, I, like, never thought of that."

Neither had I, and I didn't much care for it. Particularly because the Lazy L was isolated. We chose it to keep us away from the noise of other campers, but now, even with the morning sunshine coming through the screen, I wasn't sure that was a good thing.

I took a deep breath. "We don't have enough information to go running off half-cocked." I shot Lynn a glance. "Or cockeyed."

"That's right," Beth said.

"Jennifer, there's no need to get upset," I said. "I'll talk to Cordy and the sheriff, and I'll find out if they think we should protect ourselves. If they do, then we'll decide what's next. I'm sure it's perfectly safe in daylight and when we're together. More than likely, it's perfectly safe all the time."

"Fine, but you also need to find out if she was sexually assaulted," Lynn added.

"Sexually—?" Jennifer looked ready to pass out. "That's not, like, oh, God—"

"I think we should change the subject," Beth said with a glare in Lynn's direction.

"I agree," I said, taking a gulp of air. "Maybe everyone ought to come with me for the demonstration, and then afterward—"

"I wasn't concerned about now," Lynn said. "I don't think we have anything to worry about in broad daylight. It's later that concerns me. Tonight, when it's dark."

I said, "I'm sure Cordy and the sheriff are very aware of the safety issues. If there are any safety issues. They're not going to let anything happen to us."

Everyone considered that, and Lynn eventually shrugged, "Who can guarantee anything in today's world?"

Jennifer was as white as the pillowcase on her bunk, and Beth looked furious.

"I need to go to my demonstration," I said. "Jennifer, would you like to come along?"

Jennifer shook her head; she seemed a bit wobbly but under control. "Oh, I'm okay. I'd just rather not talk about it." And, as if on cue, Sinatra reached up and batted one of her blonde curls with his paw. She swung around and buried her face against him. "You wonderful little fuzzball."

Lynn said, "It's not like we're going to find a hook on the Lazy L door."

If I'd had something to throw at her, I would have. She

was referring to the spooky camp story about a homicidal maniac who had a hook for a hand—and the hook ends up hanging off a door handle. Luckily, it seemed Jennifer had never heard that old tale, but we didn't need any more scary stories.

I shouldered my briefcase. "I'm on my way. Lynn, why don't you walk with me?"

She didn't take the hint. "No thanks. I'm going to find something alcoholic. Preferably a Bloody Mary; that way I get my vitamins, and I still feel pretty good. Didn't anyone bring any Bloody Mary mix?"

I hadn't brought any, and if I had, I wouldn't share with her. "Sorry."

"Kitzi, give me a second," Leesa said, climbing down from her bunk. "I'll walk with you."

I glanced at Beth who gave me the slightest of nods, meaning she'd keep an eye on Jennifer until I got back. I waved a final good-bye and held the door for Leesa.

Once outside and away from the cabin I said, "That girl is scared to death—"

"I know, I know. It's that Lynn. What a mouth. We should think of a way to silence her."

"Murder isn't something to take lightly, and Jennifer is more than a little involved."

"It's not my fault Lynn is a bitch."

"No. But don't encourage her," I said, looking around. The Lazy L seemed farther off from the main camp than ever, and while the cabin did have doors, I didn't think there was a lock anywhere in camp except on the public buildings.

"She did bring up one important issue," Leesa said. "If May was sexually assaulted, then we know that it was someone from outside the camp, since there are only women here. It lets us all off the hook, and we know who not to be afraid of."

"That's not a hundred-percent accurate. Tony Campanelli is here."

"Who? Oh, the guy who does business as TonyCraft. He doesn't strike me as the violent type. I mean, he's good-looking, but in a soft kind of way. And since all the women seem to like him, why would he have to resort to violence for sex? Not that good looks and charm are a guarantee that a man is a good person. Wasn't Ted Bundy—"

"Is there anything else you could talk about?"

"Oh. Sure. Sorry. So, what are you demonstrating?" We cut down a steep trail toward the Saloon.

Nice conversational shift, but something she'd said about Tony was wrong.

"I'm showing how to make paper beads," I said. "Only I've added my own twist."

"What do they look like?"

I was still trying to catch the runaway thought. "Here you go." I pulled a small bag out of my briefcase. It contained a necklace of several paper beads interspersed with crystals and cloisonné. At the center was a large drop with oriental characters. "The drop is the main piece I'm showing how to make."

She took the necklace from the bag and studied it, like it was important. "This is very nice."

"Thank you." And then I remembered what she'd said that was wrong. "There are other males here in camp. Men." Why I hedged over Jeb's name, I'm not sure, but I did. "The men in your family are here."

"Man. Just one so far."

So, I spit it out. "Jeb."

"No, he's not here."

I stopped to look at her. "I saw him. Arguing with May Feather just yesterday."

"You can't have. That was him on the cell phone last night. Calling from New York. He isn't even in the area yet."

"I'm pretty sure—"

"I'll bet he didn't even know May. He never comes to Texas to see family, so why would he come to see her?"

Then she gave me an understanding look. "You knew my Uncle Jeb, didn't you?" she asked.

I found myself lifting my chin as if to prove something to Leesa, or maybe to myself. "Yes, I knew him for a short time. I coached him on his public speaking."

"Didn't you two date?"

Her expression was as bland as my younger brother's when he's planning to snow me. "Yes. For a very short time."

She nodded. "He's an asshole, although I'm sure I don't have to tell you that." She frowned. "But he wasn't here yesterday."

Another Jeb sighting? I couldn't believe it; I really thought I'd gone beyond that.

Then Leesa said, "Wait, I know who you saw . . ."

"Kitzi! Leesa!" Cordy was walking up from the saloon. When she reached us, she said, "Kitzi, the computer is all set up. Everything seems to be working just fine and it's already on the Internet."

"Thanks."

Leesa said, "Aunt Cordy, we need to talk. Jennifer just moved in with us, and she's scared."

Cordy rubbed her forehead and shook her head. "Damn. She's had a rough time."

"Yes, but does she have a reason to be scared? Was May Feather murdered? And by whom? And was she sexually molested?"

Cordy gasped. "I have no idea. The sheriff hasn't said anything like that."

"What did he say?"

"Not much. He found a place where the branches were broken—like there might have been a scuffle. He said that could point to homicide. I didn't think to ask any other questions. I was too stunned. But, sexual assault—God, Leesa!"

"I'm sorry, but that's the world we live in," she said.

I thought of Ron and his tryst with May the night be-

fore. What if they'd had sex before she was killed? The police would find out she'd been with someone, but could
they tell if it was consensual? Maybe Ron had used a condom. He'd had a vasectomy, but a condom would be pro-
tection against disease, if that concerned him. But if he
hadn't . . . and if the police did a DNA sample . . . and
if . . . and if. I knew way too much and not nearly enough.

"You'll get your chance to ask all the questions you
want," Cordy said. "The sheriff's going to be talking to
everyone in camp. In fact, at lunch, he's going to make an
announcement, then interview all of us."

"Good," Leesa said. "And what about the doors? Can
we lock the cabin doors?"

"I have to go," I said, gesturing toward the Saloon. My
head was whirling, and my world was sinking. I was hiding
a fair amount of information from the sheriff, and it looked
like he needed to know it. He'd have questions, and I'd better have answers.

Before I turned to leave I said, "Oh, and Cordy, thanks."

"You're welcome," she said. As soon as I was on my
way, she lowered her voice and said to Leesa, "You need to
make an airport run. Jeb's plane lands in less than twenty
minutes. Did you hang up on him yesterday? He was none
too happy—"

"I had to; they were singing some stupid song about cell
phones! And I have the Miata, so there's not room—"

"Then take the camp van," said Cordy, "but you need to
get moving."

Ten

"**A**nd you pulled all those Chinese characters off this website?"

"I did," I said.

Most of the twenty or so women who'd come to my demonstration were still crowded around the computer and me. More women were coming in all the time, which is pretty normal for Fridays at the retreat. They'd stop by next door to sign in, then dash into the Saloon before they even went to their cabins.

"So, you just cut the text and pasted it in PowerPoint?" Sande, the auburn-haired woman beside me asked. "Is that right?" Sande had gotten in for just the last half of my demonstration, but she's quick and was catching up fast. Not surprising since she's also a librarian from L.A. And the noir beader, Lynn, is her wicked cousin, not that I thought Sande would call her that.

"That's all I did," I said. "Sometimes I have trouble getting it to paste, but theoretically, it will go into any Word document, or any of those listed on the handout." I had one eye on the window in front of the Saloon, just to see if Leesa was back. There hadn't been time, and they probably wouldn't come that way, but I was still watching.

"Does it matter which program?" Sande went on.

"Not a bit. As long as you can move things around to

your liking, then it will work." I sounded like an expert, which, unfortunately, I'm not. I can maneuver around a computer about the way I can around the freeways in Houston—Point A to Point B, but don't confuse me while I'm doing it. "For these big necklace drops, I changed the size and the color to get what I wanted," I added, holding up a green-tinted bead.

"I can't believe how simple it is!" one woman said. "And we can save a fortune on beads."

"And we can print on different-colored paper or use paint mixed in with the lacquer," Sande said, holding a bead up for a closer look. "Isn't that what you did here?"

"I just aged it a bit with a wash of brown."

I knew they'd like the idea of taking the print from the Internet to make paper beads.

"Did you put that Russian web address and the Egyptian one in the handout?" Sande asked, pushing her long hair over her ears.

"Both," I said. Several women were holding pages that we'd printed. One had Arabic writing and others held characters from the Cyrillic alphabet.

"You know what else we could do with this?" Sande said. "Decoupage and card making. Kitzi, you are brilliant."

"Glad you finally realize that."

I looked around the room for more questions and saw Tony Campanelli waiting to set up his demonstration. Unfortunately, I was running a little late because the camp connection to the Internet was slow, and the women wanted to actually see the websites where I'd gotten my foreign characters.

Sande leaned over to touch my shoulder. "Can we go back to the Egyptian site? I'd like to get a sheet of that Arabic—"

"Sorry, ladies," Tony said, walking through the group to join me at the front. "But I have a surprise for everyone during my demonstration, and I need complete privacy to set up." He was smiling in his charming way, but something about the set of his jaw told me he was annoyed.

A plump woman in her mid-forties, not someone I knew, giggled. "Oh, Tony, you just want us all to yourself."

He winked at her, "You know me too well. Now, you'd all better dash off to the dining hall for something to drink, but hurry back so you won't be late." Most of the women were picking up their handouts and moving to the exit. To me, Tony said, "How much longer?"

"Let me just pack all this up."

"I'll help."

Without apology or bothering to turn off the computer, he reached down and unplugged it. A squawk stuck in my throat. I couldn't get it out before he started rolling up the power cord. I was stunned. I'd never known Tony to be rude before.

He kept on smiling as he called out to the backs of the women, "Oh, and Barb is in the office selling TonyCraft kits of the project we're going to make. To get the best ones, you'd better grab yours now."

Sande's eyes were wide with astonishment at what he was doing, but Tony seemed completely oblivious to how offensive his behavior was. He just kept on unplugging things as if this had been his demonstration.

"I'll help Kitzi," Sande said, snatching a printer cord from his hands. "So you can do whatever—"

"No need," he said. "I've already got it." He closed the computer and placed it on top of the printer.

The few remaining women were fingering the samples one more time, not paying a lot of attention to us.

"I'll leave the samples on the bar so you can study them later," I said, doing my best to act as if I weren't really pissed off at Tony's interference. "And thank you all for coming."

"Don't forget, snacks in the dining hall," Tony said. "And you need to hurry because I'll be ready for you in ten minutes."

He picked up the printer and laptop, and practically shoved them at me. "Here you go. All done." He set the few remaining papers on top.

"Excuse me," I said. "Who gave you the right—"

"Better smile."

A few stragglers were still going out the door, so I lowered my voice. "You little jerk! That was just about as rude as anyone can get, and I don't appreciate—"

"You don't seem to understand," he snapped. "Some of us make our living selling things, and I can't sell kits if you're going to hog the demonstration time."

"I didn't. We ran a few minutes over, which doesn't give you the right—"

"I was helping, okay? Sales are way down. Way down, what with May's death. Usually everyone goes for the best kits first thing but not this time."

"That's not my fault."

"Yes? Well, what about you saying that 'beads are expensive, and you can save money this way'! You shouldn't be talking people out of buying."

"I didn't. If people make these beads, they'll still spend the same amount of money, they'll just have more beads. I didn't say it to hurt your sales." I stopped to calm down. This was not a weekend to go exploding at people. With as much sincerity as I could muster, I said, "I apologize if I did."

He sucked in air, maybe storing up for another tirade, but then he let it out. He wasn't deflated, but at least he was slowed. "I'm sorry; I was overreacting, but I've got reason." His fists were clenched. "No one is buying, and I was already uptight because of this Tivolini thing. Cordy told you about that, didn't she? I mean, you two are old friends, so I figure you know." A touch of a whine in that.

"She told Beth, not me. I'm not in the running."

He began creating his demonstration space, while I stood there holding the equipment I'd used. "I don't have to tell you what the Tivolini contract could mean," he said. "I'd finally get some recognition." He laid out a black velvet cloth, and used more force than necessary to take apart a Tony-Craft kit. There were two sacks of beads, some headpins, and nylon-coated wire for stringing, some findings and instructions. From his briefcase he took the pliers he would use, as well as a crimping tool. He also had samples . . . a necklace of deep blue with cloisonné beads set at artistic intervals. There were earrings to match.

"The Tivolini contract could involve a lot of money, too," I said.

"A lot. I could turn TonyCraft over to someone else to manage. Do you know that I sit up nights putting together each and every kit I sell? Every damn one! I shouldn't be doing that. Some underpaid little women in China should be doing that. And I shouldn't be packing every box that goes to a dealer and checking the invoices." He gestured around him. "I shouldn't be doing penny-ante demonstrations at Green Clover, either." "That Tivolini contract is going to change my life—finally."

"Okay, but what happens if you don't get it?"

He turned his glare full force on me, and I had to fight the urge to flinch.

"I'll get the contract; don't worry about it."

I didn't like his tone, or his words. And I didn't like that he was dismissing the competition, especially Beth, as if she didn't have a chance.

"Then I wish you luck." I didn't say which kind.

"Thank you."

I glanced around one last time. "If you'll put the surge protector and that extension cord by the bar, I'll get them later." With my hands full, I very carefully bent down to get my briefcase. By the time I'd straightened, he was holding both items I'd mentioned.

"Here, I'll just put them in this." He shoved them in the briefcase, tilting me off balance in the process.

I straightened. "Why, thank you." I said it wishing I had the nerve to throw everything at him. It would never happen, but I could dream.

Carefully, I made my way out, muttering, "Prima donna." I had to juggle everything as I crossed the road, then down the small path that would take me to the camp office. I could understand his desire to win the Tivolini contract—he was banking on more than the price of the contract. He would also gain respect in the beading community and, with luck, from those outside of it. It would create an upward spiral; the notoriety would allow him to ask for more money for his kits. He could command higher prices for his demonstrations, too. He could author books that would sell.

Given my druthers after the way he'd acted, I druthered it wouldn't happen.

I made the last turn down the sloping path. The office was in front of me, and I got up the two steps without incident, but getting a hand free to open the door was a problem. When I finally did, I tripped over the sill and practically fell inside. A strong arm caught me, and then a warm body was against my own.

"I've got you," said a deep masculine voice that sent chills through me. "Are you okay?"

"Of course." I tried to straighten, but my briefcase slipped off my shoulder and caught on the doorknob. "Damn."

"Here, let me help." He unhooked the strap and took the printer and computer from me. Our arms brushed and a tingle careened through my body from toes to nose hitting some hot spots along the way.

"Oh, damn," I said again, this time softly. I knew that touch—and the voice. I even remembered the sizzle.

"Now," he said, turning to me, so that for the first time I saw his face. "Are you really okay?"

The face was similar, but not the same. The eyes were a deep warm brown, the cheekbones high and wide, and the hair a dark brown with streaks of silver. Not exactly Tom Cruise, but damn close, if you like men older and a little wiser, which I do. But it wasn't Jeb.

"I'm fine," I said. "Who are you?"

He smiled and held out a hand. "Nate Wright. You must be Kitzi, since you're returning the computer. Cordy had me set it up for you."

"Oh. Thanks. Yes, I'm Kitzi Camden."

We shook hands, and I felt the kind of electricity that Nate's brother Jeb had sparked in me. I didn't have anything to say; instead I stared at him, hoping I'd closed my mouth.

"I'm surprised we haven't met before," he was saying.

"Yes."

I thought of the crazy article I'd read about scientists determining if basic genetics governed attraction between men and women. The women were given T-shirts to sniff, but they never saw the men who had worn them. They didn't know age, weight, hairy or bald, short or tall. Each woman selected a favorite shirt, strictly by smell, and every single woman selected the shirt of a man whose DNA was most unlike her own.

Apparently, primal attraction is real, and it assures strong offspring for the survival of the species.

My DNA had to be polar opposite to the Wrights.

"How did the demonstration go?" he asked.

"What? Oh, fine. It was fine."

"I didn't get to see what you made."

"Beads."

The Wrights are tall and long-legged with dark eyes and dark hair, and I'm under five-five, and I'm what I like to call full-figured with eyes that are mostly green, sometimes blue. I'm also fair. Formerly blonde, with natural silver highlights that look just like the kind some women pay a lot of money for.

"What kind of beads?" he asked.

"Beads? Oh. Paper beads."

The Wright men, despite their name, were also trouble with a capital T; they were worse than Sinatra. At that moment they seemed a more immediate danger than a murderer on the campgrounds.

"Nice meeting you. Thanks again for your help." I swung around and squarely hit the edge of the open doorway, nearly knocking myself senseless.

"Hold on!" He caught me with one hand and moved the door with the other. "You're not having a good day."

He turned me slowly to face him and we were inches apart, as another voice said, "Pardon me. Seems I'm interrupting." It was Sheriff Gonzales.

I was still blinking. "I bumped into the door." I realized that Nate's arm was steadying me and I shook it off, although I did so with care to avoid hitting anything else. "I'm fine," I said to Nate.

The sheriff said, "You've been running into a lot of things lately."

Did he know about the Lexus? Or was he referring to how I'd run into him that morning?

"Are you sure you're okay?" Nate asked.

"Fine," I repeated. My forehead hurt, but I wouldn't have rubbed it for all the beads in China. "Thank you, again." I looked at the sheriff, then at Nate. "If you'll excuse me, I need to get back to Sinatra."

That gave them pause, but I didn't explain—I merely left.

Eleven

The sheriff was going to talk with us, and if the rumors were true, interview us, which put me and everyone else off their beef tips and rice. I was desperately hoping for a quick resolution to May's murder, because I didn't want to have to lie about my whereabouts the night before. And I surely didn't want to tell the truth. In Texas, that's called being between a rock and a hard place.

I got up with the rest of the group at our table, and headed for the big trashcans to scrape plates, drop off silverware, and throw away the trash. I nodded at Tony as I passed him, but neither of us spoke. I hadn't yet come up with a plan. Unless you call falling back on good-ol'-boy-speak a plan.

I'd use just a little, then I'd pass the buck, and finish up with a quick shuffle off to Buffalo. Or the Lazy L.

Cordy rang the brass bell, calling for attention, and we all took our places in silence. It wasn't a good omen. During more normal days the bell would signal the beginning of announcements; who had the best times at swimming and who was doing a skit at the campfire. After that would come songs, so that we left the dining hall energized and ready for more fun. Except it wasn't that way today. Today there was sorrow and anxiety.

Sheriff Gonzales came out of the private dining room

and walked directly to the spot where the bell was. He was all serious business.

After a solemn glance around at us, he said, "Good afternoon. I have some disturbing news."

"First, May Feather's death does not appear to be accidental." Careful phrasing or not, we knew what he meant—she'd been murdered. "I'm going to need your help."

Word had spread that we were supposed to bring photo identification to lunch, which isn't a regular part of getting a meal at Green Clover. Sande, who runs across lots of facts in her job as a research librarian, explained that legal ID was standard when giving an official statement. That was a tidbit I never thought I'd learn at camp.

As the sheriff went on, I played with the arrangement of artificial bluebonnets in the center of the table. They were stuffed in an old boot with a bright red bandanna tied around it. They were too cute for this kind of occasion.

The sheriff said, "I have already brought in DPS, the Department of Public Safety. They are working on the crime scene and forensics—"

A male voice from the back of the room cut him off. "There are fifty women here at Green Clover; are they safe?"

My heart stopped, and luckily the boot didn't contain water because I knocked it over. The voice that challenged the sheriff was one I knew well—it belonged to Jeb Wright, long-lost love and breaker of hearts. He was here, not just in camp, but in the dining hall, somewhere behind me.

Damn. It took every bit of my will power not to say it out loud. And to keep my eyes forward, focused on the sheriff.

The sheriff said, "Yes, we believe that they are safe—"

"How can you guarantee that?" Jeb's voice had a snappy ring of authority, and it wasn't near as pleasant as some other tones I'd heard him use.

The sheriff swallowed. "When a person is killed, it's

usually for a personal reason by someone close to them. You hear about it in the news. Boyfriend, girlfriend, family member, someone like that. That means the rest of you aren't in any danger."

"What if it was a serial killer?" Jeb pushed.

"Then he's long gone." Funny, I hadn't noticed the Hispanic accent before, but the sheriff was using one now. I wondered if it was because of the pressure, or if it was his equivalent of good ol' boy. "I understand your concern, so to make you feel better, I'm going to leave a deputy here on the grounds tonight."

"One?" Jeb said. "One is hardly going to be sufficient. We need several men. If you don't have that kind of manpower, who can we hire?"

I swung around to look at Cordy, to see how she was taking Jeb's interference.

Not well. She looked like a hostess who'd had barbecue sauce spilled on her white carpet and was trying to be gracious about it.

The sheriff ran his hand over his thin brown hair. "Mezner is the best."

"Are they located in Austin?" Nate asked from a far table.

"Yes, sir. They're in the phone book."

Cordy said, "Here's the most important thing: everyone has to be safe."

"They are. As much as anyone is anywhere," the sheriff said. "It's always smart to be aware of your surroundings. Especially women. And don't go walking alone at night. If something does happen, scream loud."

Was he talking about here at Green Clover or downtown New York? It wasn't the camp I knew.

"What about carrying some kind of weapon?" Sande asked, slipping her straight auburn hair behind her ears. "Do you recommend that?"

"Depends on what kind. This is Texas, and if you were thinking of putting a .357 under your pillow, I don't recommend it."

I have several guns at home, including two rifles and a revolver. That's legal in Texas. In fact, you can carry a weapon openly if you are traveling over county lines.

I've been shooting since I was a kid, and I've never missed a rattlesnake, no matter the distance. Of course, I couldn't hit a deer or a rabbit for the life of me. When the concealed carry laws went into effect I considered getting a license, but my son convinced me that with my temper, I just might use the gun and then I'd be sorry. He was right, so my weapons were all locked up at home.

Under cover of the audible response from the women I said to Beth, "Guess I could loan out my guns to people." She raised one eyebrow at me.

Jennifer's eyes got wide, and Angie said, "We'd end up shooting each other."

"I'm from California," Sande said to the sheriff. "We're peaceful. I meant Mace."

"Never carry a weapon you're not willing to have used on you, Mace included." He looked around at us. "I don't think any of this is necessary—"

"What if your wife or daughter were here?" I asked before I realized I was going to do it. "Would you be comfortable with them staying overnight?"

He gave me a tiny shake of his head. "Ms. Camden, I never feel comfortable when my daughter is out of my sight for very long, but she's seventeen and I'm a typical father." The tension shifted like mercury, and there were even a few small laughs. The man was a heck of a lot quicker than I'd given him credit for, and I wasn't sure I was glad.

"Was she raped?" Lynn asked from another part of the room. There were gasps, and heads swiveled to glare in her direction.

"We have no reason to think that. Ms. Feather was fully clothed when she was found."

That brought another of those group responses, only this one was an audible release of air. Then Lynn, true to form said, "Well, I'm getting in my Hummer and getting out of here."

"No. No one is to leave until we get statements." Sheriff Gonzales had lost his good-ol'-boy easiness.

"Are we officially being detained?" It was Jeb again. The sheriff gave him a hard look from dark eyes. I couldn't hold myself still any longer—I turned to look at Jeb.

He was standing near the back door, his body taut, but there was something else in his expression. He was doing battle and enjoying it. For him this was a testosterone-filled game.

I looked him up and down. He was in his 'business-casual attire' of khaki pants with a gray-and-green golf shirt. Must be the way he got off the plane. Even his hair looked sleek with its razor cut, and I could see he had manicured nails. Yes, Jeb had grown up since he'd left Austin, but it hadn't all been good. Over the years since I'd seen him, his skin had turned sallow, and his eyes had sunken. Either he'd had a bad flight, or Jeb Wright was taking a beating in his life with the big boys.

I looked at the sheriff again in his uniform. His face was craggy, his hair windblown, and I knew from our handshake that his hands were rough and calloused from hard work. City Boy vs. Tough Country Sheriff. I hoped Jeb would lose.

When the sheriff spoke again there was power in his voice—this was his territory. "If you just got here and you want to go, that's fine with me. But if you were here last night and you don't help," he grazed us with his look, "I'm going to wonder why."

Then he explained the drill. We were to be interviewed by law enforcement personnel. Those who hadn't been at camp last night were to go with one of the Department of Public Safety officers to the Saloon, and the rest of us were to wait our turns in the dining hall.

At some point I stopped breathing. I had lied to Sheriff Gonzales once, and now I either had to admit the lie, or tell the truth. How could I say I had caught May and Ron together last night? That I had rammed Ron's Lexus? That I had withheld information?

"Answer every question fully and volunteer what we don't ask for," the sheriff said. "Don't talk about this with each other. You could change your memories. We want to be the first ones you talk to."

There were additional instructions, but I wasn't listening.

My father, straight arrow and straight-laced, would have been angry at my lack of cooperation with law enforcement. I could hear his voice from years before, "We have to set an example, Katherine." He didn't believe in breaking the rules or stepping out of line. We weren't above the law; as Camdens, we stood for it and upheld it.

My grandfather might have been more understanding. He was a bigger, more freewheeling personality. Protecting a friend was important, and in some ways, I was saving time for law enforcement. They wouldn't be going off in directions that wouldn't lead anyplace. And I was positive neither Shannan nor Beth had anything to do with May's death. Yes, my grandfather would buy that, and maybe even support me in it, but I didn't think I could pull it off like he would have.

I kept thinking of those two heads, Ron's and May's, popping up in my headlights. What if that had started an argument between them? I couldn't see Ron getting angry enough to kill, but then I couldn't imagine anyone willingly having sex with him, either.

Mo-Ron.

No, Ron wouldn't kill someone. I was almost positive, and the little doubt I had wasn't sufficient to make me tell all to the police. Not when it would throw suspicion on everyone in the family.

I debated and must have mumbled something, because Beth touched my arm. "Are you okay?"

"Me? Oh, sure. Fine. Fine." I wrestled with my conscience some more, then took in air and made my decision.

Regardless of how bad I would look, I had to tell the truth about last night.

My insides shriveled along with my courage. And then would everyone find out? Jeb? Would he have to know? Cordy? And Nate.

And how would it be for Beth when she found out?

People were beginning to exit the dining hall, and I turned my head. A moon orbiting a planet doesn't have as strong a gravitational pull as I have toward Jeb Wright. He looked straight at me. I have no idea what he thought when he saw me, and it's probably better I didn't know. He nodded noncommittally. Like I was a stranger, or like we'd just seen each other last week.

He was the one who turned away. I had to admit his face was still handsome, but the smooth glow of youth was definitely gone, replaced by dull skin and the beginnings of bags under his eyes. There was the slightest stoop to his shoulders, but he caught that and straightened. I was betting that he ran a difficult race in his career, and I wondered if he was winning.

Then I remembered he was married. I stood up, just to stretch, and tried to catch a glimpse of his hand to see if there was a wedding ring. I was too late, he was already outside the screen door. I looked around him on the off chance I'd spot his wife, but all the women near him were regular camp attendees. His wife could be at Cordy's house or at a hotel.

And then Nate moved across my field of vision as he walked over to say something to Cordy. He bent down and spoke quietly. I couldn't hear what he said, but she seemed to relax for a moment before frowning and nodding. He said something more; she caught his hand, and I could see her lips form the words "thank you."

Others were standing and stretching, too. Jennifer, still pale, rose from her spot a few seats down the trestle table. "I've already given my statement, so I'll go take care of Sinatra."

"Thank you," I said. "Are you okay?"

She gave me a halfhearted smile. "I'm fine. I'll be better when I can play with Sinatra."

"I wonder if we'll still be doing demonstrations?" Beth asked.

Jennifer looked toward the outside. "I don't think the Saloon will be available. And who would come?"

There weren't many of us left in the dining hall. Jennifer gave a small wave and headed for the door. That left only Beth, Shannan, and me at our table. Beth rose. "I'm going to see if they have any leftover dessert—I didn't eat lunch, I can justify the calories. Do either of you want anything?"

"No, thanks," I said.

Shannan shook her head.

"Okay." And Beth left us alone.

Shannan looked at me. Either the effects of the hangover were still with her, or she needed another drink to settle her nerves. She kept her voice low, "They're going to ask all sorts of questions. And we're going to have to make statements. Sworn statements." She waved her driver's license. "And we can't tell the truth, can we?"

"Yes, we can," I said. "In fact, we have to, and afterward we'll handle whatever problems come up."

"But what about my mom? They might think that she . . . she . . ." she looked around but there was no one close to us in the almost empty hall. "Had something to do with May's death. Or my dad. Or . . ." She dropped her gaze to the table and became silent.

Or her. "Shannan, you didn't see May after we got back, did you?" I asked. "Did you say something to her? Maybe have an argument?"

"No! Of course not." But her eyes were down, looking at the scratched table. She wasn't near as convincing as I wished she were.

"Honey, listen, you—"

"Can't you pull some strings and get us out of here?

Fix it so we can go home? At least not have to make a statement?"

"No, I'm afraid I can't. It's called obstruction of justice, which is why Nixon had to resign."

"Who?"

"Like Bill Clinton, only in the seventies."

Shannan's eyes got bigger. "Could we go to prison?"

"No." This whole thing had gone too far, and there was only one way to pull it back. "We are not going to prison. We are going to tell the truth. We have to. Maybe May and your father had a fight, and she went off with someone else." I thought of Nate and the argument he'd had with May. "A lot of things could have happened, and we don't know what."

"Who else could she have been with?"

"I don't have the least idea," I said. But, maybe I did.

Nate Wright and May Feather had been arguing just yesterday afternoon and it hadn't come to an easy conclusion, either. May had flipped her long, dark hair, jerked away from Nate, and dashed off.

So, how did Nate know May? I felt a little disappointment at that.

"Maybe," Shannan said without conviction, "maybe the sheriff won't want to talk with me. I'm just a teenager; won't that mean they'll skip me?"

"I wouldn't think so. You're seventeen, and that seems to stick in my mind as some kind of important age. You might be able to have a parent with you. Maybe your mother—"

"No! I can't do that. I don't want her to find out that way. We have to tell her. Right after we finish—"

"How was your trail ride?" I asked loudly as Beth arrived back at our table carrying a plastic bowl of strawberry shortcake.

Shannan looked surprised, then saw her mother. She waited only a beat before saying, "Uh, terrible. That new woman, the wrangler, treated us like two-year-olds."

"Tell Cordy," I said. The sheriff came out of the private dining room and gestured in our direction. I almost lost my balance when I stood up. The sheriff shook his head and pointed to Shannan. "Will you come in, please?"

"Oh, no—" she turned even whiter.

"Shannan, it's just fine," Beth said. "Think of what a great story this will make at school."

I took Shannan's hand and said, "Just tell them the truth and nothing but the truth."

She looked at me. "You're sure?"

"I'm sure."

On shaky legs, she walked toward the sheriff who was waiting for her—and watching her.

I jumped forward. "Maybe I'd better go with her."

I'd almost caught up with Shannan when Sheriff Gonzales shook his head. He asked Shannan, "How old are you?"

"Seventeen."

To me, he said, "She'll be fine." Except I knew his curiosity had been piqued. He escorted her inside the private dining room and closed the door firmly.

The truth and nothing but the truth, I told myself. *Dear God, let Shannan be okay*.

"Kitz," Cordy said, touching my arm. "Do you have a minute to talk with us?"

I must have looked mute and none too bright.

"Nate and me," Cordy explained.

"Oh. Sure." I exhaled carefully. "Where did you have in mind?"

She gestured toward Beth and led us to the table. "Beth, I need a war council."

Beth pushed aside her untouched strawberry shortcake. She was more upset than she wanted me to know. "Sure. How can I help?"

Cordy sat across the table with Beth, and Nate took Shannan's seat beside me. "Do you both know my brother Nate?"

Beth introduced herself, and I nodded, but I wasn't

making eye contact with him. He seemed to generate some kind of heat, and it was just more trouble on a day that was already filled with it.

Cordy said, "This is a nightmare, and I'm afraid it's going to get worse."

"Worse?" Beth's worry made her look even more like Shannan. "You think someone else could be killed?"

"No, no! If I thought that I'd shut this place down and we'd all find hotels." She shook her head. "I think we're safe enough. Sheriff Gonzales has five or six officers here from DPS. They've even got a mobile crime lab. Crime Ambulance they called it."

"The problem is," Nate said, leaning forward. "Several of the women say they are leaving as soon as they give their statement."

"Could be as many as half," Cordy added. "And you know what will happen from there—pretty soon everyone will be gone."

We took it in, and Beth said, "Maybe that wouldn't be such a bad thing. Just this once."

"You don't understand," Cordy said. "It will kill the retreats from here on out. Oh, damn, I didn't mean kill. Wrong word. You know what I meant. It will put an end to them. Or we'll get ten people and have to start building all over again. I was just making money on them, too. The last two years they've been profitable, but they won't be if I have to start over. Or if we have to refund everyone's money."

Nate said quietly, "The real problem is that Green Clover hasn't been profitable the rest of the year. With the economy down, the summer sessions the last two years were barely half-full."

Now I understood the other part of Cordy's worry. "If it's money, I can—"

"No." Cordy snapped.

"I've already offered," Nate said, the hair on his arm brushing mine.

Cordy said more gently, "I'm sorry; I don't mean to be rude, but Nate's been a silent partner all along. He helped me get started, and if I can't pull it through this there's no point in keeping the camp."

Lose Green Clover? Beth and I exchanged a stunned look. It would be like someone foreclosing on a part of our childhood—the happiest part. The Craft Retreats were the only way I knew of to regain the fun of our youth.

I looked at Cordy. "I'll do anything I can to help. I've already told you that."

"Me, too," Beth added.

Cordy glanced at Nate, then at each of us in turn. "Thanks." She took a deep breath. "I want the retreat to go on. We have May's memorial tonight, and then two days that could be close to normal. If both of you stay, then maybe others will, too."

"I'll stay," I said.

"I appreciate that, but take some time to consider first," Cordy said. "I want a disinterested second opinion. If you think there's a danger, I'm shutting this place down now, and I mean right now."

"But you just said you thought it was safe; I don't get it," Beth said.

"I do think it's safe, but I'm prejudiced."

"We are, too," I said.

"Oh, Lord," Cordy said. "I guess I want someone to read the future and tell me it's okay to keep the retreat going. I'm just not willing to put people at risk."

If the sheriff was right, May's death was the end of the danger. *If* he was right. I tried to weigh what he'd said with my own experience of crime, which was limited to what I read about in the papers or saw on television. I'd never heard of a murderer coming back to the scene of the crime and killing someone else. That only happened in movies or books, and this was real life.

In the end I exchanged a long glance with Beth and then a brief nod.

"Well?" Cordy asked.

"I'm staying," Beth said.

"Me, too," I added. "The sheriff says it's safe, and he's a professional."

"But you have your daughter," Nate said to Beth. "Are you sure?"

Beth nodded. "I'm trusting my instinct on this one, but I'm not naïve. I still want locks on the cabin doors. All the cabins. And maybe if we put out a flyer reminding everyone to stay together it would help."

"The newsletter," Cordy said. "I have one prepared with tomorrow's schedule, only I was going to skip it. It's in the computer, so it wouldn't take long to add some things. What do you think, Nate?"

"I'll call Mezner security and have four people stationed on the grounds overnight. That, by the way, is your birthday present, Cordelia, so don't say a word about paying me back."

I liked this man; too bad Jeb wasn't more like him. But which brother was Nate? To the best of my recollection, one of Cordy's siblings was a minister, or had been, and another had some kind of security company that sold Mace and fire ladders by mail. Leesa was Zeke's daughter, and she didn't seem like a preacher's kid . . .

Beth snapped her fingers. "And remind people to close the wooden windows."

I had almost forgotten those heavy wooden pieces that came down and sealed the cabins off from the outside. They were used during storms or when the camp was closed.

"We'll have to turn on the overhead fans or we'll suffocate," I said. Air-conditioning at Green Clover meant real, breathable, created-by-the-good-Lord air and a few ceiling fans.

"Okay. And I'll get someone on those locks first thing," Cordy said.

I added, "The Tivolini contract is serious inducement for the best artists to stay. If you announced the buyer would be meeting with artisans tomorrow morning, you couldn't make people leave."

Nate and Cordy exchanged glances before Cordy said, "I think we can do that. I'll find out."

Which made me think Nate Wright was the buyer in question. After a glance at his worn jeans and his old Green Clover golf shirt, I reconsidered. His shirt was the kind male counselors wore on Parent's Day. He just didn't look like someone who selected bead designs.

I started to ask, but the private dining room door opened, and Shannan emerged from her interview. Her skin was pasty, but the look of relief on her face was hard to miss. I wondered what that was about. Beth and I were both headed toward her when the sheriff stepped out and said, "Ms. Camden. If you'd join us."

I nodded, but I was much more intent on Shannan. "Are you okay?"

"Fine. No problem."

Beth was there, slipping an arm through Shannan's. "You look pale."

"I'm fine, really." She stared at me, her eyes sending a message I couldn't read. Damn, damn, damn.

"I have to go," I said.

Shannan shook her head, *no*. What did that mean?

Sheriff Gonzales said, "If you would bring your driver's license."

"Oh, sorry," I said. "Let me get it." I turned and hurried toward the table. Nate spotted the license and picked it up to hand to me. Somehow, Shannan managed to get in between us and she mouthed, "I couldn't do it."

I felt my stomach plunge at the same time a wave of relief hit me. "Last night?"

"I didn't tell them."

She had lied to the sheriff. And now, if I told the truth it would be worse for her.

"Here you go," Nate said, pressing the license into my palm, and wrapping his fingers over mine. "Good luck."

I couldn't look at him; I was too stunned to move.

"Ms. Camden?" The sheriff said.

"Coming."

"Good luck," Shannan said.

"Thanks."

"You don't need luck," Sheriff Gonzales said as I started toward him. "You just need to tell me everything you know."

"Certainly."

Except that was the one thing I couldn't do.

Twelve

"Hop, hop
little rabbit, hop.
The hunter's
blown his top.
He'll come for you,
and you'll be stew.
So hop
little rabbit,
hop."

Camp Green Clover song

My good-ol'-boy plan felt pretty lame as I took a breath and entered the private dining room. The room held two oblong tables that were a bit less camp-worn than those outside, and the sheriff was seated at one.

"Howdy," I said, with a weak smile.

"Come in," he said.

And then I saw another man on his right. He was also in uniform, except he was younger, rougher looking, and somehow sleeker. Maybe it was the tight skin and tight muscles under his tight shirt. He completely ignored me while the sheriff gestured for me to take a place across from him with a microphone in front of it, along with several sheets of paper.

"Ms. Camden, if you'll make yourself comfortable." The sheriff's voice was still slow and gentle. The other officer finally looked up, and his eyes were as hard as his body and they took in every inch of me, assessing, determining, and then dismissing. The rise in my blood pressure was probably visible.

"This is Officer Peterson," the sheriff said.

"How do you do," I said politely. Then I sat and held out my driver's license. "I think you need this."

It was the sheriff who rose to take it from me. "Thank you." He looked at it quickly, then handed it to Peterson who read every word and even checked the back to see if there were restrictions. Not only a tight body, a tight ass, too.

"Are you ready?" the sheriff asked.

"Yes, of course." That was my first lie. Problem was that plan A was not going to work on that young Peterson, and I didn't have a plan B.

The sheriff started a tape recorder, then took me through the preliminaries, asking my name, my age, address, how long I'd been coming to the Craft Retreats, and when I'd arrived at camp for this event. The questions were easy, but he wasn't near done.

"How long have you known May Feather?" he asked next.

I told the truth about shows and the Bead Society meetings, and how we were acquaintances, but not close friends.

"And tell me about seeing May at this retreat."

If I'd been attached to a polygraph, the needle would have jumped across the room and smacked that Peterson in his broad shoulders.

"This time?" I took a breath. "I was at her demonstration, but I left early."

Peterson leaned forward and asked, "And why was that? Why didn't you stay for the end of May Feather's demonstration?"

It was the first time he'd spoken since our introduction. "I'd heard her stories before," I said. "Also, I knew I would never make the bracelet she was demonstrating. She was working with tiny seed beads doing a stitch that takes me forever."

"Where did you go when you left?" he asked.

"All over the camp. I told you, I've been coming here since I was a child. Last night I went down to the river and to the barn to see the horses. Then I went back up to the cabin to wash my hands and get my keys."

"Why?" Peterson asked.

"Because my hands had horse slobber on them." Which was one of the most dim-witted statements I'd made in my life, but the man scared me.

He let me wallow in my own stupidity before he asked, "Why did you get your keys?"

"Oh. Because I was going to lock my Land Rover. We don't usually do that, but it was near the road and all."

"Where on the river did you go?"

The man didn't think in a straight line. His questions also weren't out of idle curiosity, not that I thought Peterson was capable of anything so normal. He was asking because May had been found in the river.

"There is a trail that goes down from the campfire area. It's out there." I pointed, but I could have been gesturing in completely the wrong direction. "Wait. I don't know which way that is. The campfire is . . ." I'd never get any geography awards with that performance. "I'm mixed up now. It's straight down from the campfire. I listened to the water for, oh, I don't know. Awhile. Then I came back up."

"Did you see anyone else?"

"No."

"Are you sure you didn't see anyone at all when you were on this walk?"

He said, "this walk" as if I were making it up.

I thought about the night before, the empty trails and

how pretty the camp had looked under the stars. "I didn't see another person. Just horses."

"Who were you looking for?"

He said it as if he knew about Jeb and that I was hoping to run into him.

"I wasn't looking for anyone. I was getting reacquainted with Green Clover. It was a homecoming."

"Did you hear anyone?"

"When I went to the barn I could hear people up the hill at the saloon, but just background voices. Nothing more."

"And you got your keys to lock your truck." Peterson was staring at me as if his eyes were lasers. I didn't remember seeing him blink. Lizards hardly ever blink, either, and I don't much care for them.

"That's right."

"Except you left the camp," he said.

I had expected they'd know that, and still it upped my heart rate. "Yes, I did. How'd you hear?"

"Someone mentioned it," the sheriff said.

"Someone?"

"Someone who looked for you and was worried," the sheriff continued. "They mentioned it this morning to me."

I wanted to think about that, but I didn't get the time.

"So," the sheriff said, "where did you go? Who were you with?"

There was nothing to do but tell the story that Shannan and I had concocted earlier.

When I was done, Officer Peterson said, "Why Weldon and Company?"

"Because they were the closest hardware store that was open."

"You have vendors here." It was an accusation.

My foot was tapping, and I carefully stopped it. "Yes, and I will end up getting Beth's present from one of them. But they shut down all the booths at six o'clock. They didn't reopen until this morning."

"While you were at Weldon and Company, what did you look at, specifically?"

That was not a question Shannan and I had discussed *specifically.* "Obviously, Weldon doesn't carry beads or findings, but we looked at pliers and some wire." I know better than to go off and improvise. You try that when you're in public office and some smart-mouth reporter will hang you. So, instead I prevaricated. "In beading we use needle-nose pliers and rounded pliers for bending head pins. I'm going to get her present later, once she decides what kind of beading she wants to do. The demonstrations will help her with that."

"But she didn't stay for Ms. Feather's demonstration," he said.

I nodded slowly. "No, I guess she didn't."

There was a challenge in every question the officer asked. "Why didn't she?"

"I don't know."

"And what time did you return to the camp?"

"Good question." I was stalling because my breathing was ragged, and I didn't want him to hear that in my voice. After one more slow nod that I hoped looked thoughtful, I said, "I didn't check my watch, but Beth's demonstration was over, so I know it was after nine. Oh, wait, I saw the clock in the Rover; it was about nine-twenty when we got back here."

"And what did you do then?"

"We went to the cabin and visited with some other people. Later they went to the Saloon, and I took two Tylenol PMs and fell asleep."

"Did you hear or see anything during the night?"

"Nothing."

"What about when the others in the cabin came in and went to bed?" Peterson was making the headache come back.

"I slept right through it."

"Did you see Ms. Feather any time after the demonstration?"

I took a breath in anticipation of the big lie coming up. "No, I didn't."

"When else did you see Ms. Feather this weekend?" he asked.

I looked straight into his lizard eyes. "I saw her walking toward the Saloon right after I got here, but I didn't speak to her. She was quite a distance away."

"Was she alone?"

"She was talking to someone." I scrunched my face up and thought about it. "I didn't pay much attention."

That was lie number two and there was no reason for it, except I didn't like Officer Peterson. I didn't think I was protecting Nate Wright; more like I was just being obstinate.

Peterson turned to Sheriff Gonzales. "Do you have any more questions?"

"No," the sheriff said, with a shake of his head. "That pretty much covers everything."

I let my shoulders drop for the first time since the interview had started. The release of tension felt wonderful. I stood. "If there's nothing more, I'll—"

"No," Peterson said. "Be seated. I do have another question or two." He moved until he was sitting straight in his chair like a military recruit.

I sat down. "What can I tell you?"

He cleared his throat and threw out the question. "Why did you leave the camp this morning?"

My muscles tightened back up. This guy did an interview like a bridge player laid out a hand. Or maybe he did an interview like Freddie Krueger went after his victims.

"I left to pick up Sinatra." I was rewarded with blank stares. One small step for me . . . "My friend, Beth Fairfield, has a kitten who's been wreaking havoc at her house, and on Thursday," I paused. "Was that really just yesterday?" It didn't seem possible.

The sheriff nodded. "Yes, ma'am, it was."

Peterson wasn't quite glowering, but his expression held no warmth. "Go on."

"Oh, sorry. It just seems like so long ago." And that was the truth. Surely a lifetime had passed since I'd gone to pick up Beth for camp. "Anyway, yesterday Beth gave me the kitten. Unfortunately, I couldn't take him right then, since we were leaving for Green Clover, and I couldn't drop him at my house because I live a good twenty minutes in the other direction. Anyway, after I heard about May, I wanted some comfort; that's why I went to get Sinatra. The kitten. He's in our cabin."

Peterson stared at me and waited, but I had nothing to add. Particularly because I'd just remembered Mrs. Martin, and how I'd told her I was picking something up for Beth's demonstration. I was getting tangled in my lies, which is what happens when a basically honest person strays off the straight and narrow.

Finally Peterson blinked and said, "Is there anything else you'd like to tell us?"

Not to that man, I didn't. I shook my head no.

Officer Peterson was still staring when Sheriff Gonzales leaned forward. "Okay, do you know of anyone who might have wanted Ms. Feather dead? Or any reason someone might have for killing her?"

I considered it. The more I went over the options the less viable they seemed. No one would kill over the Tivolini contract. Love was a classic motive for murder, but from what I'd seen, May and Ron weren't having a lover's quarrel. Just the opposite.

Between the two subjects, it was better to talk about the contract.

"I know that competition for the Tivolini contract has people a little tense, but it doesn't seem important enough to kill over."

Sheriff said to Peterson, "That's what Cordelia Wright was telling us about. That contract."

"Oh. Sure." Peterson looked at me. "Are you up for it?"

"No. I'm not what you would consider a designer."

Peterson took his time, but finally he nodded. "And you didn't leave the cabin after you went to bed last night?"

"No."

"Anything else you'd like to tell us?"

"Nothing."

The sheriff requested that I not leave the camp until the retreat was over. However, he added that it was merely a request. If at some point I did need to leave, it would be appreciated if I told them where I could be reached.

He added there would be a transcription of the interview, which I would have to sign. He also said I was not to talk to anyone about my interview, since it could prejudice what they had to say. Then I was free to go.

And I went. I was out of there in a flash, almost tripping over Lynn who was sitting suspiciously close to the door. She tried to smile sweetly, but sugar wasn't in her nature. I had the worst feeling that she'd heard every word of my interview.

I turned my back on her and started toward the table where Beth and Cordy were now sitting alone, but then I remembered that I wasn't supposed to talk to anyone. Beth saw me and waved. I pointed to the outside door, to let her know that I was leaving. She nodded, but she looked more worried than when Shannan had gone out on her first date—I didn't like that at all.

I needed comfort in the form of a dip cone from the Dairy Queen outside of town, or maybe a piece of fudge from one of the little stores in Wimberley. I'd just have to tell Sheriff Gonzales that I was leaving. I headed back to the private dining room hoping he didn't ask where I was going and why. It wasn't a secret, but I didn't want Peterson to know he'd rattled me.

The door was cracked open; apparently I hadn't closed it well. Lynn was watching with great interest as I put my hand on the knob. Before I turned it, I heard Peterson say, "I don't give a damn—she's hiding something, and I intend to hound her until I find out what it is."

The sheriff said, "You might want to remember who she is."

Peterson made a snorting sound. "The Camden name doesn't mean shit to me."

My head snapped up, and I saw Lynn with her snotty little grin aimed at me. Without malice aforethought, I pushed open the door. Two very surprised men looked up.

"Officer Peterson," I said. "I'm glad the Camden name doesn't mean 'shit' to you, and do you know why? Because translation is everything." Then, before he could respond, and without any forethought at all, I muttered, "Little moron."

I hadn't meant to say that out loud. I had shot from the mouth, as my son says.

Peterson's face went rigid and white with fury, then just as quickly went cold and blank. Only his eyes showed emotion, they were icy, radiating something much deeper than anger. He raised one eyebrow and tipped his head just slightly. It was the look of the samurai, and the serial killer. He was making me a promise; he wasn't finished with me, and when he was, I would be very sorry.

I closed the door and stood there shaking in the heat of camp. Lynn was still watching me, her eyes glittering with the cheap thrill of seeing me threatened.

"Same to you," I snapped, marching toward the door.

I thought of Peterson's face. My grandfather always said that if you live a full life, you'll make some enemies, and that's expected, but you had to remember that an enemy was a luxury. Sometimes a real expensive luxury.

I had just made an enemy I couldn't afford.

Thirteen

i **headed out, thinking that with my connections,** surely, I was privy to information that would get this murder solved. Which in turn would get the DPS officers out of our camp, and Officer Peterson off my back.

The more I thought about it, the faster I walked up the trails to the main road. Who did I know in the attorney general's office? I went through a list of names, but there'd been a regime change since my time in the senate. Two, actually, and I couldn't think of a single solitary person who had quite the power I was looking for.

What if I just contacted some old colleagues? Maybe a senator who had some clout. Maybe John Cornyn. No, he was in Washington. There was Kevin O'Keeffe, who was in the attorney general's office, but this wasn't his area of expertise, and wasn't he doing Sports Talk on the radio? Didn't matter, because I didn't much feel like explaining the problem to him. I didn't much feel like explaining it to anyone.

The other thing is that I don't like asking for favors. My father always said that if you were asking for favors, you were getting something you didn't deserve in the first place. The rest of the political world doesn't feel that way, but he was a straight shooter, and I'd inherited way too much of that attitude.

My feet had been moving as fast as my thinking, and I

looked up to find myself nearly at the front entrance of the camp. For the first time since I'd been coming to Green Clover, the big wrought iron gates were closed. On this side was a female deputy who was pretending not to watch what looked like a carnival on the other side of the fence.

There were two TV news trucks and one other van, and there were a couple of people looking in the gates, as if Green Clover was a great big zoo. The most animated one was the young man who was waving his arms frantically and shouting, apparently at me.

"Hey! I need to talk to you. Hey!"

I nodded at the deputy and made my way toward the gate. I recognized the yeller. He was a reporter for Channel 17 and he never seemed to know his butt from page ten. He'd covered two major events that I was part of and always blundered his way in and asked the stupidest questions I'd ever heard in my life. Once at a Bead Show he looked at Beth's booth, which was filled with incredible beaded jewelry, then he looked at Beth who was making a beaded bracelet and said, "So, you have something to do with beads, is that right?"

"Hey—you," he yelled at me again.

"Hay is for horses," I said, "And for little jackasses."

That stopped him, but not for more than a second or two.

"Well, hey, I just wanted to put you on TV. Make you a star—"

Lounging against a van was another reporter who was trying hard not to grin. That was tough because he, Lar Brill, has a megawatt smile and it sneaks out whether he likes it or not.

"Mr. Brill," I said, moving in his direction.

"Ms. Camden," he responded.

"Hey," the young reporter said, "do you know her? Who is she? I could use an interview here."

"Friend of yours?" I asked Larry.

"I've never invited him to my Christmas party," Lar responded.

"Yes, but have you ever invited me?" I wanted to know.

Larry Brill has been in Austin news long enough to make lots of friends. While most reporters operate on the theory that "if it's bleedin', it's leadin'," Larry has convinced the powers-that-be that news should also include coverage of people who aren't murderers or crooks, and events that aren't just car crashes or political scandals. What a concept. When major charity functions are in the works, Lar is the one person who will do a story on it. The nonprofits in this city have raised millions of dollars because of him, so he has entrée to any event he finds interesting. As a result, he got a personal invitation to the president's inaugural ball when his bosses couldn't buy a ticket from a scalper.

"Actually, I've invited you to my party twice," Larry said, "but you never attend."

"Conflicts," I explained. "But if you invite me, I'll be there this year. Now tell me, what in the world you are doing here?"

"The news director decided that I'm the natural for this story, since 'these are my people.'" He shook his head. "She said that with a straight face, even though we both know we're short-staffed."

I was looking around. "Is there some place that we could talk?"

He seemed a little surprised but nodded toward the van. "Will that do?"

"Too hot."

"Hey, hey—what about my interview?" The little jackass was only a few feet away.

"Not interested," I said. "Thank you for the offer."

"Well, hey, you should want to be on TV. How about if I just hang out with you and Lar, in case you change your mind—"

"We," I said to him, putting my hand through the gate to gesture to Lar, "Mr. Brill and I, are going for a private tête à tête. You don't know what that is, but you should understand the word *private*. Have you gotten that far in your vocabulary book?"

"You didn't have to get snappy," he responded. "If you don't want me to make you famous, it's your loss, not mine."

Lar was grinning full force now. "Ms. Camden, how about if I follow you?"

"This way." I turned to my right, away from everyone else at the gate, and walked along the fence line behind May's trailer, which now had bright yellow police tape crisscrossing the door. May wouldn't have liked the color combination.

There was a small path on my side of the fence, but Larry had to fight his way through sticker vines, algarita bushes with thorns, and scrubby oaks.

"Where are we going?" he asked. At least he was a good sport about it.

"You'll see."

We went on for about the length of a football field until I found a gate in the wire fence. In the past I'd never had need of it, but I thought now would be a good time to see if it worked.

Turned out the old wrought-iron gate wasn't even locked, just latched with a rusty stretch of wire. I slipped it up, and Lar crawled through a bush to meet me.

"I'm glad you opened this," he said, dodging errant branches. "Otherwise, this might be illegal entry."

"You're my guest," I said. I gestured toward the path that would take us even farther from the gate and anyone who might overhear us. "Could you use a little exercise?"

"Oh, sure. Why not?" He was brushing the scratches on his arms.

"I'm sorry about that."

"No need to apologize for the flora; it goes with the territory."

And so we walked. After a few minutes he said, "What's so secretive? Can you tell me why you're luring me off into the woods?"

"Information," I said. "No one is saying anything. I can tell you about the camp and a little about the people, but we don't know a thing about the murder. Do you?"

"Actually, very little. The woman was May Polaski."

"Feather. May Feather."

"Not legally. Her ex-husband is Gene Polaski."

"Now there's an authentic Native American moniker," I said. "Are they publicly releasing her name yet?" He shook his head, *no,* and I asked, "What about news of the murder?"

"Well, you know Channel Seventeen—I'll bet they've reported it, but there wasn't anything on the radio driving out here." The stations monitor each other like the characters in the old *Spy vs. Spy,* so Larry would know.

I'd asked the question because of my family. If one of them heard that there'd been a murder at Green Clover, they could have some bad moments before they found out it wasn't me. And that it wasn't Beth or Shannan. I needed to make some calls pretty quick to get that cleared up.

"Okay," I said. "I guess we can talk here." We were in the middle of the wide path.

Larry looked surprised. "I assumed we were going to the crime scene. If my sense of direction is still working, it's down this way; at least that's part of it. The crime scene, I mean. The other half is down on the campground, but that's sealed off."

"It was here?" I asked.

"I would bet that if we went much farther, we'd run into some police tape."

"Do you know how she was killed?"

He shook his head. "A cop friend told me that she was bruised, but that could have been from the fall. He also said, off the record, that he didn't think she drowned, even though they found her half in the river. Her neck was broken."

That made an ugly picture. "Do you know when this happened?"

"I don't think any one does."

"Well, you're not much help. Will you tell me when you find out? I have the feeling that you'll hear a lot sooner than I will."

"I can do that," he said. "And how about if you give me an interview? Nothing important, just about the camp."

"Wouldn't you prefer someone more colorful?"

He raised one eyebrow. "More colorful than Katherine Zoe Camden? How is that possible?"

"I meant a professional beader, since this is a bead retreat. I'm just an amateur, and not even a very good one."

"Works for me."

"This way." I led him back toward the trailers, telling him about Green Clover and giving him some background on the bead retreats. When we got to the clearing with the trailers we were almost run over by Angie Hogencamp, who was charging toward her own sleeping-and-schlepping trailer. She had her head down, muttering under her breath.

"Angie," I said, "What's the problem?" Her head of curly gray hair came up, and she looked surprised to see us.

"The problem would be that ass in the private dining room. Officer Peterson. I told him everything I heard last night, and he—"

"You heard something? What?" I asked. "What did you hear?"

"Now, see, that's the kind of response I was looking for. He talked to me like I was either demented or lying, neither of which is true at the moment. Tomorrow, maybe, but not today."

"Consider the source," I said, remembering what he'd said about the Camden name. "If you want, in a little bit, we could commiserate together."

"Sure. When did you have in mind? I was planning on getting something to drink, and then hitting something. I haven't decided what."

Larry was listening all too intently, but the man was a reporter, so it was expected. I said to her, "How about if I meet you at the tetherball clearing? You can beat that ball into submission, and I'll help." First I had those phone calls to make. "Say, in twenty minutes?"

"You're on." She started to give me a high five, but I was slow and she missed, smacking empty air, instead. "You see?" she said. "That's the way my day has gone." She shrugged and went into her trailer.

"If," Larry said, "she tells you something important, you will call me, right?"

"*Quid pro quo*," I said, walking up to the TonyCraft Fifth Wheel. "And now let me get you someone to put on camera."

I knocked on Tony's door and noticed that it took only a second for him to appear. He was wearing a pressed denim shirt with the TonyCraft logo over the pocket and his hair looked recently combed. In his hand was a ruby red beaded belt of six or eight strands of glass beads held together by seed bead loops. There were bead tassels on the ends, and in the sunlight the belt shone like a maharaja's jewels.

"Kitzi, what a surprise," he said to me, but his eyes were on Larry. I guessed that Tony'd been watching out the window, trying to figure a way to get on television. That made things easier for both of us.

"I'd like to introduce you to a friend of mine. He needs someone to interview—he's with the news media. Would you be interested?"

I introduced the two men, who shook hands. They were almost the same height, but Larry looked more substantial, like a solid person. Tony was thinner and seemed a little wimpy in comparison.

"I'd be willing to talk on camera," Tony said.

"We'll have to go back to the van," Larry said, gesturing toward the front entrance.

"No problem." Tony started to hand me the belt, but I shook my head.

"Makes a nice prop," I said.

"Oh, right." Then he said, "Why don't you wait in the trailer for me? Get yourself something cold to drink?"

"Actually, I need to call my family. Since we're going to be on the news, I don't want them worrying."

"*Mi casa es su casa.* And my cell phone, too. Larry, give me just a minute," Tony said as casually as if they were old drinking buddies.

Tony ushered me inside where it was dim and much cooler. To my left was the dining booth where he'd obviously been sitting, judging by the strands of red beads lying across the table. I went straight to them since my beading time at camp had been minimal, so far, and I was feeling deprived. "Oh, wow. More belts."

I would have reached for them, but he said, "I gather you didn't want to talk to any reporters."

"No, actually, I didn't."

He opened a full-length pantry to reveal strands and strands of beads on cup hooks. More jewel tone belts were also on hooks, and Tony casually picked up the ones from the table and put them away. I wanted to climb into the cupboard and run my fingers through them all, but Tony closed the door, shutting off my view. Next he took a cell phone from the narrow shelf beside the table. "Here you go."

I shook my head to help me break out of the glitter-induced trance. "Are you sure?" After his earlier talk about poor business, I didn't want to make expensive calls on his dollar. "I'll just run down—"

"I don't mind. I get about a million minutes a month, and I never use them all." He handed me the phone. "Help yourself to anything in the refrigerator." He started to go then turned back, "Any coaching for me?"

His personality had transformed back to Mr. Charming. "You'll be great," I said. "Just talk normally, the way you do in your demonstrations."

"Damn straight," he said with a smile. "And the belt is a great idea." He held it up. "I sort of had that intention all along." Tony Campanelli was as devious as I'd suspected. "Be back."

And he went out, leaving me alone in his lair.

The interior colors were primarily greens and browns with accents of deep purple, creating a combination that was masculine and a touch bohemian. It wasn't the usual bachelor pad, but then Tony wasn't the usual bachelor.

Directly in front of me was the couch, then the kitchen area. I moved over to the booth, sat down, and picked up the cell phone.

The air conditioner turned on with a gurgling sound, and I felt chill bumps go over my entire body.

This was Tony Campanelli's trailer. May was dead, killed by someone who'd done her bodily harm; Tony was one of the few men on the grounds.

I'd already jumped up when my better sense kicked in. I sucked in some air, then peered out the curtains. The deputy was opening the front gate so Tony and Larry could get to the news van.

I had just been handed an opportunity to take some action that might get this murder investigation over and done with. And I had no excuse not to.

After thinking it through, I decided on just a little look-see around the trailer. No reading mail or anything like that—just looking.

I started with the refrigerator.

That was something of a cop-out, as my son used to say, but I was a novice and needed to get into this slowly. Besides, Tony had said I could get something to drink. I opened the refrigerator door to discover that the inside was nice and clean and held mostly things to drink: bottled water, diet RC, regular Dr. Pepper, some V8, and a six-pack of Heineken Ultra. In a bin I found a couple of bananas, an apple, and two peaches.

This guy was squeaky clean.

Which meant I had to look further. I closed the door without taking anything and, after another quick peek out the window to assure myself that Tony was busy elsewhere, I moved to the back of the trailer. There I looked in the bathroom. The little square of space was pristine, the cap was on the toothpaste (Tom's Natural Spearmint) and the towel was hung precisely by the small shower.

Not only squeaky clean but exceptionally neat, as well.

Next was the bedroom. I held my breath as I nudged open the door. I don't know what I'd expected but what I found was a carefully made bed, a closet with a few pairs of jeans, three shirts, and a pair of loafers. The mirror above the dresser was streak-free, and the only spot that could remotely be called cluttered was the top of the dresser. There was a rose and a couple of pieces of candy wrapped in gold foil.

A rose? I edged forward to take a closer look. It was a real, red, long-stem rose wrapped in white tissue with a red ribbon holding it together. There was no card and the rose had been there a while, since the petals were limp and withering. Now that was interesting.

Then I looked a little harder at the candies and discovered that they weren't edible. Well, I actually couldn't judge that, but they weren't chocolates. They were Gold Coin condoms.

One wilting red rose and three unopened condoms. A hot date gone bad? And three condoms? At my age that seemed like optimism, but then what did I know? Feeling prurient, I looked around for a trash can, just to see what might be in it, but a strange noise came from outside.

I hustled back to the dining room table, careful to leave the bedroom door at the same angle it had been before. Then I peeked outside. Apparently it was the air conditioner that had made the noise, but it didn't matter; I was relieved to have an excuse to stop snooping. In my many years of life I have done some things that were illegal, and to my regret, a few things that were actually immoral, but poking around in Tony Campanelli's bedroom felt downright tacky.

I filed away what I'd learned and checked the window again. Tony had his back to me, still fingering the belt, and they were recording. It was going to be a few more minutes.

I picked up the cell phone. I could make my calls and with luck be out before Tony returned. Then I'd think some more about what I had found.

First I called my son, who is an upwardly mobile techno-marketing whiz. At twenty-nine, he's working for one of the large firms in town, and by everything I can see, doing rather well. The reason I called him first was that if my mother heard anything about the murder, he'd be the one she'd turn to for reassurances.

"You've reached the voicemail of Will Camden. I'm in meetings most of the day, *blah, blah, blah* . . ." My son is single, bright, and I think very dear, but he is going through a very "busy" phase of his life.

I left a message explaining that there'd been a death at the camp, someone I knew but not well, and while we were upset, everyone else was fine. Including Beth and Shannan.

To Will, Shannan fills the role of the adoring younger sister, one that his real sister, who is older, does not. He calls Beth his "other mother," so both of them are important to him and he needed to know they were safe.

I added that it would be good if he called his grandmother or maybe stopped by to see her after work. I didn't say that it would be nice if he could arrange to do that before nine o'clock when his workaholic day ended. The original suggestion was *should be* enough. He doesn't like suggestions any better than the rest of us. I did tell him I loved him, and that I'd be checking messages on my cell phone if he wanted to call back.

Considering the circumstances, I had to figure Green Clover's cell phone rule was temporarily suspended.

Next I called my daughter. Katie is thirty-one and has three of the most adorable and brilliant children I've ever seen, but I'm not in any way prejudiced. What grandmother is? Clifford Camden Brewster, aka Cliffie, and his twin sister, Shelby, are five. He can read pretty well, feeds their dog in the evening, and informed me on his last visit that moths are nocturnal. Shelby is an athlete who swims, plays T-ball, and can outshoot her father at basketball. She's also into beading. I baby-sit them as often as possible, but I always wonder who's in charge.

Their little sister, Gabrielle, just turned three. She is the seductress of the family, and to balance that out, has the temper of a dictator. Gabrielle doesn't need a keeper, she needs staff, but I love her just the same.

Once more I heard the click of an answering machine, and I repeated much the same message I'd left my son.

Last, I called my mother, and wonder of wonders, she was out, too. Probably gardening. "Mom, it's me, Kitzi."

"It's after lunch on Friday, and I just wanted you to know that I'm at camp and doing fine." The problem was that my mother forgot things. Not all the time, but often enough that she worried herself and me. I didn't want to frighten her. "Remember when I used to send you letters from camp? 'Dear mom, my broken leg doesn't hurt but my poison ivy is killing me'?" I laughed. "Well, I don't have either of those. I did my demonstration and it turned out great. I'll tell you about it when I get home Sunday evening. If you need anything call Will or Katie. I love you. 'Bye."

I was looking for the button to end the call when Tony returned. I'd been hoping to be gone before he got back. "How was it?" I asked.

He smiled. "I made them promise to say that I was Tony Campanelli of TonyCraft. I also held up the belt as a sample of what I'm teaching at the retreat."

"Good going," I said. His portion would be edited to seconds, and precious few of those, but you could never tell what Larry might leave in.

"Did you get your calls made?" Tony asked, placing the belt on the table.

"Yes, thank you." I handed back the phone. "Well, I guess—"

"Can you spare a minute?"

"Oh. Sure. Okay," I said, my hand automatically going

for the belt. My fingers caressed the sparkling beads. "Do you live here full-time? In the trailer?"

"You must be kidding. There wouldn't be room for me." He opened a cupboard above my head, and I leaned out enough to see bags and bags of bead kits.

I hadn't looked in the cupboards; now I didn't have to. "Oh, wow."

"This is my storage and my office. I do sleep here when I travel to shows, but I'd go nuts if I had to live here all the time. I have a house in Clarksville." That's an old section of Austin where things are kind of funky and way overpriced. Made me wonder again about how bad his business was. "You don't have anything to drink," he said. "What can I get you?"

"How about a bottle of water?" I asked. "Do you have any of those?" I was playing the innocent, like I hadn't checked things out.

"Sure." He reached into the refrigerator behind him and brought one out. "Do you want a glass?"

"Oh, no." I pulled open the top and took a drink. He was being awfully nice. "You wanted to talk to me?"

Finally, he slid into the booth to a spot across from me. "Look," he said. "I owe you an apology. I was a little over the line when I shut down your computer this morning. I, well, it's just that I'm so stressed. And now with the police here . . . anyway, I didn't mean to be a jerk."

It was a nice speech, but he hadn't apologized. He'd merely stated there was a need to apologize. "I understand," I said.

Tony's eyes, rimmed in curly, dark lashes, were on mine. "Thanks. I didn't want you to be pissed at me. You've always been someone I admire, and what with the cops and everything, we all need to stay friends and stick together."

"Right." Which would be the equivalent of sticking to a prickly pear. He was definitely up to something.

"You're better with people than I am," he went on. "If the police were going to talk to anyone, I figured it would be you. Did they? Talk to you? Tell you anything about how May died?"

"No, nothing. Sorry," I added. "Obviously, they haven't said anything to you, either."

"Oh, well, they're pretty closemouthed." He fidgeted with the bead belt in front of us, and I dropped the end I'd been holding. He seemed more than mildly curious about May's murder. "I'm not trying to sound like a complainer," he added, "but this is the last thing we needed, what with the Tivolini contract and all. How is Beth holding up?"

"She seems to be doing fine. We haven't talked about it today, but then there hasn't been time to talk about anything." Another aspect of Green Clover that was notable by its absence was conversation.

"Her husband's a lawyer, isn't he? Is he with one of the big firms?"

"Not too big." And just where was Tony going with these questions?

"But he's successful, right? He's a partner?"

"Yes, with Ruff, Gonzales, Bailey and Burnett. Why?"

Tony shrugged. "I just worry about Beth. She doesn't seem equipped to handle all the demands of a company like Tivolini. The design work is just the start of it. I'm sure they'll want promotion, too, and that's not Beth's forte. I don't mean she's not good at little workshops or demonstrations, because she is; I'm not trying to put her down. I just can't see her at a dinner party given by Ivana Trump, and that's the kind of thing that Tivolini would expect. Big charity functions . . ."

He stopped, maybe realizing who he was trying to snow. I could think of at least one evening when Ivana Trump had attended a charity auction in my home, and Beth had been there, too. They'd gotten along very well, exchanging horror stories about remodeling, if my memory served me.

I didn't mention it to Tony. "I don't think that's an issue," I said.

"It's not that she couldn't do it," he amended. "It's just that Beth may not be the right representative for Tivolini at those kinds of functions."

Beth wasn't 'right' because she was fifty-seven years old, seventy pounds overweight, and had frizzy hair. Maybe glamour wasn't Beth's forte, but neither did she stoop to Tony's precious kind of backstabbing.

"And another thing," he went on, apparently taking my silence as agreement. "I worry about her health. Beth hasn't been well this year, and added stress could make it worse."

She'd had gall bladder surgery six months earlier and was up and beading within twenty-four hours. Obviously, she wasn't in shape to run a marathon, but then what percentage of people in this world are?

"So," I said, "you think she shouldn't talk to the Tivolini people? Is that where this is going?"

"Oh, no, I'm sorry, I would never suggest that. Her work is good, and I think Tivolini will like it, too, but that's not the only criteria for the contract." He took a breath and said, "I've done a lot of thinking about this, and I'm sorry I'm coming at my point backwards. Here's the thing, Kitzi." The use of my name alerted me to the onset of a major snow flurry. "Beth and I together have much more to offer Tivolini than either one of us separately. Collaboration is what makes sense. She and I could form a partnership outside of TonyCraft, and we'd be unbeatable, No one else would have a chance."

I nodded, thinking about it.

He went on. "Before you say anything, give me a minute to explain; this could be fabulous. Instead of competing, we double our strengths. I can run in the high-powered world of Tivolini, so I would be the front man; I'd attend the various functions, schmooze with the high and mighty, whatever was needed. You know. Things Beth would just hate. Meanwhile, Beth can stay in the background, doing what she does best, the design work. Oh, I'd have some input there, as well, I am a pretty good designer even if I do say so myself, but that would be Beth's primary function. I'm not sure how we'd work it all out financially, but I'd be amenable to an even split."

I didn't doubt that one bit; to me it sounded like he'd be getting a free ride on Beth's coattails.

"Why are you telling me this, Tony?" I asked.

Voices, female and angry, were coming from outside the trailer, pulling my attention from the absurdity of his proposal.

"Because," he said, ignoring the distraction, "I know that you and Beth are close, so I thought this idea might be better coming from you instead of me. She'd be more open to a suggestion from you."

Tony was right about my friendship with Beth, but he seriously overrated the friendship I had with him. "That's not my place," I said. One voice was getting louder. "I'm also not convinced that it would be in Beth's interest—"

I stopped as the voice outside yelled, "Damn it, do something."

Fourteen

i was immediately up and out the door with Tony behind me. Across the way Jennifer was yelling at the deputy; she even shook her fist, making her blonde curls bounce. If she hadn't been so intense, it might have been amusing.

"You have no right to keep my things!"

The deputy who'd been at the front gate earlier eased back a step or two. Her voice was calm. "You're right, and I'm sorry if you think we are trying to do that."

Jennifer saw us and made a visible effort to compose herself. She spoke again, this time more evenly. "Then let me in there."

"I would, ma'am, but it was the DPS forensic team that sealed the trailer, and once we've called them, we need to accept their judgment. I've already radioed for one of them to come up here and talk to you—"

"And that was a long time ago! I went back to the cabin, I got a soda, and now I'm here again. I told you, I'm going to need clothes and a toothbrush. Makeup. My purse. When I left the trailer this morning, I didn't know you were going to lock it up." She turned to me. "Look what they did." She pointed to the crime scene tape covering the door. "All my things are in there and now it's sealed. It's so stupid! I was in there this morning. I slept in there last

night! I've moved stuff and touched things; what does it
matter if I get my underwear?"

She was in the midst of one of those irrational furies—
the kind usually brought on by hormones or men, although
I could see that murder might cause it, too.

I stepped closer. "Jennifer, is there some way I can
help?" The red rims of her eyes made the irises turquoise.
Veins showed under her translucent skin.

"She's just being rude." Jennifer jerked her head to indi-
cate the deputy who seemed perfectly polite to me. "They
can't believe May was killed in the trailer. They just can't.
That would be stupid. I was in there all last night."

"I think it's the crime scene tape; the deputy isn't allowed to break it," I said.

"It's ridiculous," Jennifer said, now arrogant as well as
angry. "They don't know what the hell they're doing."

Tony was in the doorway, taking the conversation in but
not adding anything.

The deputy spoke to all of us. "I'll call the forensic team
again and see if they'll get someone up here. I'm sure
they'll cooperate as best they can." She spoke into a microphone on her shoulder, using some ten-code along with
some understandable English. What I got from the ex-
change was that she needed someone at the trailer ASAP,
and they responded with a stall. "How long will that be?"
she asked in an official voice. "I have people waiting for
you."

I thought the garbled response was "ten minutes."

There was more ten-code before she rehooked the
walkie-talkie to her uniform and said to Jennifer, "It won't
be much longer."

I took Jennifer by the arm. "Why don't we take a
walk, and by the time we get back, they'll have the trailer
unlocked."

She looked at her watch, then at the deputy and said,
"We'll be back in ten minutes. Please, be ready for me." To
Tony she added, "Are you coming, too?"

He shook his head. "No, thanks. I ran last night, so I'll stay here." He gave us a quick wave before reentering the trailer.

"You've had a rough time," I said, turning toward the path.

Jennifer threw one last dirty look at the deputy and then came with me. "I'm okay. And I'm not trying to be rude, but they're pissing me off. I didn't sleep very well, and then they woke me up early this morning, and they've been asking me questions——" She sounded like a tired five-year-old. She must have realized it, too. "I'm sorry. I'm really sorry."

I could identify with that feeling of exhaustion, anger, and impotence. Anyone who's ever dealt with bureaucrats can.

"It's tough," I said. "You've done very well so far. You just need some rest."

We were going back the same way Larry and I had come. Jennifer was walking fast, her legs in the heavy jeans slapping against each other with every step. I kept up as best I could.

"It's not like I don't want to cooperate," she said, pulling a leaf off a low-hanging sycamore branch. "Really, I do. It's just that I'm tired, and now they won't let me get my stuff."

"When did they seal the trailer?" I asked, quick-stepping beside her.

"I don't know. It was like that when I came back from lunch. I've been trying to get someone to let me in there ever since. All I want is my stuff—not May's."

She yawned. The fight was going out of her, and I was glad of that; no sense having the officials mad at all of us. If we stayed on the path we'd end up on the backside of the Lazy L, and with a little luck it would be quiet enough that I could get her to take a nap.

"You know," I said. "If you rested for awhile, I'll bet you'd feel a lot better——"

"But I want my stuff! I need a hairbrush——"

"I have a brand new brush that I bought for Sinatra——"

"You used it on Sinatra?"

"No, it's new. No one has used it. You can have that—"
I stopped talking. The scrub was thicker here. There was a
quick bend in the path, and suddenly I was facing crime
scene tape blocking off an area on our left. It meant that we
were very close to the place where May had been killed.

Jennifer saw it, too and started to cry. "Oh, God, I hate
this. I want to go home."

I put an arm around her and let her cry for a little, and then
I got her walking. "Maybe we should call your parents—"

She jerked away from me. "No. We can't."

"They don't live nearby?"

"We don't talk to each other. Besides, I don't need
them." And she stopped talking. In fact she stopped making any sound, and she walked with a rigid precision.

"Let's head for the cabin," I said. "I think you need a
fuzzy little buddy to make you feel better."

She softened and nodded, sending a few more tears
down her cheeks. "Shannan was playing with him. I didn't
want to butt in."

"Well, that's just silly. We can all play with him. Come
on," I said, picking up speed. "We'll jog."

I was late meeting Angie, but she was still there, sitting
on a fallen log and reading a book. It was a beautiful little
spot, a clearing tucked away with tall trees protecting it
and a tetherball pole in the middle of it. It was a great place
to deal with frustrations.

"Sorry I'm late," I said.

I'd gotten Jennifer back to the Lazy L, and the place had
been deserted. Apparently, everyone was beading away
their worries in the dining hall. Shannan was nowhere
around, but Sinatra was in his cage, probably where she
had left him. The situation looked good on the surface, until Jennifer let Sinatra out and he decided to attack. First he
went after me, leaving some bite marks on my hand, then

he crawled under a bunk and wouldn't come out. Until, that is, Jennifer had her back to him. Then he leaped out and up, sinking his claws into her jeans.

She let out a scream and whirled around. I had to catch Sinatra before he was flung off into space.

It had taken a few minutes to get them both settled, Jennifer on my bunk, Sinatra in his cage on the floor beside her. I just couldn't let him loose or he'd attack again, or run off while she slept. At least she could put her fingers through the wire and pet him.

"You want to play?" I asked Angie, gesturing to the pole. The ball and rope were already attached.

She held out her hands. In one she had a bottled wine cooler and in the other a half-eaten oatmeal cookie. "You missed all the good stuff," she said.

"That's a disgusting combination."

"Some woman came by with a cooler, and she was handing these out. You know, that weird woman with the Hummer."

"Ah." I said. "Lynn." The noir beader. "Seems like her kind of meal."

"I brought the cookies, she had the wine coolers." Angie stuffed the last cookie in her pocket and put the drink on the ground. "I think she's making up for last night. Which side do you want?"

"Either side. I'll draw the line." I took a stick and drew a straight line across the space around the pole. "What sins did she commit that she has to atone for them with wine coolers?"

Angie pulled the ball out and smacked it hard; I let it go around the pole once before I pounded it with both fists, sending it flying back at her and unwinding the rope in the process. She'd been right, hitting something did feel good.

"You didn't hear? I guess everyone forgot, what with May's death. Lynn, is that her name?" she asked and I nodded. "She showed up in the Saloon about ten-thirty drunk on her butt."

"No kidding? What did she do?"

Angie hit the ball back to me. "Well, she didn't dance naked on the table or anything like that, but she was pretty obnoxious. First she was badmouthing women. Not anyone in particular, but the entire sex. Then men. She said that sex was the root of all evil, or bad times, or something like that."

"Bad divorce," I said, thinking of her comment the day before. Or was this more recent? "Did she mention any names?" We got into our stride with the tetherball, smacking it back and forth with enough vigor to work out some pent-up aggravation.

"None. Just men in general. And then, she started insulting us."

"Nice way to make friends. Anyone in particular?"

"Me. I was making beaded bookmarks, you know, I'm always giving books to my cousins, so I thought they would be a nice addition. It's not like I claim to be a beader." Angie was a rubber stamper and a vendor who sold supplies for stampers. "So, there I was, talking, drinking a beer, and she looks at the bookmark I'm making and says, 'Well, doesn't it take a lot of talent to put beads on a string?' Like I said it did."

"The woman is obviously a moron," I said. "Did you see the pieces she makes?"

"Oh, yeah, and I was dying to say it doesn't take much talent to stick a bead up a mannequin's nose, but I controlled myself. I didn't want to insult anyone else who might do that. Besides, I really do like those pieces." She hit the ball with some real force. "Sorry. I'm still a little pissed, even if she did bring me the wine cooler."

"At least she apologized."

Angie shook her head. "No, she didn't. She just said she'd been a bitch, and to make up for it, she thought she owed me a drink. No apology offered."

"There's a lot of that going around. So what happened with Officer Peterson?"

"Oh, that." She waited until we'd both hit the ball a couple more times before she said, "Maybe I shouldn't say anything. Didn't they tell us not to talk about it?"

"At that point I wasn't paying attention—I had my eyes on the door like a horse eyeing the corral." I caught the ball with the side of my hand and it bounced off the pole twice before I got it going again. "I'll change the subject and ask you a question, instead. Ready?"

"Sure." She hit the ball and it made a half round before I sent it back.

"Let's say that a man, a man you know, invited you to his cabin."

"We don't have men here. At least not many." We had a rhythm going with the ball again. "Except Cordy's brother. Whew. Now there's a man."

"Which one?"

"The one who was here last night. Nate. He can eat crackers—"

"Wait for my question." I hit the ball a little harder than necessary. "This man invites you to his cabin. You show up, and on the dresser you see a red rose wrapped in tissue. Presumably for you. And three new condoms."

"Three?"

"Three. So, what do you think?"

"I think that man's been overdosing on his Viagra."

"Seriously."

"Seriously, I hope he took his Viagra. I also hope I don't fall asleep." She let the ball wind a bit, then struck it so hard it flew over my head. Then she said, "Actually, a woman was killed last night, so I wouldn't be going to any man's place around here." Practical. "So, what did you think?"

"Me? It wasn't me. In fact . . . I don't know who it was for. And I can't even tell you who the man was." I waited until I could reach the ball, and then I grabbed the rope and swung it to fling it back.

"That's cheating," she said.

"I never said I play fair."

"At least tell me if it was Nate. And who the woman was."

"It wasn't Nate, and I don't know who the woman was." I thought about it. "Maybe she showed up, saw the condoms, they got in an argument, and she left. I don't even know if she showed up." Now that was an interesting possibility. Maybe she never went to Tony's trailer. Maybe she, whoever she was, was in the backseat of a black Lexus with Ron Fairfield.

"But, wait, now I've got it. You saw the rose and the condoms in Tony's trailer," Angie guessed. "That's who you were talking to, and I saw you go inside."

"If I tell you, will you tell me about the argument you heard?"

She rolled her eyes. "Were you like this in the senate?"

"Angie," I said, "I think I was soft as a baby's smile. Of course, *Texas Monthly* said I could be mean as a rattlesnake and sneaky as a TV evangelist. They seriously overestimated my political talents."

"I'd believe their version, rather than yours. Okay, I'll tell you. It started when I was in the trailer taking a shower."

There wasn't much to her story. After Lynn had been rude to people in the Saloon, Angie had decided that she was no longer a happy camper and had gone back to her trailer. While she was showering, she heard an argument outside.

"We're talking about thin, thin walls on that trailer; you should be inside during the winter. Anyway, back to last night. As soon as I turned off the water, the voices got quiet. And then it was more like a kid's argument. 'Did not.' 'Did, too.' But those weren't the words."

"What were the words?"

"I couldn't actually make them out. More hissing sounds. It was the tone I'm talking about." She stopped the ball and looked at me. "I've got it figured out."

"What?"

"What happened last night. Here's my idea: Tony has the hots for May, so he invites her to his trailer. Right after her demonstration she shows up, and they're having a glass of wine or whatever, or who knows, maybe they started out with five condoms and used up two. Then, at some point Lynn knocks on the door, because she's got a thing for Tony. She spots May and makes a big scene. May leaves, and Lynn ends up in the Saloon cussing about all men and sex being the root of all evil." Angie nodded, her expression pleased. "And later, when I'm in the shower, I'll bet Lynn went and woke May up, and that's the arguing I heard." She turned serious. "Which means either Lynn or Tony killed May. That's pretty terrible."

We stood there a minute and thought it over. She could have been right, except I knew that after her demonstration, May was in the Lexus, rather than in Tony's trailer. There were a few other little problems, too.

"It's your turn to hit the ball," I said. She did and I went on, "Maybe I'm missing something but Tony has never appeared to be madly in love with May."

"In lust. He's always looking down her blouse." Angie frowned. "Okay, everybody does. Did. You couldn't help it."

I concurred with that, at least up to a point. "Tony doesn't seem too upset about her death. Not like he's missed a meal or shed a tear."

"I told you: it was lust, not love."

"Maybe. But I'll still bet you it wasn't May in his trailer last night." I hit the tetherball.

"Do you know something you're not telling me?"

She was dead-on with that, but I hedged, "Well, I can't say how I know . . ."

"I don't care if you were hanging from the flagpole eavesdropping—just tell me what it is."

"May was not in Tony's trailer. At least not then."

"And you won't say where she was?"

"I can't. But I know it for a fact as sure as I'm standing here."

Angie smacked the ball hard. "I just thought of something. That quarrel I heard? That's the first time I ever remember people arguing at Green Clover. Ever. We're always happy to see each other."

I hit the ball back, wondering if that meant whoever was doing the arguing, was the one who murdered May. "Bad times," I said.

"No shit." She used two fists to send the ball wrapping around the top of the pole several feet above my head. I watched, my hands on my hips, as the ball made the final two loops and touched the pole.

"You won," I said.

"I know that."

"I thought you were the one having the bad day? Mine appears to be slipping from lousy to worse," I replied. "Thanks for the information."

"You don't have to go off mad."

"I'm not. I'm just going off. Oh, and thanks for the therapy, too."

"You're welcome. It was mutual."

I turned onto the path that went up to the road. I had lots of new information to digest, and I was thinking I'd head toward the Rover so I could finally get my chocolate dip cone, which ought to help me digest it. That's when I heard my name called.

"Kitzi? Kitz. Do you have a minute?"

My stomach did a little leap at the voice I'd waited so many years to hear.

I slowed, but I couldn't get my legs to stop. It was still full afternoon with hot sunlight pouring down through the trees, and after the tetherball my body was sticky and my face sweaty. I was also lightly coated with dust.

Naturally, this is the way I'd look when Jeb and I finally came face to face. Isn't life just that way?

Fifteen

"When a Clover gal goes walkin' with her one and only man
Rest assured she'll do the most official thing she can
She won't let him hold her hand,
For he might not understand,
That a Clover gal's an angel in disguise . . .
Ha, ha!"

Green Clover camp song

i turned toward where Jeb Wright was standing.
Damn, he was cool looking. He had one hand in the
pocket of his khakis. His sage knit shirt with the polo
player on the pocket was tucked in just right, not a wrinkle
on it nor a drop of sweat anywhere on his body. At least
that I could see. And I wasn't looking at his body.

"Jeb," I said, hoping my smile looked like I was pleased
to see him.

"Hello." There was a good ten-second pause before he
added, "Well."

Apparently, Jeb wasn't feeling as cool as he was looking.

"Yes?" I said. He was the one who'd started this conversation, and he's the one who could get it moving in the
right direction.

During the pause, I studied his face. Those dark brown eyes were missing the fire they'd once held—in fact, they appeared downright wary, and I wondered if that was because he was looking at me, or if that was the way he faced life. In the bright sunlight his skin was pale, as if he spent too much time indoors. Beyond that he looked tired. I was almost at the point of feeling sorry for him when he finally spoke.

"It's been a long time," he said.

"Yes, it has." The last time I'd seen him had been when he'd dropped me off at my townhouse. That was before I'd moved back to the Camden Manse—my son, Will, had still lived with me, and so Jeb and I had said good-bye on the porch, kissing like a couple of teenagers.

We'd had a blissful day. He'd rented a convertible, a bright red Mazda, and we'd driven to the lake, then out to Johnson City, and on to Purple Sage where we'd had lunch. It was almost like a movie, with the wind blowing our hair and us singing along to the oldies station. We'd remembered all the words to "Satisfaction," and Jeb had tried an English accent for "I'm Henry the Eighth."

At the end of the day, I'd thought my heart would break when he kissed me one last time and said he had to go. I remember his face in the dim light of the full moon . . .

And now here he was, all these years later, standing in the sunshine at Green Clover. He was scrutinizing me, probably seeing some of the same changes I'd recognized in him. I thought I looked better than he did, but then I'd watched the years and the transformation come about gradually in me.

"You're still as beautiful as ever," he said.

"Liar."

He smiled. "Actually, I'm telling the truth. You look wonderful. How do you do it?"

"Living by the Golden Rule," I said.

I was doing unto others as I wanted them to do unto me—probably the total opposite of how he lived—but I suspected he didn't know what the Golden Rule was. The puzzled look told me I was right.

Finally, he laughed. "Don't tell me you've given up causing problems and having fun? Can't be the same Kitzi Camden I know."

I wanted to say that he didn't know me at all, probably never had. Instead, I raised one eyebrow and forced myself to smile. Too many years had passed by, too many times I'd wondered why he'd hurt me so, but I could see now that I'd been hurt by someone else. Someone of my own creation. I didn't seem to know this man.

He added, "I can't imagine you going for sainthood."

I thought about explaining, but there was no explanation in me. There didn't seem to be many words, either.

"Well . . ." Jeb said. When I still didn't speak, he glanced at his watch, then looked up to study me intently. "You've changed."

I nodded slowly. "I imagine I have." And then I did start feeling sorry for him. He'd been a rat and a brat, and I supposed he deserved to be told that, but who was I to do the telling? Instead, I dug down to find my manners and maybe even a little charm. "How is your wife?" I asked.

"My wife?" He let out a short, sardonic laugh. "Which one?"

I blinked. Obviously he hadn't spent any time pining away for me if he'd found time to marry more than one woman. "The one you married right after you left Austin," I said.

"Oh." His half-smile wasn't having an effect on me.

"You've had more than one?" I asked.

"Two. The first was Phoebe." His voice turned sad. "Just six months after the wedding, she left me for the minister who married us." He took in a breath. "It was unexpected, and quite a learning experience."

I recognized that as my cue to make sympathetic noises, and because, like most women I'm well trained, my mouth was already open when I realized what I was about to do. It

was pretty ironic that he was looking for some sort of consolation from me.

He wasn't going to get it.

"Here's what I tell myself," I said, "on those rare occasions when I have problems with the opposite sex: number
one, you picked the jerk. And number two, at least you
aren't stuck with the jerk now." I hoped he saw the double
meaning. "Words for you to remember," I finished.

He hesitated before saying, "I'll think about it."

"Good idea. Well, I'd better run. I've got some things to
get done before dinner."

"Oh?"

"Yes. Nice visiting with you." I hadn't meant to say that,
because it wasn't nice and he wasn't nice. "*Ciao*."

"Kitzi—"

In spite of myself I stopped and turned to look at him.
"Yes?"

"Maybe we can get together later . . ." He waited, like
maybe he was looking for me to fall for him again, melt into
a puddle at his well-shod feet, and utter rapturous little
whimpers. I could hardly breathe, so I wasn't about to waste
any air whimpering. When I stood as still as Lot's wife, and
probably about as happy, he finished with, "We can catch
up on each other's lives. Maybe this evening?"

"Of course. Sounds, uh, sounds good. Let me know
when." And I set off up the hill like I was training for the
Olympic walking event.

I turned onto another path and because I wasn't paying
attention to where I was going, almost ran into a tree. I
might have slumped against it but the way my luck was
running, Jeb would find me. Or Officer Peterson.

Instead, I cut off a side trail, and then around to another
wider path. Ahead of me was a tree trunk with several
rough wooden boards tacked to it. Each of the boards had
painted arrows pointing in different directions. A few were
useful and showed how to get to the Saloon and the horse

barn. One said *Wall Drug*. Another pointed upward, with the word *heaven*.

I didn't seem to be going to any of those places.

My steps were slower now as I assessed the damage to my psyche after my meeting with Jeb. Looking back I saw that I hadn't fallen apart, fallen back in love, or even fallen over my words. I had been calm. I had been the Kitzi Camden my friends and I don't recognize when reporters write about her, instead of the klutz who broke her heel and almost sat in the fountain at the governor's ball. Or the one whose daughter gripes at her about being more responsible.

My alter ego—every public person has one—had performed admirably.

I let out a shallow breath. I felt a little like the alcoholic who could finally drive by the liquor store without stopping. Doesn't mean you don't notice the liquor store, or react, but you do keep going. It meant I had grown beyond Jeb, but there was a sad side to that, too, because it meant I had left behind a little of me. Particularly the me who was naïve and more sweet than sour and believed in fairy tales. I suppose at my age it was well past time for that to happen, but wasn't it like a stiffening of the arteries? The ones around the heart?

I didn't want that to happen.

That's when I saw Beth coming down from a path above me. The worried look was back on her face, and she was shiny with perspiration.

"Are you okay?" I asked. "Is anything wrong?"

"I'm fine. Aren't we all?" she said. "Actually, I'm just stressed like all of us. Where have you been?" She stopped in front of me.

I dropped my voice. "Having a conversation with Jeb." I was surprised at how sad I sounded. Beth looked concerned, maybe a bit unhappy, so I added, "And this time I didn't swoon or faint, and I wasn't even overly nice to him. You should be proud of me."

"Are you sure you aren't taking him to dinner? Or on your way to do his ironing? Maybe buy him a car?"

"I never did most of those things, and honestly, I'm not now."

"Really? That's a good thing, a very good thing." She touched my arm. "So, how are you feeling after that? You look a little pale."

"That's from tetherball."

Her expression questioned the excuse, but she said, "Then how is he? Is he devastated that you didn't fall into his arms? You really didn't?"

"I did not. Promise. If you don't believe me, you can turn left at the intersection down there and you might see him. He's probably still standing there speechless."

"Maybe we could bronze him, and then no one would have to deal with him again."

It was quiet except for a blue jay squawking in a tree not too far off. "Maybe that's him."

"The voice is too deep," she said, then added seriously, "I'd love to waltz up to him and say, 'Hey, Jeb, how you hangin'?' I suppose that's tacky, but he brings out the worst in me."

I could hear the faint rustling of bushes farther down the path, no doubt the reason for the jay's upset. It was probably someone walking toward us and if so, it had to be Jeb. I couldn't face him again so soon. I raised my voice to say. "I have some things to do—I'll catch up with you later."

She nodded. "Sure."

I started off, then swung back around. "Have you seen Shannan? Do you know how she's doing?"

Beth shook her head. "I've haven't seen her since lunch. I was going to the barn in the hope that she's hanging out with the horses."

The footsteps were moving closer, like the jaws of a land shark closing in; I had to get out of there or I'd be needing anti-anxiety pills. "Before dinner, we'll talk."

Then I was away again, up the path and down another

one. Shannan was probably hiding out somewhere, maybe in Wimberley eating homemade fudge and buying CDs. Although I wasn't interested in the fudge, I was ready for my own brand of comfort food and a change of scenery.

I felt in my pocket. My driver's license was still there and the spare key was still hidden on the Rover, along with my emergency stash of cash and a credit card. Everything a woman needs for a getaway. I headed for the front entrance of the camp.

My hope was that the deputy would be gone so I could slip out before anyone official noticed me.

I got to the top of the path and peered up the road. There were voices, and I eased forward to discover a whole congregation of people at the front gates. The deputy was still there and she had been joined by the sheriff, Officer Peterson, and a couple of others that I didn't recognize.

I cut back along another path, then around a bend, so I was able to cross the road without being seen. At that point, I slipped behind the Saloon and kept moving until I came to the outer perimeters of the camp and the brushy area with the secondary gate. It was trickier here, but I carefully picked through the sticker bushes to the opening—except it wasn't. Open, that is. It was closed. Even worse, as I reached for the latch I discovered that the sunlight was glinting off the shiny metal of a brand-new combination lock.

If I'd been Scarlett O'Hara, I'd have stamped my foot and said, "Fiddle dee dee!" Instead I picked up a fist-sized rock with a thought of inflicting some damage to the new lock. My arm was raised, when Nate Wright stepped out from behind a tree.

"I take it you don't care for the new hardware?"

I started guiltily. "You scared me!" I lowered the rock.

For the first time I noticed a toolbox on the ground. Apparently Nate had been off watching the confab at the main gate when I arrived.

"Security duty," he said. "Locks on gates, dead bolts on

cabin doors. That's my job, ma'am." He said it with a drawl and a tip of his hand as if he were a servant.

"The camp is now secure?" I asked.

"You can drop the rock, we've got it under control." I did as suggested and he added, "Cordy's hired some men to put on the cabin locks. My job is to secure the fence, and this and a small problem near the campfire will finish it up."

"You know how to mend fences?"

He grinned, and it might have been the shade of Clark Gable grinning down on me. As both rake and roué he responded, "It's said I'm good with my hands."

"And who says that?" I asked.

That half-grin again, "Ma'am, I don't believe this is the time or place to discuss it."

Voices came up from the gate and one said, "I'll check and see if it's closed off." It was the deputy starting up in our direction.

Peterson's voice said, "I'll come, too."

"Well, shoot," I said. "I don't supposed you know the combination to this thing?" I pointed at the lock.

"You don't want to visit with any of the officials?" Nate asked me.

"Not in this lifetime."

"Okay." He turned the dial quickly. Then it was off the gate, which he swung open. "I was just leaving in a few minutes," he said. "Want me to drive down the road out there and pick you up?"

"I'd be much obliged," I said in my best good-ol'-boy-speak.

Or was it Mae West? Then I was out the gate, picking my way through the brush.

I felt like a spy, hiding between a boulder and an al-garita bush until Nate pulled up in the Green Clover van and I jumped in. Not that I thought anyone was watching, but they could have been. And not that I shouldn't have been leaving the camp, because that wasn't an issue either, really.

"Didn't want to report your plans to Peterson?" Nate asked, once I was buckled in and he was piloting us toward town.

"I don't like that man."

"He's only doing his job . . . to protect you." Nate flashed the grin that could captivate any woman.

Then he reached over and pulled something out of my hair and held it up for me to see. A small bunch of dry leaves. " 'Long live the weeds and the wilderness.' Edward Abbey," he said. "He wrote—"

"I know who he is. *The Monkey Wrench Gang*."

"Did you like Edward Abbey?"

"Absolutely. I was practicing using a chain saw—for billboards and such—when I moved on to another phase of my life. Ayn Rand, I think. Probably a good thing."

"Very likely." He tipped his head at me, smiling, then went back to watching the road. I watched him.

Now why hadn't I met Nate earlier? Say, twenty years or so?

"Tell me again which brother you are," I said.

"Nathaniel Samuel Wright. Older than Cordy, younger than Jeb or Zeke."

"That's not what I meant. Are you the former preacher, or the one who sold security things by mail?"

"Zeke was, and still is, the minister. I'm the other one. Oh, and is there any place special I'm taking you? I assume you don't want to shop for baling wire."

"I don't mind. I mostly just wanted away from all the hullabaloo." I thought about what I'd said. "Hullabaloo. Now there's an old word."

"Winston Churchill said that old words are best."

"How nice of him. Of course, he was probably old at the time so he might have been just covering his rear."

Nate was grinning again. "Didn't Cordy tell me you're a communications trainer? Who do you train? Politicians?"

"Some. Lots of computer people, too. They love jargon,

and when that's not overwhelming, they take real words and garble them. They'll say things like, we should 'incentivize the sales staff.' Or just 'incent the salespeople.' I can't convince them *incentive* is a noun and there are no verbs related to it." We hit a bump and the van flew up into the air, landing with a metal groan.

"Sorry," Nate offered.

"Not your fault. Talk to the county commissioner, he's in charge of roads." I stared ahead of us for a moment and then let my gaze rest, quite easily, I might add, on Nate. "I wonder where the word *hullabaloo* comes from?"

"Sounds like it goes with, 'when the hurly-burly's done, when the battle's lost and won.'"

"The Scottish play!" *Macbeth.* A favorite of mine, and Nathaniel Wright had just quoted it. There is nothing that can sweet-talk me faster than a man quoting Shakespeare or some really fine poetry. And he'd been quoting people ever since I got in the van. "Are you a patron of the arts?" I asked. "Libraries? The theatre?"

"Sometimes I am."

But it seemed the tips of his ears were suddenly awfully pink.

That very expressive face and the sexy voice added up to something more. I had a suspicion . . . "I was a theatre major at UCLA for a time," I said.

"You went to college in Southern California?"

"For two years, but that wasn't my point. I was working up to ask where you studied acting. You did, didn't you?"

"Ah. A leading statement to get me to reveal my youthful indiscretion."

"I wouldn't call it that."

He flashed me a quick, sheepish, and absolutely irresistible smile, this time with no undertone of the leer he'd used earlier. "I majored in Radio, Television, and Film at the University of Texas. Now, my question is, why weren't you there? With your background, I'd think your family would have insisted that you stay in Texas."

We were turning onto a paved road, and the van settled down to a more sedate shimmy. "Have you ever known kids who were accepted to universities solely on the merit of their family connections?" I asked.

He thought about it for a moment. "No, I haven't."

"Well, I have. Too many of them. I know several who didn't make it past the first year. One little blonde got into Texas Tech on her uncle's name when she wasn't smart enough to fill out the paperwork for the dorm let alone the SAT." I shook my head. "I refused to be one of those, especially since I was a little blonde when I started college, so I spent two years out of state proving to myself, and anyone else who cared to know, that I was smart enough to make it on my own. Then I transferred back."

"And gave up acting at the same time?"

"Yes, and that was a real shame, too, because I'd have been good. Instead, I majored in business with a minor in Poli Sci. It wasn't so bad. I used the acting when I was in the senate." I started looking around. "Oh, and you asked where you could take me. See that hamburger place right there, the Dairy Queen? You can take me through the drive-up."

"Ah, something to revive your spirit. Think it will help you get through the current rough spot?"

"At least until the hurly-burly's done."

He glanced sideways to give me a smile. "Or the battle's lost and won."

My heart did a flutter step. Nate Wright was good looking, witty, and down-to-earth enough to wear an old Green Clover knit shirt. His clothes were no longer sprinkled with leaves from his fence duty, but they didn't have the pristine look that Jeb's had. I liked that. I liked a lot about Nate.

And then I remembered when I'd first seen him.

Yesterday, he'd been arguing with May Feather just hours before she was murdered in a particularly violent way.

He pulled up to the large outdoor menu, but now my

stomach was quivering with something other than anticipation. Nate Wright had known May Feather well, and now
he was here, flirting with me.

No, that wasn't right. He'd known May Feather, but I
didn't have any more information than that about their relationship. Except that they'd had some kind of disagreement, and it had ended when he reached for her. She'd
jerked away and flipped her hair back before racing off.
But what had they been arguing about?

I needed to find out, but how do you phrase a question
like that?

Nate was being asked for our order. He turned to me.
"What would you like?"

"A chocolate dipped cone," I said. I needed comfort and
I needed it now.

"What size?" Nate asked.

I didn't hesitate. "Better make it a large."

Sixteen

By the time Nate was getting the baling wire, my tongue was firmly clenched between my teeth so I wouldn't pop off and ask a few accusatory, or at least uncomfortable, questions. There was a reason that I was being so unnaturally uncommunicative; I was alone with Nate, and no one on this planet knew that but him and me. A question that might provoke him seemed akin to slapping a rattlesnake. When I think it through in advance, I avoid such maneuvers.

The van rocked as he slammed the back door. His final purchase had been a small amount of baling wire for the job he needed to do. He put it beside the flowers he'd bought earlier, then he was climbing inside.

"Back to Green Clover?" he asked me.

"That suits me fine."

"I assumed it would."

"And what does that mean?" I asked.

"You haven't spoken a word to me since you got your ice cream. Unless they're dipping it in some kind of drug, there's something on your mind."

"There is," I said. "Murder."

He had the van out of the parking space, and now he put it in forward and stepped on the gas. "May Feather's murder."

"That's the one," I said.

He remained silent, apparently very intent on his driving. He didn't say that May's murder was a terrible thing, or that he was sorry it happened, or that he hoped they'd catch the SOB who did it. Nothing. And that in itself seemed pretty suspicious, until I realized I hadn't made any of those comments, either.

We rode on for a few miles before he said, "Why did you get out of politics?"

"I beg your pardon?" I'd been stewing on his silence and when the question came I missed it.

"Politics," he repeated. "Why did you leave office?"

"Oh." I gave him my stock answer. "Because I discovered that almost any jackass can get elected, and way too many of them had been." Nate started to smile. I added, "Especially if they wear pants and bray real loud."

He laughed.

I scowled. "Aren't you going to tell me that's sexist? My brother always says it is."

"Not if it's the truth—and if you're saying it, then I suspect it is."

It's hard to argue with that kind of logic. "Thank you."

"Do you still run with the politicos?"

"A few, but only those who were real friends, not the ones I just had alliances with."

"Do you know Liz Carpenter?"

"I do. A generous and charming woman who says what she means, even if it isn't popular."

"Not like anyone else I know," he said. Then he asked, "Do you think Ann Richards will ever run for president?"

"I have no idea, but I can't think of anyone who'd do a better job in the office."

"You really think that?"

"I do. When she took over the governorship of Texas, the state was six billion dollars in debt, but she worked hard, and when she left, it had a two-billion-dollar surplus," I said. "Now that's responsible government."

"I bet if she'd known she wasn't going to get reelected, she'd have spent every dime."

"So? A lot of important programs didn't get funded after she left. Having been in the senate, I can say without a qualm that the boys in the legislature like spending money on roads, but rarely on schools or social programs. They like putting funds in their little 'pet pots,' too, just to make sure that the people back home name buildings and such after them."

Nate didn't even try to hide his grin. "It's pretty obvious why you decided to get out."

"Back when I was in office my mother kept saying, 'Now, Katherine, you can attract more flies with honey than with vinegar.' Problem was, that I was almost diabetic from too much honey, and I was damn sick and tired of flies."

"I'm afraid I'd have to agree with you, rather than your mother. Not that her sentiment isn't correct, but some niceties aren't much more than bribes." He said that like he knew what he was talking about, which made me wonder again who this man was. Thinking back, he'd said more about his brother than himself.

The van turned down the dusty caliche road that would wind us back to Green Clover. "Almost home," he said.

"So I see. Guess that's my cue to get serious."

A puzzled and slightly amused look crossed his mobile face. "Serious about what?"

"I wondered what you were arguing about yesterday. With May Feather."

The amusement disappeared and his skin washed with red. He took in a breath, carefully, as if he didn't want me to see. "I'm not sure where you got your information."

"You didn't answer."

He turned the wheel quickly to avoid the pothole I'd seen last night and kept his eyes trained on the road. His voice was even. "Who says that I argued with May?"

"I do."

"I see." He drove carefully but we were almost at Green Clover, and I realized that I'd waited a tad too late to start this conversation. Nate slowed as he turned onto the private road that belonged to the camp.

"Do you want me to drop you off at the front or at the little gate?" he asked.

We were close enough I could see that the TV vans were gone, and even though the gates were still closed, there was no one guarding them. "The front will be fine." He turned into the parking area, then rolled up to the entrance. I added, "You still haven't answered my question."

He appeared intent on getting us lined up absolutely at a right angle with the wrought iron. "Why would you think I argued with May? I hardly—"

"Because I saw you."

He stopped the van and kept his focus on the view outside the windshield. "Then you must have heard what was said." His voice was calm, controlled. He turned to me, "The truth is I feel bad about that argument; it didn't have to happen. I'll let you off here, since I have to pull around to the barn."

And he still hadn't told me what it was about. I raised an eyebrow, but he was studiously looking out the window again.

"Well, since you insist," I said, "I expect I'll just head up to the cabin."

I opened the door and had stepped out when he said, "By the way, thanks for coming with me. It was the nicest part of the day." He didn't look cocky now.

I walked off, knowing that as a detective I had just bombed, and in the future I'd have to allow for the learning curve.

As I went on past the trailers, the crime scene tape was still on May's. I had to wonder if Jennifer had gotten her underwear yet. And if she'd had that nap she'd needed so badly. And where Mr. Sinatra was at the moment, and who he was terrorizing.

First stop was the Saloon, where I found half the women at the retreat jammed in at tables, working away on various projects. It wasn't the mosh-pit atmosphere of the night before with lots of cross-table talk and laughter. In fact, the women were so quiet it was almost eerie. I stepped inside and realized that there was a lot of sighing going on, which I suppose is natural when you think about someone you knew who has just died.

Finally someone talked, and I looked over to see Angie at a long table with about ten other women. They were making greeting cards, mostly in an oriental motif. I'm not much of a stamper, but I dabble, about like I do a lot of things, so I slipped into the group to watch. Angie was working on a card with dark teal paper and an origami kimono that had Asian characters printed on it. It had the antique look of an artifact that had been unearthed from some ancient emperor's tomb.

She'd added a small tassel with gold threads beside it, and then began fiddling with the placement of a Chinese coin.

I leaned in closer. "I hope you're planning on selling that; it's nothing short of amazing."

"Why? You want to buy it?"

"I want to buy a dozen, but you're going to tell me it's one of a kind. Where did you get your idea?" I was watching as she used a glue gun to attach the coin in the spot she'd selected.

"From your demonstration. Recognize the Chinese characters?" She held up scraps of paper, and sure enough, they did look like what I'd taught the women to find on the Internet.

"I'm glad I was useful. Now can someone teach me to do that origami kimono?"

"No need." She picked up the card, inspected it for last-minute flaws, then handed it to me. "With my compliments. In appreciation for the tip. Oh, and there's an envelope that goes with it in my trailer. I'll get it to you later."

I didn't even hesitate to take the card. When someone

makes a generous offer, I accept. "Thank you. This is beautiful and I promise to mail it in good health."

"You do that. You find out anymore more about those—uh—" she dropped her voice before she said, "Those items that we discussed earlier?"

"Not a thing. Did you think of anything else?"

"Not that I'm telling." She smiled, but I wasn't buying it. If she had something new, she'd be dragging me outside to tell all.

"Angie, can you show me what I'm doing wrong with this kimono?" Sandra Borders was folding a piece of paper into something that I had mistaken for a hibachi; apparently it was supposed to be a kimono. "I think I missed a step."

"Here," Angie said, pointing. "Take this and wrap it back. See? Then slide this into here."

"Oh, right."

I watched, then said to Sande, "Where's your cousin Lynn?" The noir beader was nowhere in evidence. Not that her absence was a bad thing. "I thought you came all the way from L.A. to spend time with her."

Sande shook her head as her fingers fumbled with the paper. "I was coming here anyway, but then I invited Lynn to the retreat since she lives in Austin. I'm spending two days with her after we leave here." She was still wrangling with the origami trying to get the sleeves inserted when it ripped. "Oh, sugar!" She held up the two pieces so Angie could view them. "I don't suppose a one-armed kimono could be considered my contribution to Asian art?"

"Maybe next week," Angie said, picking up a fresh sheet of paper that was stamped with tiny chrysanthemums. "Here, start over. A new look."

"So, Sande," I said. "Have you enjoyed seeing your cousin after so many years?" Angie gave me a look behind Sande's back, but I kept going. "Has Lynn changed much?"

"She looks different," Sande said, starting to work on a

fresh kimono. "But, then it's been almost ten years since we've seen each other. We mostly e-mail."

"She told me she'd had a bad divorce."

"Bad isn't even the word. But she got her revenge—she made him pay. Big!"

There's no alimony in Texas, only settlement. "I suppose she got the house and half the bank accounts."

Sande snorted. "That was the least of it." She lowered the paper that she'd been folding, as well as her voice, and said, "He swore there wasn't anybody else, but he did start dating pretty fast, and Lynn . . ." she looked around to see if anyone else was listening. There wasn't, or they were smart enough to pretend they weren't. "Lynn didn't stand for that."

Angie leaned forward. "What does that mean?"

"Well, he was renting some big place on the lake, and she decided to stake it out. Like some kind of detective. Only nothing much happened until a lady came to clean; Lynn decided that was her chance, and she just waltzed in behind the woman. She said she was Carl's wife, which was true, and when the woman was in another room Lynn swiped the woman's key and raced down the road and got a duplicate made." Angie and I stared, rapt. "By the time she got back, the woman was frantic looking for her keys, so Lynn 'helped her look.' And found them—surprise, surprise."

"But what did Lynn do with the key?" I asked.

Sande said just above a whisper, "First, she did a lot of research on the Internet." Sande dropped her voice even more. "I thought she was going to make a nuclear bomb— she scared me to death, but finally she found something that was almost harmless. She found a way to make a stink bomb that was rigged with a timer. Can you believe that? She put it under his bed. And when it went off . . ." Sande was grinning now. "Carl was furious, and he called Lynn from his cell phone because he couldn't stay in the house. He said he'd been alone in the bedroom, but Lynn thinks he had company, and it must have been worse than farting under the covers."

Angie let out a snort of laughter, then stifled herself, as she realized she was getting a lot of curious glances.

"Did she ever find out if there was a woman?" I asked, thinking of May.

"I don't know. At the time, she was just after revenge."

Angie was still grinning. "Think she'd tell me how to build that bomb?"

"You can't tell her I told you about it," Sande said, "but I'll see if I can get the web page."

Lynn might be tacky and rude, but I had to give her credit for ingenuity. "Very tricky."

"I mean that about not letting on that I told you," Sande added, "She's not someone to cross."

"Promise," I said, exchanging a look with Angie.

"Me, too," Angie said. "Here, give me that paper—"

"I know. I'm still doing this wrong," Sandra said, "It's the collar."

Angie helped her while I thought about Lynn. An anonymous stink bomb wasn't nearly the same as sending a woman over a cliff, but I'm no psychiatrist. I had no idea if a woman who would make a stink bomb was capable of murder.

I looked around. My fingers were itching for the feel of beads and the total absorption of making something. All of my supplies were in the Lazy L, and I wasn't in the mood for the hike. Who might stake me to a few beads? Beth was at a large round table, and she signaled me to come over. I was on my way when I saw that she was working with wire.

They were doing the dreaded wrapped loop.

It's a standard in some types of beading. You take a piece of wire or stiff pin, make a loop at one end, then take the tail of the loop and wrap it around the rest of the wire. It was something I could never master, and it looked like the women on either side of Beth were having their problems with the technique, as well. I didn't recognize them, so I assumed they'd arrived while I was gone. They also seemed to be new to beading.

"I've been looking all over for you," Beth said to me. "Give me just a minute."

Even though this wasn't an official demonstration, Beth was helping the two women just as Angie was helping Sande. I've noticed that's how crafters are—supportive—and they love teaching each other new things.

I ran my fingers over the beads in Beth's design tray. All I needed was ten minutes of bead therapy—

"You need to hold the loop firmer," Beth was saying to one woman, as if it was something anyone could do. "You had it just right on that last one."

And that's the problem with the wrapped loop—unless you know what you're doing, you end up with one well-shaped loop and one that looks like a trapezoid. Beth can crank out a chain of wrapped loops like a machine, and so can most good wire workers. Not me. Maybe someday when we have an ice storm and I'm stuck in my house with no electricity and I'm working by candlelight, I'll spend hours perfecting the art of the wrapped loop.

Or maybe I'll take a nap. Depends on my mood at the time.

Beth made encouraging comments about grip and such, but it all seemed futile to me. In the corner Leesa with two *es* was watching a woman create a delicate beaded cover for a needle holder. Leesa seemed entranced. At a table near me several women were making beads and medallions of polymer clay. If Beth hadn't requested my presence, I could have gone to play with clay.

Through the door to the vendor's room I could see Tony Campanelli and Cordy Wright. Cordy was fingering some beautiful pink quartz beads while Tony spoke earnestly to her.

"Ready?" Beth said, moving me toward the door. "Where did you go?"

"Long story. I feel like I'm missing the whole retreat, and I have the need . . ." She didn't join in as I said, "The need to bead." A bad sign.

We were outside by then. "I know the feeling. Did you see the newsletter?"

Cordy's daily camp newsletter. "No. Should I?"

"Not unless you were planning to submit to Tivolini."

"Not me."

Leesa came out the door, "Hi."

"Hi," I said. "How did you like those needle covers?"

"Magnificent," she said. "People do such amazing things. Well, I'll see you at dinner." And she hurried off toward the Lazy L.

I turned back to Beth, "So, what did the newsletter say?"

Beth took a long breath, making her large bosom quiver. "We had to sign up for appointments. I'm meeting with the buyer at nine o'clock tomorrow morning. I have the first slot."

"Beth, that's great."

"How can you say that? It was distant before, but now there's urgency. It's tomorrow. It's winner take all, life or death—no, I didn't mean that. I don't know what I mean. I'm stressed."

"I see that, and for no reason at all. You are a wonderful designer, you've already done all the work, and now you'll get to bask in the glory when you are selected as the new Tivolini designer."

"Sometimes," Beth said, "I think you live on another planet." She shook her hands to shake out the nerves. "If you were me, you'd be just as nervous as I am. Admit it."

"As I said, there'd be no reason for it."

A bell sounded at the dining hall. It was the fifteen-minute warning, telling everyone to pack up their materials and head for dinner.

"I've got a bunch of things I need to put away," Beth said, turning back inside.

"I'll help." I followed her. Cases were being brought out from under tables, and projects were being carefully packed up in towels before they went into boxes. "Where's Shannan?" I asked. "I haven't seen her since lunch."

"I don't know. I thought maybe you two were together." She looked at me. "But she wasn't with you, was she?" I shook my head, *no*. "Oh, dear, you don't think—"

"I think she'll be in the dining hall in just a few minutes."

"But I haven't seen her in, it must be a couple of hours."

"She's probably sleeping off her hangover." I sounded sure of myself, but that was for Beth's benefit. I didn't like Shannan's absence, either. "I'll go poke my head in the cabin, just to make sure she heard the dinner bell."

"That's a good idea." Beth was nodding, but I could almost see her stress level rising.

"I'll see you in a few minutes," I said. "And I'll have a beer for you, because you need it."

"I'm on a diet."

"Won't matter what your weight is if you keel over with a stroke."

I took off to hunt for Shannan.

Seventeen

This wasn't the time for Shannan to be off by herself. Especially with the sun starting to dip and some clouds sliding out to darken the sky. It made me nervous. Concerned, as anyone in their right mind would be.

First thing, I went up the path toward the Lazy L. "Shannan?" I called out as I neared the cabin.

There was no answer, but I did hear a sound like something moving across the concrete floor, then bed springs creaking.

"Shannan?" I said again, as I stepped inside the dim cabin.

"Not here," Leesa said. She was lounging on her bunk, her head propped on her hand as she peered down at me. I'd have sworn the girl just climbed up there, but I couldn't say why I believed that.

"Have you seen her?"

"Not since lunch. She's probably on her way to dinner. The gong's already gone off."

"I thought you were going down to the dining hall."

"Oh, I am. I just . . ." She looked around the cabin. "I was playing with Sinatra. He's the cutest thing."

The little guy was curled up in the corner of his cage with the baby blanket half over his tiny body. He *was* the cutest thing, but if she came up to the Lazy L to play with him, then why was she on her bunk ten feet away from his cage? And why was Sinatra sleeping?

"Do me a favor," I said, reaching down to pet Sinatra, "If you see Shannan, tell her I need to talk with her."

"Where should I tell her you'll be?"

"Looking for her." I pulled my hand out of the cage, as he reached a paw to nudge me.

Leesa remained on her bunk, which made me even more curious as to why she wasn't moving.

"Are you all right?" I asked.

"I'm fine."

"That's good." She was up to something, but I was more anxious to find Shannan than I was curious about what it was. "See you at dinner."

I grabbed a zip-up sweatshirt and headed down the hill toward the campfire. On the path I got behind a slow moving group of women who were putting on jackets and juggling flashlights as they went. I couldn't quite get around them, so I turned back to get my own flashlight from the Lazy L, since I'd need it after dinner or after the memorial service. Funny thing was, in just the few minutes it took to get back to the cabin, Leesa was gone.

I grabbed my flashlight and started out again. At the rate I was going, I'd put in enough miles for a marathon before bedtime.

I caught up with the group of women just as they entered the dining hall. Under their cover, I poked my head in, in case Shannan had beat me there. The dozen or so campers who were already lining up for food didn't include my goddaughter. Beth wasn't there yet, either, but I wasn't surprised since she had supplies to put away.

I left my flashlight and sweatshirt at an empty place then slipped out again. As I'd told Beth, this is a big camp, and Shannan could be in a dozen different places, and maybe even having a good time in one of them.

I was passing the camp office, still trying to convince myself that I wasn't really concerned when I heard someone moving around inside the small building. It wasn't likely that the someone was Shannan . . . still—

"Hello?" I opened the door and stuck my head in. I blinked a couple of times in the bright light before I realized that it was Nate Wright standing there. "Oh. Hello," I said.

He didn't seem as surprised to see me as I was to see him. "Kitzi, hi. Come in."

I stayed on the step. "Thanks, but there's no need. I was looking for Shannan. My goddaughter, Shannan Fairfield. A little taller than me, auburn hair, seventeen? Very pretty."

He thought for a second. "Sure, she was at your table at lunch." And then his eyes widened. "Is she missing? Do we—"

"No, we don't," I said. "She could be on her way to dinner, but I haven't seen her in several hours and neither has her mother. I'm just making sure she gets to dinner on time."

His dark eyes were intent on my face. I got the feeling he was trying to believe there was no reason for concern; kind of like I was convincing myself. "If you don't find her," he said, "Let me know. Or I could go with you now."

"I appreciate that, but there's nothing both of us could do that I can't do on my own."

"We can get a group—"

"If we started a search, we'd scare everyone half to death."

"I don't see that it matters. I'm not an alarmist, but I'd prefer to err on the side of caution."

Damn, I liked the way this man thought.

"I've got two more places to check, and then I'll be in the dining hall," I said. "I'll let you know." Without waiting for an answer, I made my way down the steps and along the trail. Too bad I hadn't met Nate instead of Jeb. I'd have to have a chat with Cordy about that.

The path forked, and as I cut right I thought I heard voices. I stopped, but there was nothing but a lot of silence. I started again, moving as softly as I could. The talking came again, from farther down the hill. I was practically tiptoeing, hoping to tell if it was Shannan's voice, but even my breathing was clouding my hearing. Finally, there was the unmistakable sound of something punching a ball. I recognized the *whomp* of the tetherball being hit.

"Shannan? Shannan? Is that you?" I took off moving at a lope, which wasn't smart since at twilight the shadows can be tricky.

I raised my voice, "Shannan?"

The sounds of tetherball stopped. "Tante Kitzi?"

I roared into the clearing. She was there, holding the tetherball in her hand, and on the other side of the pole from her was Jennifer.

"Shannan," I said. "Why don't you let someone know if you're going to go off by yourself?"

Except she wasn't by herself; she was with Jennifer, who said, "We've been right here."

"Yeah," Shannan said. "What's wrong?"

"I'll tell you what's wrong—someone was murdered last night. Someone female and beautiful, just like you."

I was close enough now to see Shannan's face, and her expression went from mild annoyance to swift comprehension. "I just, I guess I just didn't think about that."

"Well, you should. We're all at risk, and when I couldn't find you, I had some very bad moments. The dinner bell has already rung. Why aren't you two on your way to the dining hall?"

"We didn't hear the bell."

She looked genuinely contrite, and Jennifer looked curious. I hadn't said a thing about her, so I rectified that oversight. "And what about you, Jennifer? You didn't tell anyone where you were going, either," I said.

"I'm not afraid," she said. "I've taken karate."

I swung closer to her. "Well, that's just fine, but you'd better be very good at it to defend yourself against a murderer."

She opened her mouth to say something, then seemed confused. "Well, I'm pretty good, but I don't see the big deal—"

"I left you napping," I said. "I didn't expect you to sleep all day, but you weren't in the Saloon, and you didn't show up in the dining hall, either."

Was that a wary look on her face? It was hard to tell with the shadows so deep. "I didn't think anyone would care."

"If something happened to you?" I asked. "That's the stupidest thing I've ever heard. From this moment forward, you and Shannan are under protective custody. Mine." She nodded, maybe pleased that someone cared. "Now," I said, moving forward, putting an arm around each of the girls. "We need to get up to the dining hall. And we need to work out some kind of plan to look after each other. All of us."

"But how?" Shannan asked as we started walking. "This is a big place."

"That's my point," I said. "You don't have to let us know every time you go to the john, but if you're going to be gone long enough for me to start worrying, then you better see that I don't."

"Yes, ma'am," Shannan said.

"And you, Miss Jennifer? That goes for you, too," I said. Jennifer nodded. "If you're sure."

"I am very sure."

"Okay."

"Good." I gave them a little shove as we started up the hill to the shortcut that would take us to the dining hall. "Then I won't have to track you down, because it's wearing."

"Is my mom looking for us, too?" Shannan asked.

"No, I sent her on to dinner." I made the last turn toward the dining hall, where the final bell was being rung.

"But what about you?" Shannan said. "I couldn't find you this afternoon . . ."

It was a good point. I'd been off with Nate, and at the time I hadn't been sure if he was one of the good guys or the bad. For that matter, I still wasn't sure.

"I'll make the same deal," I said. "Does that work?" The girls nodded. "Then it's settled." I sniffed the air. "And unless I'm mistaken, we're having barbeque for dinner.

Lucky for you two I didn't miss that." Just ahead of us I could see the lights of the dining hall.

"Smells good," Jennifer said a▮▮▮▮moved forward. "I guess I'm hungrier than I thought."

Shannan shrugged. "I'm not."

Something weighty was being manhandled in her very clever mind.

"You two need your flashlights for after the memorial service tonight. Shannan, why don't you—"

"I'll get them," Jennifer said.

"No, I don't want you alone now that it's almost dark. It's what we just talked about, remember? You go on and get us some places at a table, and Shannan and I can run up to the cabin."

Jennifer and Shannan exchanged glances, but they agreed and Jennifer veered up toward the dining hall.

As Shannan and I turned to our left, I said, "What's up, Miss Priss? You're worried about something."

"It's nothing."

I touched her arm. "It's something. Maybe I can help."

She slowed her pace and fumbled with her words. "It's, well, you know. I feel stupid about the way I acted, and the things I said last night."

"Oh?"

"When we saw May in my dad's Lexus." We were walking side by side, and the only sounds in the camp besides those we were making seemed to be below us where everyone had gathered for dinner. "I said some terrible things about May. I think I even made it sound like I was going to, well, do something to her. But I wasn't, really."

"I know that."

"I was just mad. Really furious that she was, you know. We shouldn't have hit them," she concluded.

Can't worry about hindsight, although I imagine we all do. "Maybe not," I said. "We couldn't predict what would happen to May. I think that's one you'll have to let go of, since you can't change the past."

"That's only a little piece of what I'm worrying about. I'm mostly worried ⬛⬛ut my dad." I remained silent, as wind ruffled the t⬛⬛⬛es overhead. "It's not that I think my dad could eve⬛⬛⬛nyone," Shannan finally said. "Especially since he re⬛⬛eemed to like her. He did like her, didn't he? Maybe even loved her."

"Seemed to."

"Well, there couldn't be any other reason he spent so much time with her. Could there?" I heard hope in her voice.

"Could have been plain old sex."

Shannan made a small gagging sound. Why is it that humans always think their generation invented sex and anyone older than them shouldn't be having any?

We reached the Lazy L and I turned on the light. The sleeping porch was empty, and Sinatra blinked in the brightness. Then he meowed. Repeatedly.

"You get the flashlights and some jackets; I'll take care of Sinatra."

"Okay."

Under cover of our busyness, I said, "So what's the other part of your worry?"

"Peterson." She had the flashlights from the window ledge and was taking a sweatshirt off the foot of her bed.

"Do you think he'll find out we didn't tell the whole truth?"

"So what? What's the worst he can do?"

"I don't know but look at what happened to Martha Stewart."

I personally didn't think that was a good idea, so I plopped Sinatra in his litter box and turned around to say, "No one is going to put us on trial for misleading Officer Peterson. He doesn't have that kind of clout. Why are you worried about your dad?"

Shannan sighed and sat on my bunk. "Tante Kitzi, I know he didn't do anything to hurt May, but there have to be people who know about what they were doing. If someone tells

Peterson, then my dad could be arrested. He doesn't have an alibi for that night, since Mom and I were here. Maybe he'd go to jail—"

"Do you hear yourself? *If* someone . . . then he *could* . . . and *maybe* . . . Shannan, ninety-seven percent of what we worry about never happens. That's fact."

"This could be the other three percent."

"*Could* be. Could *not* be." I turned in time to see her lower lip quiver. I sat down and put an arm around her. "Honey, there is nothing we can do to protect your father. We've already lied. Now all we can do is pray."

She sucked in a big breath of air and straightened. "I know you're right."

"You're a good person and a wonderful daughter. That's partly your dad's doing, so let's give him credit for being able to take care of himself. And he's a lawyer, too. You're forgetting that." Sinatra was poking in his empty food bowl. "You need some food, and so does Sinatra. Let me feed him, and we'll go down to dinner."

There were six of us at one of the small round tables, Beth, Shannan, Jennifer, Sandra, Angie, and me. We had done our best to get down our portion of the barbeque and now we sat with greasy plates in front of us, waiting for our turn to scrape and stack them before we could get our dessert. Not that I was all that interested in banana cream pudding with vanilla wafers.

It was a relief to note that around us the talk was about the appointments with the Tivolini buyer for the following day. Tivolini had upstaged murder.

"Ten in the morning, and I not only have to rise, but shine, as well," a woman behind us was saying. I recognized her from the Austin Bead Society, but I couldn't recall her name. I seemed to remember a beautiful butterfly bracelet in shades of pink and orange that she'd shown at a recent meeting. When I turned to look, she was holding up the next day's schedule of events, which also had a copy of the appointments. There were still a few available slots to meet with the Tivolini buyer.

"If anyone wants one of these, just let Cordy know," she was saying to some women in the dessert line. "I'll even give away my place!"

"Don't need it," one of them said. "I don't have that kind of talent."

"Sure you do," another added.

"Let the beads shine for you," a woman advised.

Beth leaned forward. "And I'm up first."

"Why did you want to go first?" I asked, reaching for the schedule on our table.

"First impression. I set the standard, and everyone else has to do better." Then Beth shook her head. "Or maybe it was 'first to get it over with.'"

I was looking down the list, recognizing the names of the best artisans. Beth was listed first, then Donna Hawk. Tony Campanelli. Mary Newton, Valerie Felps, Barbara Formicelli, Wing Feather—

Wing Feather? It wasn't May, she'd have put her name. And she'd been dead before the appointments had been set.

"Maybe," Beth was saying, "I should give up my slot. I'm sure someone else could use it—"

"Mom," Shannan said. "Why would you say a thing like that? You'll be the best."

I looked up to see Shannan's concern and Beth's unhappy expression. Sandra and Angie had started their own side conversation and Jennifer, who was nodding along with Shannan, looked less than comfortable with Beth's insecurity. But then, the young think the world is all about them and the rest of us should just maintain holding positions.

"You," I said, leaning closer to Beth. "do incredible work. In-frigging-credible." I looked at Shannan. "And it's not about the best, either. It rarely is in this world. This is a particularly subjective submission. *If* the buyer is looking for work that can be replicated, *if* the buyer likes your style of work on that particular day, *if* the buyer—"

Beth cut me off. "You're getting radical."

It was our turn to get in line to scrape our plates. The others were up in a flash, Jennifer and Shannan first, then Angie and Sandra who were deep in a discussion of new types of paper. Beth and I were at the end of the line.

"I don't mean to get pushy," I said, my voice pitched low, but still insistent. "It's just that I get frustrated. You just go out there and do your best."

Beth stared at me for a minute before dumping the scraps from her plate. I noticed that she was doing so with a lot of vigor. When our plates had been put in the bins and we were facing the dessert table, she picked up a beige plastic bowl of pudding and said, "The rest of the world is not like you, Kitz. A few too many kicks, and the rest of us wear the scars."

"I wore the scars, too." Two tables away Jeb had his back to me. He had finished eating and was involved in a conversation with Nate. I nodded toward Jeb and said as quietly as I could, "I wore the scars from that experience for years."

Beth glanced at Jeb, then back at me. "I know. I'm sorry," she said as I followed her back to the table.

The girls had gone, leaving only Sandra and Angie a few chairs away. Beth sat down and said, "I'm being a wimp—ignore me. There's just so much riding on this."

That's when I realized that Beth knew about Ron and May Feather. And we couldn't talk now because Nate was ringing the bell to signal the end of dinner. I wondered why Cordy wasn't doing it herself; it was her camp, and she always gave the announcements. I sensed someone behind me and turned to find Cordy.

"Can you come with me for just a minute?" she asked.

"Now?"

"Right now. In the office. Hurry."

I leaned over and whispered to Beth, "After chapel, we need to talk."

"And drink," she added.

I took off after Cordy, but I didn't catch up to her until we'd run down the path and were at the office. She beat me inside and immediately started futzing with the computer. "What's up?" I asked.

"I have to show you something—"

The door opened, and Officer Peterson stepped in almost on my heels. "Don't let me interrupt," he said. "Especially since you seem in such a hurry."

"Oh. Hello," Cordy said. Her face went blank, as if his appearance froze her brain. I knew the feeling. Finally, she said, "Is there something I can do for you?"

"No, no. I can take care of it myself. You go ahead with your business."

"Sure. Things are just running a little behind, and we're trying to catch up."

Peterson went to the copy machine, but he didn't touch it. He just waited, watching us. Cordy nodded at him then reached into a desk drawer to pull out a jeweler's display box.

"Kitzi, this is what I wanted to show you. It was donated for the Bead Tea. I thought we could hold a raffle to raise some additional money."

I tried to look interested, but there was something odd going on here.

"What is it?" I asked.

Not that it mattered, if whatever she had would help out with the tea. Cordy and I had organized the charity event to raise money for ovarian cancer.

We've put our hearts and souls into it because the cause is one that touches a lot of us, and there isn't a cure. Instead, there's chemotherapy to keep the cancer at bay with the hope that they'll hit the right combination to kill it. There doesn't even seem to be a lot of research on new drugs, either.

Cordy and I have personal reasons to give our time and effort to ovarian cancer. We both have dear friends who have it—both going about their lives as if they had acne, not cancer. Two amazing women named Carol and Rebecca.

Rebecca came up with the idea, and I approached the Travis County Bead Tamers to work with us on what is now going to be a huge three-day Bead Tea. There will be dozens of artisans selling their work, tea will be served in the conservatory of my home, and we'll also have demonstrations. I think it will be a great start on raising awareness, if we can find the hook to get enough media coverage.

Cordy opened the jeweler's case and I gasped. Now she had my attention. Inside was a necklace like nothing I had ever seen before. In the center was a large, square-cut gem of a clear and rich teal. Teal is the color used for ovarian cancer awareness.

The large central stone was held in place by delicate gold leaves, and the rest of the necklace was formed by three strands of delicate gold links, interspersed with smaller stones. They were like a rainbow of gems in pink, green, and teal, with just a few black.

"That's stunning," I breathed.

"Very nice," Peterson agreed. It seemed even he was impressed.

"It was donated," Cordy said. "And I think we can make some real money off it if we can promote the raffle right and sell tickets in advance."

"Watermelon tourmaline," I said, finally placing the smaller stones. Tourmaline is rare and expensive. It's also beautiful. "But what's that middle piece?"

"Tourmaline."

"I don't believe it." I'd never seen a piece so large or so clear. "It must be worth a small fortune. Or is it a large one?"

"Not as big as your trust fund, but I should have the appraisal by next week, and then we can publicize it."

Peterson snorted as he reached into the copy machine and pulled out a piece of paper. He held it up toward us. "I thought maybe you'd found this. Lucky for you, you didn't."

He smiled. "You ladies can go back to your jewelry; I have work to do." And with that, he left the office.

Cordy dropped the necklace to her desk and let out a huge breath. "Thank God, he's gone. I thought I was going to have a heart attack when he walked in." She flopped into her desk chair. "And I'm sorry I made that crack about your trust fund; now he's got one more reason to dislike you."

"I don't suppose it's a secret that I have one," I said. Most people don't know that I only use it to maintain our family home. I support myself, and my mother, with the income from my training.

Cordy put the jeweler's box with the necklace back in a drawer. "Okay, now you can forget you ever saw this."

"What do you mean? Are you saying it isn't for the tea?"

"The necklace isn't important." Cordy dismissed it with a wave as she continued to suck in gulps of air. "Peterson's what really matters."

"Forget it? Is it real? Where did it come from?"

"It's real, and it was donated to us for the ovarian cancer tea, but I wasn't supposed to tell you about it until next week. Then we'll have the appraisal—"

"Who donated it?" I had a suspicion that it was Jeb, and I didn't want charity from him even if it was for a great cause.

"Look," she said, "I really wasn't supposed to say anything; I just pulled out the box when Peterson came in. I wanted to show you something else." She swung around to face the computer. "Keep an eye on the door in case he comes back."

"Then will you tell me about the necklace?"

"Next Wednesday—don't ask anymore questions." I would have argued, but she was hurriedly moving the mouse around the screen. She tapped a few keys and pretty soon she had a scribbled document on the screen. "Can you read this?"

I leaned over her shoulder. It was handwritten, not typed like I would have expected, and the writing was atrocious, worse than my brother's. As I stared I could make out that it was a list of names. Including mine. "Sort of. What is it?"

"A page of Peterson's notes from this afternoon." She glanced nervously at the door. "He came in here to make copies, and what he walked out with just now was the page he left in the machine earlier."

"How'd you—"

She pointed to the copier. "It's one of those all-purpose things. Copies, faxes, and scans. During dinner, I was going to make some more of the activity lists, and I found it. I thought about taking it, but I was pretty sure he'd come back. I didn't even want to get fingerprints on the paper, so I scanned it into the computer and pretended like I didn't know he'd forgotten it."

My head was buzzing with all this as I stared in admiration. "Quick thinking; you're amazing."

"Yes, I am, but here's the bad part. From what I can figure out, these are the only people who can't be accounted for during the time that May was killed."

"Oh." I looked again at the computer screen.

There were only nine names on the list, and the first three were Beth Fairfield, Shannan Fairfield, and Katherine Camden.

Eighteen

"Oh, my Lord, Oh, my Lord
I have placed my trust in thee
Though you have so many children,
You are always there for me.
Now the day is almost over
And the sun has gone to hide
Keep us safe here at Green Clover
Oh, my Lord, please be my guide."

Green Clover good night song

Y ou can take me to a funeral, but you can't make me listen.

The first funeral I ever attended was when I was just eight, and it was for a friend who had died suddenly of spinal meningitis. The minister said that God must have wanted a beautiful little girl in heaven, and so He picked Charlotte.

That made me think God was selfish and not to be trusted. Especially since He'd made so many people cry. It was lucky that after the funeral I went to my grandparents' house and had a talk with them about it. My grandmother explained that the minister might have misunderstood.

Maybe it wasn't God's idea that Charlotte should die; instead, Charlotte might have prayed very hard, asking God to take her to heaven, and finally He agreed. Or maybe we didn't know the reason that Charlotte went to heaven when she did.

I didn't much like that answer, but it was better than the one the minister had given. One of the things I took away from the talk was that God does answer prayers, which made me more careful what I prayed for. Also, I never said the "Now I lay me down to sleep . . ." prayer again. I worried that the line "if I should die before I wake" might be misconstrued as a request.

During the memorial service at Green Clover I tried not to think about what the minister was saying, which was fairly easy since that list Cordy had shown me was causing me considerable concern. I hadn't trusted my memory to recall the names, so I wrote the initials of everyone on a piece of paper; I used initials in case anyone else saw it. Beth Fairfield, Shannan Fairfield, and Katherine Camden were the first three he'd written, but I knew for a fact that none of us would kill anyone.

CW was next. Cordelia Wright, and I put her in the same category as the first three. May's death was hurting Green Clover, which was like Cordy's baby. Besides, I'd known Cordy almost as long as I'd known Beth, and while she might get stressed, I'd never seen her get radical over things. Murdering someone was radical.

AH. Angie Hogencamp didn't seem very likely as a murder suspect, either. Angie, my tetherball buddy, seemed way too smart to push someone over a cliff. Besides, she didn't live in the area, so I doubted she knew May all that well. She didn't have a husband that May could have stolen, and Angie wasn't even a beader. She was a vendor who came to sell us paper goods. I supposed a little research on her wouldn't hurt.

Then there was JW. Jennifer Webster, May's assistant, who was too young for the role of murderer. Not that young people don't kill, but normally it's to get away from something, like an abusive parent, or to prove they aren't nerds. Or when they have something to gain. What would Jennifer gain? May's old trailer? Her leftover beads? And May's death meant Jennifer didn't have a job, and she wasn't likely to get severance pay, either.

I looked down at the slip of paper in my hand to see the rest of the initials and lost my concentration. The words of the minister caught me.

"May Feather was born in Oklahoma and grew up in Clovis, New Mexico before moving to Lubbock, Texas for her teenage years. There she excelled in art. In high school she was already working with the theatre group to create beautiful sets and costumes for the shows they put on. After high school she realized she wanted to be in a larger artistic community where her talents could flourish. That community was Austin, and she moved here just twelve short years ago."

The minister was standing alone in the spotlights shining down on the wooden stage of the outdoor chapel. She was wearing khaki pants and over them a dark blue choir robe. She was doing an admirable job considering she hadn't known May.

The women seated on the wooden benches were paying rapt attention and several were sniffing into tissues, while a few were openly crying. My heart hurt for them, but my feelings for May were convoluted. On the one hand, I hated that she had been murdered. I felt sorry for her and didn't want to think about what the last moments of her life might have been like. On the other hand, I had been royally pissed at the woman for taking what didn't belong to her. Beth's husband.

I went back to my list. I could barely make out the letters in the dim light. TC. Tony Campanelli, a definite possibility. In fact, I could almost believe Tony would methodically kill off all his competition if it would move him closer to success. As for the method, pushing May over a cliff seemed in character. It was quick and it was neat, which appeared to be Tony's style. Although, until this weekend I'd always thought Tony was a pretty nice guy. Even this weekend, most of the time he was a nice guy.

I glanced around and spotted him sitting up front with Cordy and Jennifer. As I watched he put his arm around Jennifer, which I assumed was for comfort. Or was it something more? Was she the intended recipient of the red rose and the condoms? Jennifer was a good fifteen years younger than Tony, and to my mind a romantic relationship between them didn't bear thinking about. Still . . .

Beth, who was sitting beside me twitched uncomfortably. I turned to glance at her, and she looked stiff as an old wooden Indian. I had no idea what she was going to do about Ron, but I knew I would help in any way I could.

In my limited experience, long marriages, like the one my parents or grandparents had, can be rich and full of deep love that sometimes doesn't show to those on the outside. I didn't think Beth's was like that. I suspected that Beth was a convenience for Ron that allowed him to feel superior. He also got his meals cooked, his house cleaned, and his child cared for without any effort on his part. He certainly didn't display great passion toward Beth, nor had he ever.

As for Beth's feelings—I could only hope she was ready to move on.

I'd had one rat of a husband, and I suppose anyone who lives long enough is bound to date at least one of those, if not marry one, but Beth was just facing the realization of what Ron had been up to. That initial discovery can be devastating, and I figured things were going to get worse for her before they got better.

Tomorrow, I would get some supplies from Angie and make a card with my favorite saying, "Everything turns out okay in the end. If it isn't okay, then it isn't the end." At least it would give her a quick, if temporary, smile.

My eyes roamed over the backs of the women in front of

me. Angie was slumped like this was one sad occasion, and I thought what a nice person she was, and I was actually glad that someone felt that way. A row behind her was Sande Borders, who kept swallowing hard as she brushed her long auburn hair over her shoulders. I wondered if she knew May all that well, or was just feeling sorry that all of us have to die some day.

Beside Sandra was her cousin Lynn. I saw her stifle a yawn and if I'd had popcorn or a pebble, I'd have pitched it at her. I was betting that she'd had something to do with May's murder, more because I didn't like her than anything else, but it was a sufficient reason for me. She was on Peterson's list as Susan L. Donaldson. He'd put Lynn in parentheses. It had taken me a minute to figure out that she was now plain Lynn, our noir beader.

I turned around to see who was behind me and found none other than Officer Peterson staring at me. The man was a menace. And he had a list with my name at the top of it.

I turned back around. Beside the minister a table held May's picture. It was the headshot we'd all seen in her brochures and in the camp flyers. Cordy had taken it to the copiers and they'd blown it up as large as they could make it. Now it was in an antique silver frame that set off May's dark beauty perfectly. Also on the table was a bouquet of flowers; not the stilted roses I would have expected on short notice, either. There were red gerbera daisies, yellow mums, and purple irises. With all the greenery and in the tall milky white vase, they made an exquisite statement.

They were the flowers Nate had put in the back of the van.

NW. Nathaniel Wright was the last name on Peterson's list, and I had no idea what I thought about that.

"Talent is a gift of God," the minister was saying. "But the way we train talent, nurture it, and allow it to grow makes the difference between a crafter and a skilled artisan. May Feather honed her talents. We shall all miss seeing her beautiful—"

Someone from the front row jumped up and began to run along the benches to my left. In the darkness, and with the added shadow of the trees, it took a moment for me to realize it was Jennifer. I couldn't figure out what she was doing until she ran into the bushes almost directly beside us and I heard her retching.

I was up and ready to go to her when Cordy slid past. I sat back down to let Cordy play the gentle stranger and take care of Jennifer. I needed to stay here for Beth who was absolutely rigid beside me. At one point I'd patted her arm and Beth had jumped a good four inches off the wooden bench.

I could hear Cordy's voice saying something soft and soothing to Jennifer. In a few minutes they both appeared, Cordy helping Jennifer along the path and back toward the cabins. Sheriff Gonzales said something to Cordy. She nodded and kept on walking. Officer Peterson watched them. Both of the men had put in a long day and it wasn't over yet. I felt a little sorry for the sheriff, but not for Peterson.

"Wherever she went, there was beauty. She will be missed."

Beth dug her fingers in my arm and I yelped before I could stop myself. It was lost in the sound of everyone rising for a final prayer. As soon as we said "amen," all the camp lights went out.

For just a moment we were in darkness with those glittering stars looking over us. Then the flashlights started to go on, and someone began the singing. Slowly everyone turned toward the cabins, and those in the front row filed out as we all sang the good-night song.

Days at Green Clover had ended this way for as long as I knew. Even when I was eight I loved the dark night, the wind rustling in the trees, and all our voices raised up together. When I was a counselor it had been my favorite time of the day. Of course, that might have been because it also signaled the end of the planned activities, so we could put our charges to bed and finally have some time to ourselves.

When we'd started the bead retreats, there had been no question but what we would sing on our way back to our cabins. I listened to the voices, probably sixty or so of them,

> *"Oh, my Lord, Oh, my Lord,*
> *I have placed my trust in thee*
> *Though you have so many children,*
> *You are always there for me."*

I stood in place, watching as the women walked past. I saw Nate and heard his voice as he sang. The man could even sing. He saw me, and nodded, but he didn't miss a note. Seemed just right, and I found another reason to like him. Jeb was behind him, but Jeb wasn't singing. He was pushing buttons on his cell phone, probably checking messages. I couldn't believe I'd wasted so many years yearning for him. I was beginning to wonder how I'd ever been attracted to the man in the first place.

> *"Keep us safe here at Green Clover*
> *Oh, my Lord, please be my guide."*

The words took on different meanings at different times. When I was eight and new to camp, the God of the song wasn't the same one who had taken Charlotte away. This God was like my grandfather, and even though He was in heaven, I was sure He heard us. I also figured He was watching out for us.

In recent years, I thought the song referred to the danger of one of us tripping and breaking a leg in the dark, or at the very least, spraining an ankle.

Now, I hoped that God would keep everyone safe from the murderer.

As the women filed past, some were singing, some were sniffing away tears. I thought about the eight-year-old Charlotte, and how I'd been told she wanted to go to heaven. It made me wonder again what comes after death.

Oh, the ministers can talk about heaven and hell, but they never tell us what heaven looks like. Are there trees? And if there are, then what kind of trees? Do we live in houses, or do we just float around on clouds all the time?

I'm afraid I have to agree with Mark Twain, who was highly disparaging of all of us going to a place where we played musical instruments and sang for the rest of eternity. Not only does it sound more than a tad improbable, it also doesn't sound like a heck of a lot of fun.

As too many people have pointed out, I'm a here-and-now kind of person, doing the best I can in the moment. I couldn't do anything about May's current whereabouts, and I certainly couldn't deal with anyone's future residence. Right at this very moment, I had to take care of something more immediate, and that was Beth. She was going to need comfort and a sounding board. She'd also said she wanted a stiff drink, which was fine, but I didn't want her blurting out any accusations about May to the wrong person.

Finally, our row was able to leave, and Beth and I walked side by side, following the beams of our flashlights back toward the cabin. On the way we passed a man in a Mezner Security uniform. I nudged Beth and pointed him out.

"I think it's good news that he's here," Beth said. "I think."

"I feel the same way."

Finally we reached the Lazy L. "It's good to be home," I said.

"I'm making margaritas," Beth said. Ours is one of the few cabins with a refrigerator, and Beth went to the party room to get some of the ice she'd stashed in its freezer. While she was gone, Jennifer came in.

"How are you doing?" I asked.

Jennifer covered her white face with her hands. "I'm so embarrassed. I can't believe I got sick—practically in front of everyone."

"It happens to all of us at least once in our lives, and you had a good reason. It wasn't like you were drunk." Of course, she had been drunk the night before, and the cause of her stomach problems could have been barbeque on top of a hangover.

Jennifer took Sinatra out of his cage and climbed up to her bunk. "I keep telling myself that at least I was in the bushes, but still—I threw up! And everyone heard me." Sinatra wasn't a happy kitten—he bit Jennifer. "Ow. You little monkey."

"As you get older, Jennifer, you'll discover that bodily functions become less offensive and more routine." I began to pet Sinatra who started to purr. "My mother's friends talk about bowel movements—"

"Gross! That's like disgusting."

"What is?" Beth asked, returning with the ice.

"You don't want to know," Jennifer said.

Beth began making the margaritas, and I went to the cooler and got out my bottle of Muscovito. I sipped a plastic cup of it as I sat on my bunk watching the parade of women coming in from the service, and those who were already leaving. The ones going out were heading for the Saloon carrying bead boxes and design boards for a night of their favorite activity. We treated several to margaritas on the way out, and we collected some iced sugar cookies in return. They were not going to be eaten with the margaritas.

Shannan came in long enough to get a jacket and some money for the vendor's room, then Jennifer put Sinatra into his cage and the two young women started to leave together.

Beth stopped them at the door. "Go straight to the Saloon and straight back. No wandering around the camp. In fact, stay with a crowd—"

"Mother!" Shannan said.

"I'll watch her," Jennifer said as they scooted out.

"Why am I not secure with that?" Beth asked.

"Because of their behavior last night," I said. I pointed to the newest batch of margaritas. "Now, are you going to drink any of that, or are you giving it away?"

"Are you in a hurry?"

"No, but I can't sit here and watch you feed the entire camp."

"This isn't food."

"Manna. Nectar of the gods . . ."

She poured out a drink, started to stash the pitcher in the cooler, then said, "Oh, to hell with it, I think I'll drink it all."

"I'll bring my bottle." I grabbed an extra blanket in case the combination of the frozen margaritas and the night air was too much for Beth, shifted my wine under my other arm, and followed her to the rock above the cabin.

I put the blanket underneath us, and Beth put the pitcher on the ground. I leaned back with a sigh, holding my wine. The camp lights were back on and it was like a fairyland. "It's always so pretty from up here."

"The whole world is like that, don't you think?" Beth asked. "You just don't want to get too close, or too involved, because then it can get ugly."

That was my cue. "How long have you known?"

She paused but only for a beat. "About four months. I think I got in around the beginning. At least, I think that's when things started for them."

"How did you find out?"

"Oh, you know, he'd get strange phone calls on his cell phone and say he had to go out. He started having a lot of dinner meetings with clients, and he hadn't done those in years. Pretty much the usual, I guess. It wasn't confirmed until a week ago by Mr. Jack Pomrey, Private Eye."

I turned to stare at her. "I beg your pardon?"

"I didn't want to believe that Ron was having an affair, so I waited forever, and then I hired a private detective. You didn't think I followed Ron around, did you? I wouldn't stoop that low. How did you find out?"

"I followed Ron around."

"Nice going, Kitz. Why didn't you just ask me? I'd have shared Mr. Pomrey's report with you; I'd have let you see the video."

This time I almost choked on my drink. "A video?"

"It was dark when Pomrey took it, so you can't see much. Thank God, because it wasn't easy to watch." She drank some more margarita. "Now, why were you following my husband around? Surely you had more interesting things to do." I didn't say anything. "Well?" she asked. "Why were you following Ron?"

"Does anyone else know? About the affair?" I asked.

"You're doing it again."

"I can't answer until you tell me."

"How should I know? I haven't talked about it with anyone except Mr. Pomrey, and Mr. Pomrey doesn't chitchat."

I hesitated. "You'd better drink up, I may have more bad news."

"Now what?" She took a big swallow from her cup. "Darn, this is cold."

"Here, warm it up." I poured wine in the frozen margarita. "That ought to melt it."

She sipped. "Luckily, I'm not after taste . . . just effect." She took another swallow of the melting slush. "You might as well tell me; after the past two weeks I think I can take anything. I cope well. In fact, I'm getting damn sick and tired of coping."

"Boy, do I know that one."

"Would you stop mincing around and tell me? I can't sit here all night."

"Okay, okay; I'll tell you. I found out last night, and it wasn't my idea." This was the part I dreaded. "Shannan wanted to borrow the Rover, and since I couldn't let her, I volunteered to drive. She said she saw Ron's car here at camp . . . and she wanted to know for sure."

I could feel Beth slump beside me. "I was afraid she was suspicious. My poor baby. I wanted to talk to her, but I thought I should confront Ron first. And, I just couldn't. I couldn't do it." She picked up the pitcher and refilled her cup. "You saw Ron with . . . her last night? What were they—no, don't tell me."

"They weren't doing much. Just talking." That's the kind of lie I can get behind.

"But it was enough to upset Shannan, which, I'll bet, is why she got drunk. I'll go talk to her—" She started up, but I pulled her back down.

"I wouldn't worry about it now. She's coping today," I said. Laughter floated up from the Saloon. "At the moment, she's probably having fun for the first time in months."

"You're right." Beth let out a long sigh. "I feel so sorry for her. Poor Shannan."

"Poor you." I started to drink some wine and discovered my cup was empty. "Want more?" I asked, holding up the bottle.

"A splash." She poured in margarita, and I topped it off with Muscovito.

I realized I was leaning against Beth. "Sorry." I sat up straight. "The big question is, what are you going to do about it? Or have you thought about that?"

"It's all I've thought about."

"Have you done anything? I mean besides hiring Mr. Pomrey?"

"First, I cried a lot. Then I planned to murder Ron, but I decided it would upset Shannan, so I didn't do it. Then I thought about killing May—but, I didn't." She looked at me. "Really, it was just a mental exercise to make me feel better. And that was weeks ago. And now she's really dead; I can't believe it. You do know that I didn't have anything to do with her murder?"

"I know. But that doesn't answer my question; what are you going to do?"

Beth scooted back and almost fell off the rock. When she had her balance she said, "I don't know. I wanted to get the Tivolini contract so I could support myself and Shannan. It would have made it a lot easier to leave Ron."

"And if you didn't get the contract?"

"I thought about trying to talk Ron into couple's counseling. That's what it's called these days. It's not marriage counseling anymore, because the marriage doesn't get counseled, the couple does." She took a sip of her drink, made a terrible face and said, "Here, taste."

I did. "Fruit punch gone bad." I handed her back the glass.

"Let's chugalug," she said. We did, and she added, "Whew. That'll send you to the super bowl. Where was I? Oh, counseling. I know Ron's never been your favorite person, but for a long time, he was mine. When we first dated, I loved how logical he was, and how he thought I was cute and funny." She laughed, then the sound turned into a sob. "I'm sorry. It's just hard. It feels like my whole life has been false. Maybe he never loved me. Maybe I was never good enough. And then when I gained all the weight—"

"That's crazy!" I stood up. "Okay, you loved him. *And,* he loved you. Ron is way too selfish to marry someone he didn't love."

"Yes, but then there was May. And maybe others—"

"You don't know that, and you don't know that he loved May. It's possible he was just in lust with her. And now she's gone, never to return."

Beth wiped her cheeks as more tears fell. "I know. Murdered, which doesn't make things any better because he didn't give her up voluntarily. And the police might decide he murdered her. Did you think of that?"

"Of course." I sat back down, half on the blanket and half on the rock, which was very cold. "Scoot over, please." She did, and I sat down again, although my aim wasn't much better. "One more time." This time I hit the blanket and leaned back. "You know it's worse than you thought. Think. The police could suspect Ron, but they could also suspect you." I didn't mention Shannan. "So, what about Ron? I know it's bad to question his integrity—or do I mean morals? But you know he could have had an argument with May and blown up. Could he have killed her? I just wondered. Think he could have?"

"After all these years, I know Ron, and he's not that explosive. Of course, I never thought he was that passionate, either. Damn." She took a gulp of her drink. "I'm beginning to like this stuff. Maybe we should bottle it."

I shuddered. "I don't think there's much of a market."

Her head came up. "I just figured out where you went today. And why you came back with Sinatra. You went to tell Ron. About May." She turned and looked at me. "That was nice of you."

"I wasn't being nice to Ron," I said. "I went so you wouldn't have to tell Mo-Ron."

"I knew that. You were being nice to me. Good ol' Mo-Ron." She shook her head. "You really shouldn't call him that. To Mo-Ron." We clicked our plastic cups together in a toast and drank some more. Finally, Beth said, "You know, if Peterson finds out about that affair, my whole family could be in trouble."

"Absolutely." The word came out *absoluly*. "My tongue must have frozen," I said. "From the night air. The cold night air."

"Right."

"Most important," I said. "We have to make sure no one knows about the affair. Shannan won't say anything. But she does have few choice words for her dad."

"Oh, good. Someone should."

"Are you getting cold?"

"A little." She raised her glass. "Whatever happens, happens." She took a drink. "Maybe Ron will stay now. Or maybe I'll get the Tivolini contract. Or maybe— Oh, to hell with it." She drank, and I followed her lead. "So, tell me about Jeb."

"What's to tell? I came, I saw, and I think he's a moron. My heart has mended."

"Yes, but is your brain better?"

"My brain?"

"The number-one sexual organ."

"Well, he did screw with my head." Beth laughed and I added, "My brain doesn't like him, either. He is self-absorbed. Rude. And you know what else? He never liked me. He married two other women, did you know that?"

"Actually, I did."

"And you didn't tell me? Oh, who cares. Wait, I do. Not that you didn't tell me, but that he could marry two different women, and he couldn't even bother to call me on the friggin' telephone. It could have been on his cell phone, and it wouldn't even have cost anything. What a sumbitch." I took a sip of Muscovito. It tasted soft and warm, so I re-filled my cup and sipped some more. "I suppose it's a very good thing Jeb didn't call, because I'd have hauled up to New York, left behind my family, given up the manse. Jeez. Talk about a moron. I win the moron of the decade award. Moron of the century—"

"Enough. It's over now. Done. Finito. You don't think you're growing up?"

"I sincerely hope not." I shivered. "Maybe we should go back to the cabin. I'm chilly."

"Good idea."

I tried to get up and finally had to roll off the rock. "You can show me what you made for the Tivolini buyer. You promised you would."

"I didn't promise. I just said I would." She bent down to get the pitcher, and almost missed as she swayed. Beth's never been much of a drinker, and she doesn't hold her liquor all that well. I wasn't steady, either. I don't hold my liquor any better than she does.

I picked up the blanket. "I feel the need—"

"The need to pee!" She laughed, and so did I.

"Take me to john!" We stopped at the john and finally got to the Lazy L, holding each other up so we didn't fall off the path.

"You're lurching," she said.

"I did not 'lurch.' I tripped over the tip of the blanket."

"Blankets don't have tips. They aren't stockbrokers—"

"In, madam." I opened the door. "Get your creations." I tossed the blanket on the foot of my bunk and sat down, holding onto the rail to keep myself upright. Beth put the almost-empty margarita pitcher in the cooler and brought one of her bead boxes out from under her bed.

She stood in front of me. "Are you ready?"

"Ready."

She unclicked the latches and popped the top, "Ta da!"

I looked inside the box, then looked up at Beth. We both peered in the case again.

It was empty.

Nineteen

"**T**his isn't possible," I said. I glanced at Beth, then back at the case at least three times, as if the jewelry might be there the next time I looked. "You must have put it someplace else."

"I didn't."

"Well, then . . . it's . . . close by."

"Where?"

"Somewhere," I said. "Be reasonable. Jewelry can't walk off on its own."

"Appears it did." Beth sat down on her bed, still holding the empty box.

"First," I said, trying to think logically, or just think at all. "When did you last see it?"

"Friday, when I packed it."

"We need to look in your other bead cases. Maybe you moved things."

"You already said that. I didn't."

"You might have—"

"Right." She was too stunned to move.

"Don't get up," I said. "I'll look."

Beth's loose beads were in a large plastic box with five sliding trays, all with lots of compartments and tight-fitting lights. It was on the floor under her bed, and I pulled it out.

"They're not there," Beth said.

"You don't know; they could be." I carefully took out each tray. There were beads, findings, tiger tail, pliers, and things I didn't even recognize, but no completed jewelry. "Maybe you should tell me what I'm looking for."

Beth stared at me blankly.

"Sober up," I said. I felt stone-cold sober already, which was a good thing and a good waste of wine. "What did the pieces look like?"

"There was a set," she said. "Not to brag, but it was different."

I waited, but she didn't add anything. "How was it different?" I asked.

"There were chandelier earrings with blue beads, and to go with them, there was a necklace. It looked like one of the earrings, only big. The circlet went up on the neck, and then the chandelier was, oh, four inches across and it fell a good six inches. There were sixty-five Swarovski crystals on the dropped portion. I spent forever making chain."

"Just the earrings and necklace?"

A little color was coming back into her face. "No. There was a bracelet, too. The circlet went around the wrist, and the drop covered the back of the hand. A band slipped over the middle finger to hold it in place. It was very delicate."

"What size beads?"

"Small. Four millimeter."

I could picture the elegant pieces and the hours of work that went into making them. It would have won Beth the contract in a minute, a flash, less than an eye wink, only now they were gone.

I stood up. "Okay, I'm not worried, because we'll find everything," I said.

"I called it Empress Eugenia. I was really proud of it. What is it the Bible says? Pride goeth before a fall?"

"Yes, and it means when your pride goes, you fall. Next,

I'm going to look through your suitcases. Were the pieces in a box?"

She was up now, the dead blank look being replaced by confusion. "Yes. Maybe you'll find it. A gray linen jeweler's box with a clear cover." She glanced around the small sleeping porch. "Maybe Shannan took them out to show someone and put them back in the wrong place. Do you think that could have happened?"

"Absolutely," I said. "It absolutely could have happened."

"I'll look under all the beds." She wobbled but finally got down on her knees to look.

"Good idea." I dug through her suitcase, then through mine. "Not in any of those. Wait! My bead box." I have a plastic case similar to Beth's only mine is blue where hers is red. And I don't have as many beads, but I don't spend as much time at it as she does. I pulled my case out and looked through every tray. Nothing.

"Not under the beds," Beth said with a sigh, getting to a sitting position.

"Okay, what do you think? Should I?" I was holding out Leesa's designer duffle. Beth looked uncertain. "Oh, to hell with it," I said. I swung it up on Leesa's bed and almost fell over with the weight. "I'm checking it."

"If you think so, but I'm not helping."

Leesa's designer duffle held smaller designer cases and designer zip pouches that contained things like matched makeup brushes, Elizabeth Arden makeup, and designer underwear. "I'll bet you she's got a designer toothbrush. Is there such a thing as designer dental floss?"

"Yes. They make it into thongs." Beth was looking under pillows and running her hands over the covers of the beds. When she finished she turned to me. "We'll never find my things."

I didn't quite slap her on the back, but I briefly considered it. "We are in an enclosed area. People haven't left all day, so all we have to do is tell Cordy—"

"No."

"No? What do you mean—"

"I mean no."

"Why not?"

"I refuse to have security guards digging through everyone's luggage and acting like our friends are pretty thieves. No. I won't allow it to happen."

When Beth gets stubborn, it's best to move in a different direction. "Okay, fine," I said. "We'll finish checking in here, then we'll poke around the rest of the cabin. And after that, if we haven't found the jewelry, and I'll bet we have, then we'll branch out."

She stared at me. "You are nuts. And probably less than sober, because if you were, you wouldn't be doing this."

"Maybe, but don't bet on it. At least I haven't given up, which means we can still find your things. If we quit, we won't." I couldn't stand seeing Beth so defeated, and I couldn't stand that someone stole from her. Not that Green Clover hadn't had some petty thievery in the past, but this was beyond petty. This was mean-spirited.

Beth was thinking hard, and in the end said, "I'll do these." She pointed to Shannan's bags, a large duffel and a smaller tote, and began searching them.

Sinatra started yowling. "Oh, come here, little guy," I said, taking him out of the cage. He curled up against me and began to purr. "You're cute, but unfortunately you can't help." I held him up and looked at his big blue eyes. "You didn't see anything suspicious did you? Maybe someone walk off with Beth's jewelry?" He purred but didn't answer. "Okay, here you go. You can watch, and I don't mean cause problems." I put him on the bed and gave him a crumpled newsletter to play with.

There was a paper sack on Jennifer's bed and I decided that was the next item to be searched. Apparently, the forensics' people had let her in the trailer, or maybe they'd handed things out to her. Either way, she now had clean underwear, along with two pairs of jeans, four tops, and some toiletries. No jewelry. I put the sack back where it had been and looked around the porch. There was a wooden bead case on the floor in the corner, and I hadn't seen it before. "Do you think that's Jennifer's?"

"Probably."

I opened the top and then the drawers, each was lined with green felt. "Now this is the way a bead should travel."

Beth turned. "What?"

"Nice, huh?" I opened a second drawer that held tubes of seed beads. "The lining and all."

"Very nice."

I slid open another drawer and whistled. "Oh, my—" I pulled out a necklace of teardrop-shaped turquoise, black crystals, and silver pearls. "This is stunning."

The door opened. "Tante Kitzi!" Shannan was behind me. "That's Jennifer's! What are you doing?"

"Well, we aren't stealing it, if that's what you're worried about," I said.

"I didn't think you were, but why are you in her things? She just stopped off in the john and she'll be here any minute—"

"Calm. Be calm." I put the necklace away. "You didn't move any of the jewelry your mother brought, did you?"

"No."

"Darn." Then I slid open all the other drawers. When I didn't find what I was looking for, I pushed the bead box back into its corner.

Shannan was appalled. "You just went through all the drawers."

"I know that," I said. "And I have a very good reason. The things your mother made for the Tivolini buyer are missing. We're searching the cabin; would you like to help?"

"Missing?" Shannan looked at me, then at Beth in disbelief, her mouth open, her eyes wide. "I don't understand. Where would they go?"

Beth sat down on my bunk and started petting Sinatra.

"If we knew, then they wouldn't be missing, would they?" She sounded unnaturally calm, and I couldn't decide if it was the tail end of the liquor or if she had gone beyond all rational emotion. She'd had more to deal with than seemed fair.

Shannan sat beside her mom. "Oh, mom, I'm so sorry."

Beth let out a long sigh and patted her daughter's arm. "Me, too, honey. Me, too."

I was pacing the sleeping porch. "You know, there are other places to look in this cabin. I see no reason for us not to spend a little time just poking around—"

"Peeking into other people's things?" Shannan said.

"Yes. And now that there are three of us, you can help."

"Tante Kitzi—"

I leaned toward her and said softly, "You owe me."

At that moment Jennifer came in. "Hi." She looked at each of us. "What's happened now?"

It was Shannan who told her the story, finishing with a shake of her head, and saying, "And so, now my mom can't present to the Tivolini buyer tomorrow."

"That's horrible. Do you think they're just lost? Or stolen?" Jennifer asked.

Beth and I exchanged a look. "Stolen," I said. I couldn't think of any other way that the jewelry could have disappeared.

"Why don't you just tell Cordelia?" Jennifer asked. "There are security guards all over the place, and they can—"

"No." Beth remained firm. "I will not have my friends treated like criminals."

"One of them is a criminal," Shannan said.

"We don't know that. But, even if it's true, I still can't do that."

Jennifer turned out to be a young woman of action. "Maybe we should start searching, just in case your things are still here." She glanced at her watch. "They're going to shut down the Saloon in half an hour. The guards want everyone back in their cabins to lock the doors, so that doesn't give us a lot of time."

"I'm with you, Jennifer." I stood up and discovered that there was still alcohol in my system. I spoke as crisply as I could. "As I tell people when I'm training, 'Be bold, be brief, be gone.' So, who is taking what?"

We divided up the rooms and started off. "Oh," I said. "If you see anyone coming, yell my name loud as a warning for all of us."

Shannan stopped in the party room and opened the refrigerator door. Since she was most squeamish, she'd been given the easiest place to search, and after she was done with the fridge, she had to check the sacks of goodies. Then she'd help Jennifer and Beth in the main cabin. By that time I hoped either her inhibitions would be gone, or they'd be finished. Or maybe we'd have found the jewelry.

I went outside and up the stairs to the second floor, holding onto the railing as an extra precaution, since the effects of the wine reappeared when I least expected them.

Upstairs, only six bunks were being used, and I started by looking under the blankets and pillows, sliding my hand along the covers, feeling for lumps or beads. That was the easy part. I didn't really want to snoop into people's personal belongings, but my like for Beth was stronger than my dislike for the search.

I pulled out an old, brown vinyl suitcase, probably saved for occasions like camp and went through it carefully. Clothes, more clothes, and a couple of magazines, including *The Stampers' Sampler* and a *Somerset Studio Paper Arts*. I might have slowed down to peruse the amazing pictures, but underneath them was a hairbrush with long auburn hair. This was Sande's, and I felt like a complete rodent for going through her things. As I closed the suitcase, I reminded myself that if we found Beth's sample pieces, we'd all feel terrific.

Outside, I heard the Saloon doors open and close a couple of times. I looked out the window, but thank goodness whoever went out was going in the other direction. I wanted to check with Beth and the girls in the main cabin, but the only way down there was on the outside staircase, and I didn't have time for that.

I looked through a bead box, but there was only one completed piece and it was a leather necklace with earthy African beads. A noise came from outside, and I must have jumped a foot. I pushed my forehead against the screen, but I didn't see anyone.

More bags. A green duffel came first, and I went through it in record time. Next was a black rolling bag, and I was careful not to miss a zipper pocket or the cosmetic case. A vinyl bag was filled with rubber stamps, stamp pads, and some really interesting charms that I assumed went on cards, and another similar case had beads.

The final suitcase took forever because it had boxes and boxes of beads, and I had to open each one to look for Beth's things. By the time I finished I was sticky with sweat, and I don't sweat. If I kept this up I could get a job searching bags at the airport, and I'd already be trained.

Only one or two little items left. Heads under sheets sitting on a rickety card table. Lynn's heads.

One more time I thought I heard someone outside, but the pathway downstairs was empty. Obviously, burglary was not a profession I was cut out for, and I wasn't even stealing anything.

I lifted the first square of material and saw the head that Lynn had shown me the day before. It looked more garish than I'd remembered, and as a tiny bead fell off, something inside me fell, too. I realized that whoever took Beth's jewelry could already have them apart and the beads could be in something else entirely. Or down the john. I was betting Beth had thought of that long ago, and it was only my insistence that had made her agree to a search.

Well, if she could tough it out, I could, too. And I

would. I lifted the head and looked at the bottom, just in case something could be hidden inside. It was solid and I put it back the way I'd found it. Last, I used great care to lift the final sheet and found the face of a woman staring back. She had huge eyes of deep sapphire Swarovski crystals. Four millimeters. The size Beth had used. The beaded head also wore a choker of the same blue crystals. As much as I hated to, I ran my hand over the choker looking for a loose bead. When I found one, I popped it off to show Beth.

"My, my, guess who I found snooping around my things."

I swung around to face Lynn Donaldson.

She seemed amused at my awkward position.

"Yes," I said, pointing at the head with my left hand so I could slip the bead from my right hand into my pocket. "I thought you'd made this."

"And now would you like to explain why you're up here? Or do you still just assume that you can do whatever you want and to hell with the rest of us?"

That was a shot out of the blue. "I have no idea what you're talking about."

"I'm not surprised." As she said it, I realized why her sneer was so good—she practiced it all the time. "I'll just run down and get Officer Peterson, since he said to report anything suspicious," she said. "He can decide whether you spend the night in jail."

"Fine." I put my hands on my hips. "Then get it over with."

"Darn, I just remembered that we aren't supposed to leave because of the lockdown. Guess I'll do it tomorrow."

"This is ridiculous. I didn't take anything."

"Oh, really? And what about the bead you're holding in your hand?"

I held both hands out, palms up. "What bead?"

"A thief and a magician. Do you cheat at poker, too?"

"I only play poker with my grandson, and usually he

wins." I shook my head. "I have no idea why you are acting this way."

"No, you wouldn't, because you have no idea who I am."

I looked at the woman, trying to place her. "Nope, I don't. Can't say that I've given it much thought, either."

"You wouldn't." She sneered again.

"Let me guess, you drive a Hummer Two. Hmmm, is your other car a broomstick?"

The look on her face told me that I had shot from the mouth again, and she was going to make me pay for it.

"I'm sorry," I added, genuinely sorry that I was even having this conversation. "That was rude. You don't deserve for me to be rude."

"But it's exactly what I'd expect from you."

This woman had a chip on her shoulder about the size of the Rocky Mountains, and for the life of me I couldn't figure out what it had to do with me—if it had anything. I decided that retreat was the best way to respond.

"Now, if you'll excuse me—" I started for the door but Lynn stepped in front of me. She was about the most obnoxious person I've ever met, but even so, I drew the line at pushing her out of my way. "I'd like you to move," I said. "If you don't mind—"

"Oh, but I do mind. I mind a lot." She wasn't sneering now; she was genuinely furious. She stepped closer so I could smell her musky perfume and her heavy breath. "I mind that you even exist."

What in the world was I supposed to say to that? I might have asked her, but I figured that would just give her more reason to go after me. "I beg your pardon?"

"It is way too late to beg my pardon—"

"Okay, well, whatever you say." I could hear some women coming up the pathway below us, and I recognized Sande's laugh. I didn't particularly want them to hear Lynn ranting at me. Truth is, I didn't want them knowing what I'd been doing.

"I'm leaving now," I said, stepping around Lynn, "unless

you'd like to keep me here by force?" Big talk, since I'd already opened the door.

Lynn turned to face me, and the sneer was back. "By all means, go right ahead. I'll talk to Officer Peterson in the morning. Oh, and say hi to all the girls as you pass them on the path. They'll be my witnesses that you were up here."

There is a term for women like Lynn and I'd have reminded her of it, if I hadn't been in such a hurry to leave. I took the stairs two at a time, and then, instead of taking the path, I turned the other way and fumbled along the back of the cabin in the dark. It was behavior more fitting a child or a criminal, but I was feeling like both.

Most of the wooden slats were down to cover the screens, and I had no light except the little bit that peered out through the cracks. Served me right. I should have stood up to Lynn and demanded to know why she disliked me so much. Trouble is, I've got enough sins in my past to figure she had good reason. Now isn't that disgusting?

There was a slight gully on the far side, and I held on to a prickly tree to get around the corner without mishap. By that time, I wasn't far from the sleeping porch door and a fairly even pathway to walk on. I could hear voices, Beth's and Shannan's.

I was more than relieved when I grabbed the door handle and pulled. It didn't budge. "Hey," I whispered as loudly as I dared. "Open up. It's me."

I heard a lock clicking, and then Beth was standing there with her frizzy hair outlined in the light. "Where have you been? We've been worried."

"With good cause," I said, grateful to be inside.

"What happened?" Beth asked. Her table was back in the corner with a partially made necklace on it. It looked like it would complement the flat bracelet she'd created yesterday. Beading away her worries.

Shannan said, "And why do you have pine needles in your hair?"

I pulled them out, then flopped on my bunk. "I was slinking around the outside of the cabin, hoping no one would see me."

Jennifer looked confused, "Why would you do that?"

"Not important. Did any of you find anything?"

"Nothing, and you didn't answer us, which by the way, is becoming a bad habit." Beth sat back down and picked up her beading. "Why were you sneaking around outside? And what happened?"

"Because Lynn Donaldson caught me upstairs, and I panicked." I put my pillow on my stomach, which was feeling pretty queasy. "What are you making?"

"Something to show the Tivolini buyer in the morning. It's not nearly what I wanted her to see, but on short notice, it's the best I can do. I just can't believe Lynn caught you— of course, it would have to be her. I hope you told her to stuff it up her beaded head."

"Not exactly. Who is she, anyway? She seems to have some terrible grudge against me."

"I told you all I know about her. She was married to a partner in the law firm," Beth said. "I'll bet Sande would know more."

"I'll talk to her tomorrow—maybe she can tell me why Lynn hates me so. I didn't tell you, Lynn says that in the morning, she's going to tell Peterson I was stealing."

"You've never stolen anything in your life!" Beth snapped. "How dare she talk about you like that. Oh, Kitz, I'm so sorry. Here you were just trying to help me, and now you're in trouble. What does she say you took?"

I pulled my hand out of my pocket. "This bead."

"She's talking to Peterson about one bead?" Shannan asked. "You could have found it on the floor—"

"But I didn't. I did steal it."

"Why would you do that?" Jennifer asked.

"Because I wanted Beth to see it. Could this be a fugitive bead from one of your chandelier pieces?"

Beth looked at the bead, then at me. "Mine weren't sapphire—they were pale. An icy blue."

I didn't know whether to be relieved or upset. "Well, hell."

I was going to jail for kidnapping an innocent bead.

Twenty

The one thing I can do is sleep—especially when the pressure's on. I slept hard and woke to a soft rumbling sound. When I opened my eyes, I found myself staring into a pair of big, round, light blue eyes. Sinatra was sitting by my neck, waiting for me like a furry little vulture.

"What are you doing out here?" I asked. Naturally he didn't respond; I hadn't expected him to. I sat up, and my head reminded me of all the wine I had consumed. Then came the memory of Beth's missing sample pieces and how we'd gone searching for them like a group of overaged and overzealous Nancy Drews. It actually hadn't been a bad idea, if I'd been more sober.

And if I hadn't been caught.

Add that to my ramming stunt of the other night, and I was on a roll.

If Lynn Donaldson really did decide to talk to Officer Peterson, I was in big trouble; it would be a great excuse for him to insist on another chat. I hadn't much liked the first one we'd had, and I didn't want a second. Secrets are hard to hide when you're face to face with someone like him.

In the future, I would limit my activities to those that were legal and completely, mostly, ethical. I intended to get started on them immediately.

I sat up. The bunks around me were all empty; between

the alcohol and the guilt I had slept not only hard, but long.

"So, what are you doing out here?" I asked Sinatra as I climbed out of my bunk. "I've got lots to do today, and you're supposed to be in your cage."

I fed him, and while he crunched away I caught sight of myself in the round mirror Shannan had hung on the wall. My hair looked like curly hay gone amok. Worse, my face looked like my mother's, but without her careful makeup. The expression wasn't as cheerful as my mother's, either.

I told Sinatra, "In case I get arrested or even questioned again, I'd like a little more armor than just a day's worth of dirt. I'm going to take a shower and do my hair." I opened my suitcase and fished out clean underwear. I was bent over digging out my cosmetic case when claws sank into my rear end.

"Sinatra!" He was hanging off the back of my sweatpants. I reached around and unhooked him. "That is a very bad habit," I said, "and you have got to stop doing it." He purred, and I picked up my things. "I can't take you with me to the john, but you can come along to a demonstration or two later. Deal?"

He didn't say no, so I put him back in his cage. His yowl told me he was not a happy boy. "You can't do everything your way, even if your name is Sinatra."

I went to shower, and by the time I was spiffy enough to face the day, and anyone who might be in it, a bell was ringing at the dining hall. There were no other campers around, leaving me to assume it wasn't last call, but the too-late-it's-over bell. I was right, because when I got to the dining hall, I had to go to the kitchen for leftovers. I ended up with an extra dollop of scrambled eggs to make up for the absence of bacon or toast. I did get a large cup of hot coffee to wash them down.

The dining hall was almost empty, and the clock showed that it was five after nine. I stared at it and swore softly under my breath. Beth was already meeting with the Tivolini buyer, and I hadn't said good luck or break a leg, or anything. I hoped she'd gotten an encouraging send-off from Shannan and her other friends, since I had been remiss.

If only Beth had the chandelier set to show the buyer, she'd be walking out of the meeting with a contract, but obviously someone hadn't wanted that to happen. Someone who knew that Beth was one of the best.

As I stood there, eggs in one hand, coffee in the other, I had a realization. What if May had been killed to stop her from presenting to Tivolini? We'd all dismissed that because it seemed so ridiculous, but it was really about money. People kill for money all the time. And what if the murderer had planned to kill Beth, too, but for some reason changed her mind and had just stolen Beth's pieces? I shuddered. Beth was so dear; how could some no-talent moron . . . Wait. If I'd hit on the reason, then it meant that whoever killed May was a contender for the contract, too. It couldn't be a rubber stamper or a vendor.

And then I remembered that just before dinner last night, Leesa had said she was going to the dining hall, but I'd found her at the cabin not five minutes later. She said she'd been playing with Sinatra, but that was pure hooey. I hated to think that Cordy's niece was a thief. She wasn't even a beader, was she? Which meant if she'd taken the chandelier pieces, it was to wear them and show them off. Which shot my theory all to hell and distressed me even more because despite her slightly arrogant ways, I liked Leesa. She said what she thought, and I appreciate that.

"Kitzi?" Angie Hogencamp waved a hand in front of my face. "Are you okay?"

"Oh, sure, I'm fine. I'm looking for a place to sit." The dining room was almost empty.

"Come join us. I can't stay long, but I've got a few minutes."

Angie led me to a table near the door where Tony Campanelli was sitting. TC and AH. I couldn't for the life of me see Angie killing anyone, and she didn't have a reason for wanting May dead. Tony did.

He looked tired, and there was a streak of dark stubble along his chin as if he hadn't been too attentive to his shaving. This was not our usual Tony.

"Mind if I join you?" I asked.

He didn't even look up to see who it was. "Help yourself." His hands were wrapped around what looked like a very cold cup of coffee.

"Are you okay?" I asked as I sat down. "You don't look too chipper."

He glanced at my face. "Look who's talking. I'm not an hour late for breakfast."

"Big night last night?" Angie asked me.

"No, I didn't do anything last night—I just overslept."

That appeared to wake Tony up. "Oh, right."

"What does that mean?" I asked.

"I just heard some things," he said.

"About?" I asked. His mouth moved, and it looked like a grin, as if whatever he'd heard was not going to be fun for me to hear. "Go ahead; I can take it," I said.

"Spit it out, Tony," Angie said. "Gossip and secrets are no fun if you don't share them."

He didn't hesitate. "Well, someone was telling me how Kitzi had a little too much to drink last night," he said.

Angie waved that away. "We're at camp. We're supposed to let loose."

"Yes, but Kitzi's drinking might have, hmmm, how shall I say this? It might have 'headed' her for some real trouble." He looked directly at me and grinned.

"Gee, I wonder who told you that," I muttered. Then I started eating, because I knew the answer, didn't care to hear it, and hadn't really meant to ask the question.

Tony laughed outright this time. "Well, it wasn't a little bird."

Angie looked from Tony to me. "What is he talking about?"

"Something of Beth's was missing last night," I said. "I went searching for it. Not a big deal."

"Except she was looking in somebody else's things—"

"I was looking *at* her work," I corrected. I turned to Tony. "You're making it sound like I was doing something wrong, and I wasn't."

"Whose work were you looking at?" Angie asked.

"The beader from the Dark Side," I said.

Angie frowned. "Darth Beader?"

"Pretty close. Lynn Donaldson. The lady with the Hummer Two. The one who brought you a wine cooler yesterday."

"Oh, yes. The one who says that men and sex are the root of all evil." Angie stood up and stretched. "Guess that would apply to you, too, Tony." He almost choked on his coffee, but Angie was picking up a sack of change, so she didn't notice. I certainly did.

"See you," Angie said. "I have to go open my booth. Good luck on your meeting with Tivolini," she finished to Tony, then headed out.

"So, Tony, how do you know Lynn?" I asked. "Old buddies? New friends?"

"Who said I know her?"

It was a cool response, but I'd seen the look on his face. He knew Lynn, and I didn't think it was all that pleasant an association. "I do. Among others." I sipped some coffee and kept looking at him, waiting for more.

"I have no idea what you're talking about," he said.

"No kidding. Really?"

"Yes, really."

"Then don't tell me about the two of you, just tell me about Lynn."

He seemed suspicious. "Why would you want to know about her?"

"Because the woman seems to have a grudge against me, and I can't think why. Oh, and by the way, Beth says I have an annoying habit of answering a question with a question. It seems you have it, too, and she's right, it's very annoying." I pushed my plate aside. "So what about Lynn?"

He looked around carefully before he said, "You can't repeat any of this."

"Promise."

"Well, you know I work pretty closely with the Bead Place, right?" I nodded. "That's where I first met Lynn. At a demonstration. Then about a week later, Lynn and Marcie, the owner, had a falling out. Seems Lynn thought Marcie was going to have her start doing demonstrations, except Lynn had misunderstood. Marcie had actually scheduled an artisan from New Braunfels who did similar work. When Lynn found out, she acted as if it wasn't important. She even bought over fifteen hundred dollars worth of beads that day."

"Wow. We're talking about a lot of beads."

"A lot. Then Lynn put a stop payment on her check and brought all the beads back. Dumped together in a zip-top baggie. The gallon size."

"Oh, dear."

"Marcie refused to take them, but what did it matter? Lynn wasn't going to pay, so in the end, Marcie was stuck separating them all and restocking. It took days."

I had guessed right; her other car *was* a broomstick.

"Do you have any idea why she dislikes me?" I asked.

He shook his head. "Just on general principles?"

"Maybe, but I must have done something." I thought it over and couldn't figure out what it could be. I hadn't insulted her car or her nail polish, or her heads, and that was really all I knew about the woman. No, I also knew that Tony had some association with her . . . and Tony'd had a red rose and some condoms in his trailer.

"Tony," I said. "Is there anything else you can tell me about her?"

He looked guilty. "Nothing."

"Oh, come on. I saw the way you jumped when Angie mentioned Lynn's name. Oh, and that comment about men, or was it sex? Being the root of all evil." When he wouldn't respond I shrugged. "Fine, don't tell me. I'll ask Lynn."

It wasn't a big threat, or I didn't think so, but Tony cracked faster than an egg hitting a floor. "I'll tell you." He leaned closer. "It's not a big secret—I'm sure half the people in camp already know. She came to my trailer the other night. That's all. She came to my trailer, we talked, and she left. And now it's time for me to leave. I have the Tivolini meeting coming up." He was up in a flash.

"But, Tony—" He was gone.

I finished my coffee, trying to think what it all meant. Tony hadn't bought the rose or the condoms for Lynn, that much was for sure. If he'd bought them for May, it was obvious they were never received by her. What I wondered about was whether or not Tony had designs on someone else at camp. He didn't seem attracted to older women. Who was younger? I couldn't think of anyone except Jennifer. And Shannan.

What if Tony was some kind of sexual predator trying to lure young women to his Fifth Wheel? What if—

I stopped the forward movement of my thoughts, because I was basing conjecture on conjecture on fabrication. When any of my illustrious colleagues in the senate had done that, I'd been quick to annoyance and just as quick to point out how totally untrustworthy their comments were. I needed to hold that same measure of fact up to my thoughts. What I knew for a fact was that Tony'd had condoms and a wilting rose in his trailer on Friday. Period.

I would certainly ask Jennifer and Shannan if he'd invited them over, but in retrospect it didn't seem all that likely.

Cordy stuck her head in the door. "If any of you are interested in the demonstrations, they are beginning right now in the Saloon." She spotted me and hurried inside. "Kitzi! Half the world is looking for you."

"Who?"

"Beth before her meeting with Tivolini, but that was a bit ago."

"I must have been in the shower."

"Good thing." She sat down in the seat Tony'd left and

was almost whispering as she leaned toward me. "Jeb is looking for you, too."

I jerked up, and we almost bumped heads. "What does he want?"

"I have no idea. Don't you want to see him?"

"I do not. He may be your brother, but he is, to quote your niece, an asshole. Smart young woman."

Cordy was looking edgy. "She's right. But now the bad news." Again she leaned closer. "Officer Peterson is also looking for you, and, even worse, he is looking for Shannan, too. He was really steamed about something."

"Shannan? What—" But I knew in my heart he'd found out that we'd lied to him. I couldn't guess how he knew, and I sure wasn't going to ask him. "I've got to find her," I said. "Any idea where she is? Or Peterson?"

"He was at the front gate. He asked what cabin you were in, but I told him in no uncertain terms that he was not allowed in the cabins unless he had a search warrant or an arrest warrant. Which is why he's now royally pissed at me, too."

"Great." I looked around quickly and found that there were only five women left in the dining hall and no sign of anyone official. "Do you know where Beth is?"

"Abigail's Parlour having her meeting." Next to the Saloon.

"I've got to get out of here," I said.

"Good idea. I'll clear your table. Go."

I was out and gone in a flash, careful not to let the door hit me in the butt as I went.

Green Clover has paths running every which way and if you know them, you have several ways to get almost anyplace. I had to find Shannan. Seemed like I'd spent all weekend chasing her, and I'd forgotten to ask Cordy if she had an inkling of where I should look. The best bet was the demonstration, but there was no way I could cross the road in front of the Saloon. I'd have to go down closer to the river and cut across there.

By the time I could see the dining hall again, from the other side, I was practically out of breath. If I kept up this pace, I'd either lose some weight or have a heart attack.

I stayed in the trees until I was right behind the Saloon, then I hustled inside its back door. I was behind a woman who was demonstrating some beautiful outdoor hangings of wire and beads. Shannan was in the front row.

I waved my arm and mouthed, "Shannan." Several people saw me, but not my goddaughter. The woman next to her was squinting at me, trying to figure out what I wanted. I pointed to Shannan, and the woman finally nudged her.

It might as well have been a silent movie, and a pretty silly one, but finally Shannan, greatly dismayed, made her way out the front doors of the Saloon, apologizing all the way. I raced out the back and met her at the side of the building.

"What is the problem?" she asked. "That's the first—"

"This way, quick." I grabbed her hand and started up the path to the Lazy L at quite a clip.

"Why?"

"Because Officer Peterson is looking for both of us, and Cordy says he steamed."

Shannan turned white. "But why?! What's he going to do?"

I cut between two trees pulling her as hard as I could. "Don't balk. Run. I have no idea what he's up to, but he can't do anything if he can't find you. Would you run?!"

"Fine!"

I tripped over a rock and almost pulled Shannan down. She swore, using a few words her mother would have been annoyed to hear, but personally I didn't give a damn.

We reached the Lazy L, and I threw the door open as if we were going to be safe at home. I heard a squeal and looked down to see Sinatra scooting along the floor.

"Oh, no. Poor baby." Shannan scooped him up.

"Is he okay?"

"He's fine. Why'd you leave him out of his cage?"

"I didn't. He gets out by himself. He's magic." I pulled my purse out of my suitcase and rummaged around looking for my keys. "Listen, you have to get out of here unless you want to meet up with Peterson. Take the Rover and go home. Or to a friend's. Actually, that's a better idea. Go to a friend's house. Call me on my cell to tell us where."

Shannan is not a slow young woman once she gets on track. She put Sinatra in his cage and was reaching for her purse. "What about my mom?"

"He's not looking for her; just us. I'll tell her where you went."

She only took a second to throw some things in her tote. "I'll be at Christie's house." Her expression was frantic as she peered out the screen at the paths. "How am I going to get to the Land Rover?"

I was thinking fast. "We'll have to reconnoiter the parking area. If Peterson is there, well . . . well, we'll work out a plan B." I reached down and checked the latch on Sinatra's cage. I turned to Shannan. "Come on. Run silent and run fast. But run!"

Twenty-one

he door banged and we were off. I led the way, around the perimeter of the camp until we came to the small gate. I wished I'd asked Nate the combination to the lock, but if worse came to worst, the fist-sized rock was still sitting there and we could use that on it.

"Look down to the gate," I panted, pulling Shannan toward the bushes. "See anything?"

"No." She was puffing, too. "You think Peterson is there?"

"Maybe." I breathed for a second. "Okay. Here's what we do. You stay here—"

"No. Then he'll just get you. That's not a good idea."

"Sure it is. I'm older, and I have clout."

"Not with Peterson."

"Maybe the jailer voted for me."

"That's not funny."

I nudged her. "Okay, we'll go together. But stay toward the fence and try not to make too much noise."

We dodged in and out of the brush until we were close enough to the gate and the parking area to see that the female deputy was back on duty at the front gate.

"Now what are we going to do?" Shannan asked.

"You are going back down to where we stopped. The

gate is probably steadier than the fence, so climb over
that—I'll pick you up."

"But how are you—"

"Shannan don't ask a lot of questions, just go."

I figured I could do pretty much the same trick as Nate
and I had executed yesterday, only with a twist ending.

I strode out into the middle of the pathway and kept
right on going. There was no reason to think that I
couldn't just walk out. The only thing was, I was nervous.
I've done a tad of smuggling in my past, nothing like
drugs, but a few things that I felt imperative to either bring
in or take out of a country. Things that some official or
other thought should not move across borders. There was
the Egyptian money that I took out of Cairo. I paid over
three dollars American for a small, battered, and dirty
piece of paper. You'd think they'd be thrilled to get rid of
it, but the law says you can't take Egyptian money out of
their county.

And then there was the time coming out of the Bahamas
when I was smuggling genuine fake Rolex watches. Five
of them. I had decided that they were the perfect gift for
my friends, some of whom had real Rolexes. I had even
splurged on two that had genuine fake diamonds. Beth and
my daughter, Katie, got those.

In both situations, and a few others not worth mentioning, I was nervous walking up to Customs. I had to remind
myself to smile and act natural, whatever in the world that
is. I was doing exactly the same thing here, sauntering
along like I didn't have a care in the world, looking at the
sky and the deputy. And the wrought iron gate that was
once again closed.

"Good morning," I said to the deputy, who was in full
uniform, including hat, and holding a clip board. "Beautiful day, isn't it?" Even in my state, I couldn't miss that the
blue sky was deep and cloudless.

"Yes, ma'am."

"And, seems we're lucky. I heard that no one here at Green Clover reported any problems last night."

"Yes, ma'am, so far as I know."

"I'm just going to run into Wimberley. I'll be right back." I held out my keys.

"If I could have your name. Officer Peterson wants to okay all departures."

I felt a panic start in my stomach, but I ignored it, and concentrated on working my facile tongue. "I wouldn't doubt it. That man is awfully officious, but I didn't say that."

The deputy smiled. "I didn't either."

"Problem is, I'm in a hurry. I swear I'll be back in fifteen minutes. Twenty at the most. Where is the grouch anyway?"

"I'm not sure. Let me try to raise him on the radio."

"No, no. That's not necessary. I'll be back as fast as I can." I reached inside my pocket. I'm not sure what I thought I'd find that would do any good, but there was nothing there. Not a driver's license, *nada*.

"Yes, ma'am, if I could just have your name."

"I don't mind at all." I was thinking fast. "I'm Sande. Sandra Borders. I'm a rubber stamper from California. Just got here this morning."

"Yes, ma'am," she said, writing the name. "And you'll be right back?"

"Right back." She reached for the gate, and I had to control myself not to knock her over so I could get out faster. "Thank you." I sort of loped to the Land Rover. In just seconds it was running and I was backing out, heading not toward town, but the other way along the fence.

Shannan started to wave the minute she saw me, and I pulled over. She had the passenger door open before I fully stopped.

"Get in over here," I said, jumping out.

She threw in her duffel and her purse, then slammed the

door. "Where are you going?" she asked, running around the front to the driver's side.

"Back to camp."

"How do I get out of here?" She slid in and adjusted the seat.

"Drive to the next intersection, turn right, then right at the stop sign. One more right and you'll be on Otero Road. That's this one, except you'll be about two miles farther along. Then just head to the highway."

"Will you be okay?"

"Of course."

"Tell my mom where I am. Christie's house. Don't forget."

"I will tell her, and I won't forget." I remembered that kids never have money. "There's fifty dollars under the seat. Here." I reached underneath it and pulled out the bill. "In case you need food or gas, or anything. Be sure and call."

"I will." She started to put it in gear but hesitated. "Tante Kitzi, maybe I should just go home."

"No. What in the world would you say to your dad? Now is not the time to go home. Is that clear?"

"Don't yell. Okay."

"And don't wreck my Rover! Go."

She pulled away slowly, and I watched her until she turned the corner, then I let out a breath of relief. Now that she was safely on her way, I had to get back to the front gate, and figure a way to explain why I was on foot when I'd left on wheels.

I lurked about ten minutes in the parking area, assuming the deputy would expect me to be gone at least that long. About then I saw a car coming from the other direction. It was moving pretty fast, raising a cloud of white dust in its wake. I ducked behind a red SUV and waited on the off chance it belonged to somebody I didn't want to meet up with. It was an official car, all right. I wasn't close enough to see who was in it until it turned toward the gate. The door was clearly marked *Sheriff* and, no surprise, it had the sheriff in it, but he was alone. The deputy opened the gate, and she and the sheriff spoke a minute before he drove on through and into the camp.

I waited until I couldn't see the whites of his fenders, then I hustled to the gate, and slipped through fast. The deputy hadn't seen me drive up, but then she hadn't *not* seen me drive up, either.

"I'm back," I said with as much good cheer as I could muster. "Thanks again!"

She scratched out the name on the clipboard as if she hadn't wanted anyone to know I'd left, either. "Yes, ma'am."

I turned and heard another car coming toward Green Clover. The only safe place was on the other side of May's trailer, and that's where I went. After I was out of sight, I stuck my head around the corner in time to see a DPS car pull into the parking lot. Officer Peterson. Which proved once again that timing is everything in life. While the gate was being opened, I took off, using as many shortcuts as I knew to get back to the Lazy L. I looked over my shoulder the whole way. A piece of me wished I'd gone with Shannan, but that would have been problematic. It would have looked suspicious, and she wouldn't have been as safe. Besides, I couldn't leave Beth behind to fend for herself.

I peeked in the screen of the cabin, feeling ridiculously like a voyeur, but the Lazy L was quiet, and for once Sinatra was in his cage. I slipped inside the sleeping porch.

"What's the matter? Losing your powers?" I asked Sinatra. He let out a meow, and I took him out and put him on my bed. "But no fooling around, deal?" He jumped down and went to his cat box.

I took out my cell phone and plopped on the bunk, breathing hard. This was some kind of camp, and I had lots to do before I could see it getting any better. First, I had to call Larry Brill in case he'd heard anything new. Then I had to find out how Beth had done with the Tivolini buyer; after that came another chat with Tony. I hadn't gotten to a number of topics with him, such as roses and condoms. I also hadn't asked him about his relationship with May, which seemed remiss, to say the least.

I was also stalling. I was a lawmaker, not a law breaker, and I just didn't feel good about lying to Peterson and then not telling him the truth. I planned on doing that very thing when I got my other chores taken care of. What was the worst he could do? Put me in jail? Well, yes, he could do that. Maybe I'd call our family lawyer and ask him to meet me at Green Clover.

In the meantime, I checked my cell phone which showed that I'd missed two calls, one from my daughter and the other from Larry Brill, my friendly TV reporter. Things might be turning in the right direction after all. My daughter had left a message saying that the murder at the camp was on the news, and what in the world was going on? She was very afraid that her children would find out, and then how was she going to explain that their grammy was at a camp where there had been a murder? She wanted me to call her.

Considering that Cliffie and Shelby are five and Gabrielle is only three, I didn't think they should be watching the news in the first place, and knowing Katie, they weren't. Katie doesn't want perfection, she simply wants control.

In this particular case she wasn't getting it because I wasn't calling her back. It was Larry I was more interested in and whatever information he might have for me on May's murder. The message he left said to call him. I pushed buttons until I finally heard a ringing. An answering machine came on, and my shoulders slumped until a real human voice interjected, "Hold on. We're here." The machine stopped, "This is Larry."

"This is Kitzi. What's the news?"

"Hi, to you, too. How's camp?"

"Not all it used to be. I'm kind of under the gun here, not literally, of course, but I have to talk fast. Have you heard anything?"

"I have. This isn't official, and you didn't get it from me, but according to my contact in the coroner's office, it appears May Polaski was in a fight before she went over the cliff."

"How could they tell?"

"I asked that same question. Something about place-ment and angle of the bruises. Only they call them contu-sions. Plus, once someone is dead, they don't bruise anymore, so she was hit before death." That was more than I'd ever wanted to know. He went on, "Oh, and she didn't drown. They think that she must have had a serious head injury and then crawled toward the water."

I thought for a second. "Did your contact say anything else?"

"Just that there were several bruises on the neck, as if she'd been hit by something. According to him, someone who went over a cliff would usually have injuries on their extremities from trying to stop themselves. They might have a few on the neck, but that's protected. They wouldn't have several, like your friend did. Oh, and her face didn't have a scratch. The fatal blow was on the back of the head."

"Wonder how accurate your contact is?"

"Well, usually about ninety-five to a hundred percent. Around the station our story is, if Roger says it, you can take it to the morgue," he said, and I groaned. "Sorry. Sick humor."

I stopped to think for a second. "Lar, have you heard anything about May's ex-husband?"

"Not much. They had a hard time tracking him down because he and his second wife are on a cruise in the Ba-hamas. They were at sea the night May was killed. He was pretty much dismissed as a suspect after that." He paused.

"That's all I have. What about you? Have you heard any-thing?"

I let out a puff of air. "They haven't told us a thing. Nothing."

"So what's going on at Green Clover?"

"Beading and rubber stamping. Last night we had the memorial service for May, as planned. Nothing new there. Then at ten o'clock the officials, and I couldn't tell you which ones, shut down the activities and made sure we were all in our cabins. With new locks on the doors that we locked."

"Really. No sneaking around—girls sneaking to the boys cabins and vice versa?"

"We don't have boys here. Or girls for that matter."

"Not as much fun as the camp I went to as a kid."

"Yeah, and I'll bet you didn't have murders there, either."

"You're right. We limited our crime to manslaughter."

"You're in rare form today. I'll let you go. You must have lots more people to share your gallows humor with."

"Hint taken. I'll call if I find out anything else, but that's not likely."

"Okay. And I'll do the same. And, Larry. Thank you."

"My pleasure."

I snapped my phone shut and thought about what he'd said. Some kind of fight. Angie said she'd heard an argu-ment and it was the first time she'd ever been aware of a dis-agreement at Green Clover. I hadn't asked Tony about that, either. His Fifth Wheel is close to Angie's trailer, so there was a chance he'd heard something, too.

I had to think. There were so many things in my head, they were beginning to jumble. First was that Peterson knew something about Shannan and me that had him hunt-ing for us. Like that we'd done something other than just look for pliers on Thursday night, but how had he found out? I hadn't said anything to anyone about that, except Beth, and she certainly wouldn't have informed on us.

Something wasn't right.

May had come to Green Clover to meet with the Tivolini buyer and to do some demonstrations. After her first one she'd snuck away and met up with Ron, and continued her affair. Yes, that was right, that wasn't the first time they met, not according to Shannan and Beth. So, May had left, and then she'd come back. But when was that? Did anyone see her after she got back?

And I was missing something. May had an argument with Nate Wright on Thursday afternoon, and he'd still never told me what it was about. That needed to get clear, and the only way to do that was to talk with Nate.

I picked up Sinatra. "Okay, little guy, you have to take a short nap." He yowled as I latched the cage. "Try to stay out of trouble."

Voices were coming toward the cabin from down the hill, and I stopped moving so I could better hear them. Angie'd said she hadn't remembered any disagreements here at Green Clover, but I was pretty sure I was hearing one now. It was Cordy's voice I distinguished first.

"I told you, that unless you have a search—"

"Ms. Wright, we need you to stay right here," a man said. Peterson. His voice was pitched low and soft. "Be completely silent. We don't want to alert anyone."

"I'll say again, you may not go in the cabins. Dear God! You've got your gun out! You don't need that to talk to Kitzi."

"I told you to be quiet. I was told she's armed with guns. Not one. Several. Stay here, you don't want to get hurt."

I didn't want to get hurt, either. It was time I moved. Peterson seemed to be on the path toward the sleeping porch, so I slipped through the party room to the back door. Instead of dashing out, I waited and peeked out the screens. I could see the rock, and the stairs, and the path that led down to the Saloon. Peterson could see the path, too, if he looked in this direction. The path took a bend only about ten feet beyond the door—if I could get to that point, I'd be safe.

I slipped outside as quietly as I could. I turned toward

the Saloon and had taken two steps when I heard a soft shuffling on the path below. Someone was coming up this way. Friend or foe? Someone else with a gun? I trusted the sheriff, but not one of Peterson's men.

Because of the bend I couldn't see who it was, but I wasn't willing to chance it. I was hardly breathing. The cabin wasn't safe, the stairs would land me in Peterson's hands sooner rather than later, and crashing through the woods would be noisy. That left the rock. This time there was no hesitation—I ran for it. The voices were closer, so I rolled over the top of it, and landed with an *ooph* on the other side. I hoped it had been a silent *ooph*.

There was an old coke can directly in my vision, and some kind of broken bush under my stomach. It hurt, but I didn't budge an inch.

A man's voice came soft and low. "I've got the other door." I had gotten out just in time. "Are you going in? Now? Okay."

They were apparently talking on those shoulder radios. Handy tools, but not as handy as a good pair of ears. Mine.

I heard the back door close, quietly. Peterson and his friends were inside. All those years my family had been in official positions and we'd had dozens, maybe hundreds, of uniformed officers around us, and they'd always seemed to fall into one of three types: hearty backslappers, obsequious kiss-ups or, for the most part, just good people doing a job. Come to think of it, there had been one officious moron at the capitol . . . a rude DPS officer I'd met in my later years. I was betting he and Peterson were best buds.

I'd had my eyes closed, listening intently as the men searched the cabin when I realized that this was one of the worst things I could have done. I didn't have any guns. But Peterson said he'd been told that I did. Who would do that? Why hadn't I just marched up to Peterson, hands in the air, and told him that I wasn't talking with him until I had a lawyer. That would have been the adult thing to do, but I certainly hadn't done it. And I couldn't just walk out now.

That would look really bad. My mother would tell me that one more time, I had acted before I thought.

That wasn't the kind of thing I wanted to dwell on while lying on a bush, so I opened my eyes. A centipede was crawling up over the soda can. Bad things, centipedes. They can bite, or sting, or something. It hurts, that's all I know. I blew air in its direction, and it stopped but didn't go away.

"Beat it," I whispered, "or I'll sic my cat on you."

The centipede took a neutral direction, but kept on going. So did Peterson. He was quick and efficient. He went through the downstairs like Sherman marching through Atlanta. I could hear him checking under beds, moving some chairs, telling one of his men to check behind something else. While he searched, I watched the centipede, who was now six inches from my nose, as intent on me as I was on him. The bush under my stomach seemed to be growing and my neck was getting stiff. Then the back door of the cabin opened. I held my breath, waiting, hoping the steps would turn toward the Saloon and fade away.

They didn't; they came closer. They were on the path, then silent. I was picturing him looking around. I kept thinking, *don't look at the rock*. Like anyone could miss the great big thing. Of course, who would think to look behind it? The centipede was on the move again, coming closer. I couldn't even hiss at the little creeper for fear that Peterson would hear me.

Then the footsteps hit wood, and Peterson—I was sure it was him—was going up to the second floor. Under cover of his footsteps, I scooted a little to ease the pressure on my back. I was going to have some kind of bruise on my stomach. Maybe some scratches, too. The centipede was on the ground scuttling toward me. I gently moved my arm until I could reach the old soda can. I lifted it up silently and used it to push the centipede back under the rock. My arm was stiff, and when the can scraped against the rock, echoing in my little spot like a truck hitting a freeway barrier, I held my breath.

Nothing happened, and the boots on the steps kept going, across the small landing and inside the cabin.

Slowly, carefully, I inched forward and rolled over onto my side. Ah, relief. Sort of. It didn't help my neck, but my stomach was quite grateful. Voices. I could hear someone say they were heading toward the cabin. It was tinny and probably coming from the microphone on Peterson's shoulder. Then I heard someone else walking up the steps, moving very quickly. An officer with news? Good news? Bad? The steps were awfully light as they went up the stairs, and the old door squeaked open.

"What in the hell are you doing here?" It was Lynn, and she sounded mad.

"Who are you?"

"Lynn Donaldson. Now, one more time, what are you doing with my stuff?"

I'd have been enjoying this if I didn't need a good stretch, and if the centipede hadn't been intent on finding me again.

"What do you call this thing?" Peterson asked.

"I call it art in the hands of a barbarian."

It took me a minute to get it, but then I had to grin. My, Lynn was feisty today.

I didn't hear what Peterson said next, but Lynn said, "You're twelve hours too late. That's when she was here going through my things, just about like you're doing."

"She was? Katherine Camden. Damn." There was some growl to the words. "How do you know? Did she take anything?"

"I know because I caught her—just like I caught you. As for taking anything, yes, at least one bead, maybe more. Why don't you arrest her?"

He growled something else, and I didn't catch the words, but Lynn laughed. It was the kind of laugh that could goad someone to murder . . .

"If you see her," Peterson snapped, "I want to know first thing."

"Ooh, yes, sir," Lynn cooed.

The old door opened, banged shut, and Peterson thundered down the stairs, paused for a minute, then spoke to someone else. I missed the first of it, but then the words came loud and clear.

"I don't care what it takes—just find her, now."

Twenty-two

"Sleepy Time
Sleepy Time
Oh, it's that sleepy time
When we can close our eyes
And drift off to the skies
Sleepy time at camp
Sleepy Time at camp
Good night!
Zzzz—zzzz

Green Clover camp song

"**W**ake up, Sleeping Beauty."

I opened my eyes to find Nate Wright peering at me over the top of the rock. For just a moment I wasn't sure where I was. Then I knew.

"Are you Prince Charming?" I asked.

"Prince Elano. I played Elano in the Downey Children's Theatre production one year."

That man was an amazement. I rolled a bit and had to stifle a groan. I was going to try to get up, but it seemed beyond me. I stayed down.

"How did you find me?" I asked.

"I came up here to scout the camp, and I heard you."

"I talked in my sleep?"

"Snored. Delicately."

"I don't snore."

"Then I guess you hiccupped." He leaned over to view my position a little better. "Maybe I should help you out."

"Good idea. Has Peterson given up his search for me? Or moved it elsewhere?"

Nate leaned over, and I gave him an arm. He lifted, and I lunged, and between the two of us, I got to a standing position behind the rock.

"Okay," he said. "When I lift, put your foot on the rock and come on out."

"I think I can do this myself."

He looked me in the eye, and I swear his were twinkling like some hero in an old movie. "I'd rather assist. It gives me a chance to hold your hand."

Now what woman in her right mind could resist that? I gave him my hand, and I was up and over in no time. I dusted my clothes off and looked up at the sky, as if I could tell time by the position of the sun. I can't, so I looked at my watch. I'd been asleep for well over an hour.

"Thanks for your help," I said.

"Care to sit on my private box seat?" He gestured to the rock. Well, maybe it was his, although I'd always considered it mine.

I looked at him. "I have an awful lot to get accomplished. If it's safe for me to come out."

"Maybe you'd better sit down."

"I hate it when I sleep through important events."

He gestured again to the rock, and after I sat, he climbed up beside me. His arm brushed mine causing a tingle that zipped through my whole body. "Things have been happening," he said. "Officer Peterson has gone, and he took all the other officials. We're more or less on our own."

"On the surface that sounds like good news. What's the bad part?"

"He has gone to interview a man who was having an affair with May Feather. Ronald Fairfield."

I almost fell off the rock. "How do you know? How did he find out? Where is Beth? I need to get to her. How's she taking it?" I took in a big breath of air, which is something I should have done first. "Okay. How is Beth? And where is she?"

"She left and said she was going home. She seemed to be pretty calm, under the circumstances. She started looking for her daughter, but Shannan was gone. Luckily about the same time we discovered your car was missing. We assumed the two of you were off somewhere together. Obviously, that's not so."

"No, she's with a friend, but she does have my car. Poor Beth, I'd better get over to her house." I was off the rock.

"That's not the plan." He reached out to take my arm "Beth wants you to stay here and take care of Shannan."

"But Shannan isn't here and doesn't need taking care of. Beth does. She shouldn't be alone."

"She's not," he said. "She's going to be with her husband."

I gave him a pitying look. "I call her husband Mo-Ron, and if I know him, he won't talk to Peterson. Instead, he'll start screaming for a lawyer, and the police will end up having to resort to warrants and whatever else they do. Maybe they'll take him to the police station." I liked that idea. "Actually, this could be a great thing. Maybe they won't bring him back. Except it's not good for Beth."

"She asked us to tell everyone that she could deal with her husband's situation better . . . if it was only the two of them." He touched my arm, again. "I think it's a husband and wife thing."

She didn't want me there.

And after a moment, I realized she was right. Mo-Ron

and I don't get along fabulously during the best of times. Alpha people don't, I suppose.

I leaned back up against the rock, suddenly a woman without a mission. "So how do we know that Peterson is interviewing Ron? Did Ron call here?"

"No, not as far as I know. Cordy overheard Peterson on the phone; then she told Beth."

"How long ago did Beth leave?"

"About an hour. When you sleep, it's serious business."

"It's serious stress. Some people turn to drink or heavy drugs. Me, I just sleep." I rubbed my neck and winced. "I don't believe I'm built for sleeping on the ground, though."

"How about if I rub your neck? Just five minutes and you'll feel better. There's nothing you have to do right now, since Peterson is gone, and I'm told I'm very good with my hands." He said it so innocently I didn't dare make a comment.

"Well . . ."

"Here, sit up here."

I sat on the rock facing off to the side, and he gently rubbed my neck. "Is this the spot?" he asked.

With Nate Wright, darn near any spot was the right one, but I didn't say that. "Yes. Feels good."

"And you are very tense." His hand slid gently along the top of my right shoulder, and I almost melted into the granite rock.

"Of course I'm tense," I said, trying not to sound it. "My best friend is in trouble, and I can't help. I just wish I knew who killed May. It would solve everything." We were silent while I let a hundred things roll through my brain, and Nate gently massaged my neck. The moves were great for my stiff body, but it wasn't helping my brain a bit. He did have good hands.

Then I remembered his argument with May Feather.

"Nate, we need to clear something up, and as good as the massage is, I have to be looking at you while we talk."

He stopped rubbing and said, " 'When duty whispers

low, thou must, the youth replies, "I can." ' Youth being a relative term."

I turned to face him. "You had a disagreement with May Feather on Thursday," I said, and his upper lip did an Elvis-like twitch. "I know you don't want to talk about it, but that's beside the point. I'd like to know what it was about."

The twitch disappeared as his ears turned red. "Are you sure we couldn't just skip this? I'd like to buy you dinner next week—"

"That sounds grand, but I could be in jail next week. Or you could. Or Beth. I'm not asking for your marital history," Now where did that come from? "I just want to know why you were arguing with May."

He took in a big breath and looked me square in the eye. "It's the stupidest thing in the world, and I want you to know that I'm not happy admitting it."

"You found me snoring behind a rock—how much worse could it be?"

"Worse," he said. "Here goes. May pulled her trailer in and ran over three new trees that I had just planted. In light of what's happened since then, it doesn't seem very important, but at the time I was mad." His voice became earnest. "Have you ever heard of the Weeping Cherry? Also known as the Kiku Shidare?" I shook my head, and he went on with some enthusiasm. "They're amazing. It's a weeping tree with double pink flowers that can be over an inch wide. I thought they would be a great way to greet people at the entrance of the camp, so I ordered three, and put them in the ground two days ago." His voice ran down. "It seems so inconsequential."

"Most everything does in light of murder," I said. "But she broke them off?"

"Yes. And she wouldn't move the trailer. That's what really made me mad."

"Why wouldn't she?"

"I'm sure I was being 'high-handed' as my ex-wife used to say. That's when May decided she was too busy and that she'd get to it when she was good and ready." He shook his head. "I don't think either of us could call it our finest hour." He let out a breath. "Happy now?"

"No. Darn." At least that was one puzzle solved; I didn't figure Nate had killed May because of a couple of trees. I gave him a thorough look. "You didn't kill her, did you?"

He put his hands up. "I did not," and then he frowned. "You know, I'd lie to you if I did. Miss Camden, you're a bit naïve."

"Maybe, but not innocent." After saying it, and watching one of his eyebrows go up, I could feel myself flushing. I went on faster than I might normally have. "How do you feel about gardenias?"

"I like them all, but which variety in particular?"

"Never mind, you've answered my question." I wondered if he'd like the ones my grandfather and I had raised in the conservatory, and then I felt guilty. "None of this is helping protect Beth and her family. We have some serious thinking to do."

"I have a question for you, before we finish this adult version of Truth or Dare," he said.

"I don't know if I'll answer."

He smiled slightly. "Then I'll come up with a dare." The smiled disappeared as he plunged ahead. "Are you avoiding Jeb?"

"No. Why in the world would you ask that?"

"Because he thinks you are."

"What an egotist. I hadn't thought of him at all. In case he doesn't realize it, you might remind him that I've been busy with a few other things that have been going on around here."

"He wanted to take you out to dinner tonight."

"Tell him I won't be hungry, but thanks for the offer."

Nate raised an eyebrow. "I think that's a message you'll have to deliver in person."

I remembered too late that Nate was Jeb's brother. "I'm sorry. I've had so much on my mind."

"You two have a history."

I nodded. "I like that. We do have a history. Past tense, which is why we won't be dining together." I added, "That's not really important; what I'm concerned with is Peterson."

"You should be. His intention was to charge you and Shannan with obstructing justice or some such. He was going to take you both to the sheriff's department and put you in a cell until you told him the truth about something. I never did find out what, but he was dead serious."

"I sent Shannan away on gut instinct."

"It was a good instinct."

Shannan was having to face enough right now with her father's affair and May's death. She didn't need any more upset, and she surely didn't need to be in a jail cell somewhere. What she'd done, and said, to Peterson had come out of fear. Maybe if he'd been kinder and more understanding she'd have told the truth.

Beyond that I kept wondering how Peterson had found out that Ron and May were having an affair. I knew that Shannan hadn't mentioned it, and I hadn't.

"Do you know how Peterson learned that May was involved with Ron Fairfield?"

"May I safely assume you didn't tell him?"

"You may assume that, and correctly so."

"I suppose Beth knew, too, even if they do say the wife is the last to know."

That was pretty perceptive of him. "Beth knew but she didn't tell me; I didn't find out until Thursday."

"Oh?"

"I found out by accident." He waited so patiently, I found myself starting into the story about finding Ron and May in the parking lot.

"What did you do after you saw them?"

Well, that put me on the spot again. After a long pause, I told him how I had mostly accidentally rammed Ron's Lexus. Nate started that little smile again.

I don't know why I was talking so much; maybe the old rock was giving off confessional emanations. "And then we were going to tell Peterson the truth, but that didn't happen. Long story." I wasn't about to blame Shannan. "We ended up lying, in part to protect Beth and Ron. Peterson was obviously pissed off, pardon my French, when he found out where we'd really been Thursday night. So, the question becomes, how did he find out? I'm sure Beth didn't say anything."

"May could have talked about Ron to someone. If she was really in love with him, that would be natural, wouldn't it?"

"That's true. I just wonder how many people are going to be put under a microscope because of it?"

"I'd say Ron, Beth, and Shannan, at the very least. And you."

"I'm not worried about me." I thought for a minute. "Oh, dear. What if Shannan decides to go home for something? She'll run right into Peterson." I jumped off the rock.

Nate was behind me. "Do you know where to call her?"

"Shoot! No. I only know her friend's first name."

"Let me call Beth's house. I'm pretty much in the clear, in case anyone official answers the phone."

"Are you sure?" We were already moving toward the path.

"I'm sure. What's her friend's name?"

"Christie. Come on in the Lazy L; we can use my cell."

We cut around the other side of the cabin toward the sleeping porch, and I heard a meow in the brush to my right. "What in the world?" I stepped off the path and there was Sinatra, watching me from under a dwarf cedar. "You are supposed to be in your cage. What are you doing out here?" I asked him. I bent down, but I couldn't quite reach him.

"Here, let me." I stepped back, and Nate's longer arm made it all the way into the foliage so he could scoop up Sinatra. The kitten immediately started purring, like he might have been nervous out there in the wilds of the country.

Nate held him against his chest. "You're a handsome fella." He turned to me. "Yours?"

"Yes, and I surely would like to know how he keeps getting out. First, he was getting out of his cage, and now he's gotten out of the cabin. This is more than a little worrying."

"He's safe now," Nate said, using his free hand to open the door and hold it for me. "So, what's his name?"

"Sinatra. After old Blue Eyes. Plus, as I'm just learning, he thinks everything ought to be his way."

In the distance the lunch bell rang, but I ignored it as I dug out my phone. I punched in the number then handed it to Nate. "Here you go." Next I pulled paper and a pen from my purse.

"Beth? Nate Wright here. Are you okay?" He nodded at me. "Shannan went to her friend Christie's house. Do you have Christie's number?" He repeated it along with Christie's last name, and I wrote. Then he said, "I think Kitzi wants to talk to you." And I hadn't said a thing. He handed me the phone then pointed outside and went, taking Sinatra with him. I'd forgotten the *no men allowed in the cabins* rule, but Nate hadn't.

"Beth? How are you?" I said.

"Fine." She dropped her voice. "We've got a stand-off here. Ron won't talk 'til his lawyer arrives, and Peterson won't leave until that happens."

"Sounds like a happy time."

"Not much. Why is Shannan at Christie's?"

"I thought she'd be safe there."

"Kitz—get her back to Green Clover. Peterson is out to crucify someone, and I—" Beth raised her voice. "No, we

don't want a maintenance contract on our house, but thank
you for calling." And she hung up.

Peterson must have snuck up on her. At least she
sounded okay, and maybe this adversity would give old
Mo-Ron a new appreciation of Beth.

I dialed Christie's number and after a quick conversation with her mother, was assured that Shannan would be
on her way right after the girls finished lunch.

Not nearly soon enough for me.

"Aren't you coming to lunch?" It was Sande, passing
through on her way to the dining hall.

"In a minute." She hadn't gone more than two steps
when I remembered a question I had for her. "Hey, Sande,
what is the story with your cousin? Why does she dislike
me so?"

Sande turned, a frown on her pixie-face. "Lynn? She
doesn't seem to like many people. It was better e-mailing
her than spending time with her."

"But why is she so hateful to me? She said last night,
well, never mind, but she seems to have a personal
grudge."

"I'll ask. She'll probably be overjoyed to tell me."

"And one more question; I heard her husband left her
for another woman, one with dark hair. That woman wasn't
by any chance May, was it?"

"Oh, no, it was someone named Alicia. He married her,
and I think they have a baby. You should hear Lynn go off
on that."

"No thanks, but I appreciate the info."

She started to leave, then turned back around. "Where's
your kitten?" Sande's a cat person with two of her own including an adorable Maine Coon.

"Sinatra is outside. Having a cigarette and hanging out
with Nate Wright."

She laughed. "That's quite a boy. See you at lunch."
And she was gone.

I put my cell phone on vibrate and stuck it in my pocket, because there was no telling when I'd need it next. Then I went outside to get Sinatra and put him away. I had a plan of sorts formulating in my head, and I was sure that Sinatra would only get in my way.

Twenty-three

In the dark of the night
When the moon's the only light
It's scary and I run
Cuz the darkness is no fun
So I sneak into my bunk and I eat the kind of junk
that the counselors don't allow
They would have a mighty cow!
If they caught me in the night,
when the moon's the only light
And it's scary and I run
Cuz the darkness is no fun
And I sneak into my bunk and I eat the kind of junk
That the counselors don't allow
They will have a mighty cow
Holy cow! Holy cow!
Here come the counselors now!

> Green Clover chant, said when the counselors
> return from a meeting during dinner

Cordy clanged the bell, and the talking in the dining hall slowed, then stopped. "As most of you know," she began the announcements, "Two of our premier demonstrations can't be held today. I take full responsibility—I called Fire Mountain Gems and Interweave Press and asked them not to come out here, after the unfortunate, uh . . ." she trailed off. She still couldn't say murder or death. "So, we have a special treat for you instead."

"Strawberry shortcake?" someone asked.

Cordy smiled. "No, but I'll put that on the list for next year." It was her standard reply when we made an off-the-cuff request; most of the time she even followed through. "This weekend is the Wimberley Trade Days. Merchants come from all over the state with antiques, craft items, homemade baked goods—"

"Show me the way!" a woman called out.

"I'm in," Sande said with a laugh.

"Good, then it sounds like you'll enjoy this. We have three Green Clover vans, and I've shanghaied Nate and Jeb to help me chauffeur all of you. Believe me, you don't want to take your own cars; the traffic is unbelievable. We'll load up in front of the Saloon in ten minutes."

"How do we get back?" Sande asked.

"We'll rotate the vans so there's always one where we dropped you off. When you're ready to leave, you just climb in. Oh, and if you want to stay longer at the Trade Days, you certainly can, but vendors will open their booths here at two and demonstrations start again at two-thirty."

It was a scramble as everyone jumped up and headed for their cabins.

I wasn't in the mood for shopping, and I couldn't leave anyway, since I was waiting for Shannan, so I sat and chewed my lower lip, an unattractive habit I had developed in the senate.

"Not shopping?" It was Tony Campanelli. I'd have thought the man would avoid me after the morning's encounter, but he looked a little lonely. If I wasn't as pushy as last time, he might actually answer the half dozen questions I had stored up for him.

"Shannan's at a friend's," I said. "And she's in my car, so I need to be here when she gets back."

"Hope she knows to drive around Wimberley. If not, you can add an hour to her trip."

Shoot. "I'm sure she doesn't." By now the dining hall had cleared out. "Have a seat," I said, gesturing to the empty bench across from me. "Are your sales doing any better?"

"Some, not much." He drifted to the other side of the table and sat down. "This is just the worst retreat I can remember."

"Isn't that the truth? At least we have Peterson off our backs." Instead, Peterson was squarely on Beth and Ron's backs—which I didn't like much better.

"Peterson may be gone for now, but I have the awful feeling he'll be back," Tony said. "He can't believe I wasn't in love with May, or a jilted lover or something. She was sexy and beautiful, granted, but there's more to life. The guy needs to get over it."

I had a real interesting thought. "Tony, did he go through your trailer? Or did one of the other cops?"

"They aren't cops, but actually, Peterson did go in the trailer just to use the bathroom. Why?"

Which was the perfect segue into my questions for him. This conversation was meant to be. "Because," I said. "I'll bet he poked around in your trailer and saw something that made him think that you and May were close. Anything like that in there? A picture of the two of you?"

He shook his head. "Nothing. May and I weren't close. I've known her for seven or eight years, and we've had dinner together maybe twice. We are die-hard competitors, and we never forget it."

"So, you didn't have a rose and some condoms waiting for her the other night?"

He flinched. "How'd you hear about them?"

It was time to fess up. "I didn't hear about them—I saw them," I said. "I went to use your bathroom, and well, there they were."

"Damn it, Kitzi, I resent the hell out of you poking through my trailer—"

"I wasn't. I didn't open a single drawer, and I didn't poke at anything. I saw the rose and the condoms on top of the dresser. I didn't go looking for them, if that's what you're thinking." I added. "And I didn't tell Peterson or anyone else about them, either."

He glared for just a moment before he said, "No, you didn't, and I appreciate that." He ran his index finger over his chin which had been shaved a little better since the last time I'd seen him. "But now I see why Lynn was so pissed at you for going through her things. You know, you—"

I held up my hand to stop him. "There have been very good reasons for everything I've done. Primarily to protect Shannan or to help Beth."

"Which is admirable, but not so considerate of the rest of us." He slowed down again. "How is she doing, do you know? Beth, I mean."

"She's doing pretty well, considering. Now, are you going to tell me about the rose, or not? Was it for May?"

"That is none of your business."

"I am well aware of that, however, I'm not above telling Peterson, not if it will get Beth off the hook." I stopped and let Tony fume for a minute, assuming he'd blurt out the truth eventually. Just as his internal temperature appeared to be near the boiling range, the truth hit me. "Lynn brought those things to your trailer!"

He shoulders dropped, and so did his armor. "But, Kitzi, you cannot tell anyone. You know how she is, we've already had that conversation—"

"I know, I know. Calm down."

"My brother always says that I'm in the wimpiest business," Tony said. "Since I work mostly with women who are much older than I am, but little does he know about you, and how I have to—"

"Don't say any more." I patted his hand. "You'll hate yourself in the morning."

He sputtered, "You see? You see how you are? Are you happy now that you know? Lynn brought the flowers and condoms," he said. "When she stopped by uninvited, just like I told you before."

I thought for a few minutes. Now I knew the source of the mysterious rose, and that Tony was not a sexual predator, at least not one who lured young women with flowers and condoms. There was only one more thing that I could think of to find out from Tony. I hoped it was more revealing than the rest of what he'd said.

"Okay, last question."

"I wish you'd told me this was a quiz."

"You're passing, so don't let it bother you," I said. "Did you hear an argument near the front gate sometime Thursday night?"

"Peterson asked me that. No."

"What about just a conversation? A whispered conversation? Don't say 'no' right away; think about it. It wouldn't have been that late. At least not too late." I tried to think of times. Angie had said Lynn showed up in the Saloon after ten-thirty and started insulting people. Wonder how long it took to do that? Probably not long, since Angie is patient, but not masochistic. Say, fifteen minutes. Then Angie goes back to the trailer and takes her shower. That would have made the argument at around eleven or so. "I think the conversation was around eleven."

He stopped and thought, then gave me the oddest look. "Thursday wasn't all that unusual for camp; you know what I'm talking about, Kitzi. There's so much talk, and people are excited to see friends."

"You thought of something."

"I'm not sure."

"Talk it out," I said.

He nodded. "I had the windows open, since the air is so nice out here. Lynn left around, I don't know, say quarter of ten. She'd already had two drinks, and I gave her one for the road. I took a shower, came out, and I heard a car pull in around, say ten. Two women were talking and laughing. They'd driven in from some place; you know how that goes." He was thinking again. "I told Peterson that part, but there was something else. I went to bed pretty early, and I remember vaguely hearing Angie go in her trailer, and then I fell asleep. Except, at some point I remember hearing a car door, and Angie closing the window on her trailer. It didn't register at the time, but I remember that afterward there was whispering."

"And? . . ."

A frown crossed his face. "Just whispering. Two women, I'm pretty sure, and they walked past my window and went toward the back of the camp." Toward the spot that was now cordoned off with yellow crime scene tape.

So he heard a car door. Was it when Ron dropped May off? If so, then May met someone, a woman if Tony was telling the truth, which meant it could have been a lot of people. It could have been Angie, except I still couldn't see a reason for her to kill May. It could have been Lynn, just out of meanness. Maybe she thought May had arrived in time for some kind of late date with Tony . . . Practically everyone in camp was female.

I clicked my tongue.

"What does that mean?" Tony asked.

"Sorry. It means I'm stumped."

Tony nodded a few times, looking directly into my eyes, then he said, "Well, just as long as you know that I didn't do it, I'm happy."

He actually reached out and patted my hand. Funny thing, up until that maneuver, I'd been sure. Then I wasn't so sure at all.

It was after three o'clock, and Shannan still wasn't back at Green Clover. The demonstrations had started up again, and to ease my stress I had bought a hundred dollars' worth of beads. I decided to ask Cordy if I could borrow a van to find Shannan. I was marching toward the office, my eyes on the path when I heard someone ahead of me, just around the bend. I was hoping it was Cordy, who could save me a little time. "Cordy?"

"Not even close." It was Jeb, smiling that half-smile that used to have an affect on me. "I've been looking for you."

"Oh?" I was rooted to the spot, one more time hearing the voice of the man I'd dreamed of for way too many years. He wasn't handsome anymore but that wasn't a change that mattered to me. The important one was inside, and I didn't figure that one had taken place.

"We said we were going to get together and talk over old times. I thought we could go somewhere nice and have dinner."

I smiled, and my body loosened up a little. "Jeb, I'll be honest with you. I really don't care to, but thank you for asking."

"Oh, don't be mad at me. We could have a lovely time."

"No, we wouldn't," I said. "Besides I have lots to do right now."

He did the little-boy-sad look, like I'd just stolen his teddy bear. "Don't be mean to me."

Mean to him? "You know, Jeb, maybe if you'd made the offer ten years back, I'd have been flattered. I might even have been flattered a month ago, but right now it seems like way too little, way too late. Not only that, I have a whole lot of other things that I need to be attending to."

"I know that I was a real wanker. You deserved so much better, but I wasn't mature enough to give it. I've grown since then."

"Really?"

"Really, Kitzi. I can see now that you're a very special kind of woman—"

That did it. "And I can see that your eyes are brown because you're full of shit." Those dark eyes flew open in surprise. "Sorry, Jeb, but I'm suspecting something here. Either you just got dumped by some other woman and you're thinking I would make a dandy consolation prize, or you want me because someone else does. Or maybe I'm just handy for the moment. I don't care which it is. I don't care if you realized that I am your soul mate." I took a breath. "I'm not. And the truth is," I slowed down and said with all the honesty I had in me, "The truth is, I just don't care."

He took it in, slowly, with a stiff expression. "Cordy told me you didn't have anyone else in your life right now, but I guess she was mistaken."

The man couldn't hear what I had said, and I didn't care about that, either. "Thanks for the offer of dinner, that was nice of you, but no thanks. If you'll excuse me . . ." I hurried around him and along the path to the office.

I kept expecting to feel regret that I had put him aside. Maybe some smugness that I hadn't stooped so low as to tell him what a bum he was, but I didn't feel anything.

Heck of a deal.

I popped up the steps and opened the door to find Nate Wright standing there as if he was expecting me. "I have a favor to ask."

"Ask away," he said. Something in his expression made me suspect he'd heard every word of my conversation with Jeb.

"I need to borrow one of the vans. Shannan hasn't shown up."

"Have you called her?"

I pulled my cell phone out of my pocket. "It's dead, and I don't know where to call without the number that went in the memory."

"That's probably long gone if the battery died. Here." He took my cell phone, looked at it, and then plowed through a drawer with about a dozen chargers. "We seem to collect these things."

In just minutes, we had the phone plugged in. "Thank you," I said. "Now, if we just had the number for the Nachman's."

Nate closed his eyes. "Four-two-eight . . ." He concentrated for just a few seconds and then said four more numbers before opening his eyes and reaching down to pick up the camp phone. He held the receiver out to me. "I'll dial."

"Amazing." The call went through and began ringing at the other end of the line. Sure enough, it was answered by the same woman I'd spoken to earlier. "Shannan still isn't here," I told her, "and I'm getting a little worried."

"Oh, I'm so sorry. She was running late, but she called your cell phone and left a message. She should have been there by now. Oh, dear."

"How late did she leave?"

"Maybe an hour and a half ago."

I held my breath. "And how far from Wimberley do you live?"

"Oh, gosh, we're up in North Austin. I'll bet she had at least an hour's drive. But still—"

"There's a traffic jam here because of the Trade Days, and she must have gotten caught in it. Don't worry, I'm sure she'll be here any minute."

"Have her call and let me know she's safe, won't you?"

"I certainly will."

I was breathing again when I turned to Nate. "She's on her way, and not even very late."

He took the phone and hung it up. "Finally some good news."

"Yes, and while we're making calls—let's just check in with Beth." Nate didn't look convinced. "No?"

He handed me the receiver again. "Okay, but she did say she could do this on her own."

I believed him, but that didn't mean I believed Beth was right. It wasn't so much that she couldn't handle it—just that she was in the kind of situation that called for reinforcements. I wanted to be there, at least in voice, if I couldn't be there in person.

I reached over and punched in the number, then waited through six rings until the answering machine picked up. I didn't like that at all. Even if the lawyer had arrived, Beth would have answered the phone.

Nate said, "Is something wrong?"

"I surely hope not. She didn't answer." I hung up and thought about it. Beth loves the telephone. She sometimes wears a headset so we can talk while she's beading, and I've never known her to let a phone go unanswered. Something wasn't right.

"Do you have a phone book for Austin?" I asked.

"Somewhere." He rummaged around in a bottom drawer, and I worried. Now the entire Fairfield family was not in contact, and it was concerning me more than I could stand. Damn.

"Here you go." Nate put the huge thing on the desk, and I flipped through as fast as I could.

I was looking for the number of Beth's neighbor, Mrs. Martin who knows all and sees all. If she was operating true to form, she could tell me what was going on at Beth's house.

There were dozens, no, more like hundreds, of Martins in the Austin phone book, and while I didn't know the first name, I did know the address. I searched for the street name.

"Can I help?" Nate asked.

"You can try that page," I said, pointing. "We're looking for an address on Brayton Road."

He didn't ask any questions, just started searching. A few minutes later, we had it.

Helen Martin. I dialed, and she answered on the second ring. "Mrs. Martin? This is Kitzi Camden, Beth's friend—"

"She told me you'd call. I've got a message for you."

"Okay."

"You're to take care of Shannan and be sure and keep her at that camp. Don't let her alone and don't let her come into town." Mrs. Martin took a breath. "The big thing was, don't leave Shannan alone. I expect because of the murder."

A nice guilt-inspiring message since I hadn't seen Shannan. "Where is Beth now?" I asked.

"Oh, she and Ron and some man in a flashy black Mercedes left right after the police."

That ought to tarnish Beth's reputation in the neighborhood. "Do you know who the man was? In the Mercedes?"

"Yep. It's their lawyer, but he didn't look near as snippy as Ron."

"One more thing, do you know where they were going?"

"I don't know for sure, but I expect it's some police department, don't you?"

I expect I did, except which one? Austin? The Travis County sheriff's office? And it didn't really matter, because I had to stay here. "Miz Martin, thank you. If you see Beth when she gets back, she can call my cell phone."

"I'll give her the message. Anything else going on?"

"No, ma'am, not a thing. Thank you, again." And I hung up.

"You look stressed," Nate said. "Not good news?"

I passed on what I'd been told, and then I shook my head. "Well, thank you for the loan of the telephone. And the charge on my cell. I'll be back later to collect it." He opened the door for me, and I listened for a second before I stepped out. "The camp seems awfully empty. Where is everyone?"

"We have about ten women still at the Trade Days, and the others are all in the Saloon. Oh, and some went home."

Apparently, I'd slept through that. "Is that a problem for Cordy and Green Clover?"

"I don't think so. Most of them had kids and just felt they should be with them. They'll be back next year; I don't think you need that on your plate, too. In fact, what are we going to do about your stress?"

"Cheech," I said. "I'm going for a quick walk around the camp on Cheech." My favorite horse.

"I'll help you saddle him up."

We went off to the barn, and I had the bridle in my hand before we even got to the stall. The big sorrel didn't even move while I slipped his bridle on. "You are such a handsome boy," I said to him.

"Why, thank you," Nate said.

"I meant Cheech." Then I looked at Nate and said, "But, you're not so bad yourself."

"I have been damned with faint praise. Or was I darned with faint praise?" He slipped the latch on the stall and led Cheech out into the main area. Once there he said, "Here, you go." He handed me the reins, and I held them while he saddled Cheech.

Nate was a pretty good cowboy, not to mention a pretty nice guy. I'd have to remember that when this was all over. Of course, I didn't know where the man lived, and he could be a resident of Yakutat, Alaska with a fiancée who didn't like Texans. And I'd prefer he didn't have a fiancée at all. Anywhere.

We walked Cheech out into the sunlight; the horse was hopping a little, maybe picking up my tension.

"You sure you don't want me to top him off?" Nate asked. "He seems a little skittish."

"We'll be fine." And I was pretty sure we would be.

When Nate gave me a boost up into the saddle, something I wouldn't have needed ten years earlier, I said, "Thank you. I'm going up by the front gate to wait for Shannan."

"Let me know when she gets here."

"I will. Thanks, again."

I tapped Cheech's flank, and we trotted up the path. I tried to pull him down to a walk, but he wouldn't settle. "I can't take you out on the trails today, but maybe later, after she gets back." Cheech nickered.

I reached down and petted him. He had the softest coat and sweetest disposition. If he'd been a little smaller, I'd have taken him home years ago to live in my house, even though horses don't make good house pets and I don't have a stable. But my, it felt good up so high. I wished all the problems were at ground level, and I could rise above them.

We met Cordy on the road in front of the Saloon. "Not going to the demonstrations?" she asked, rubbing Cheech's nose.

"No, I'm going to wait for Shannan. She's got my Rover, and she's late." Cheech was dancing, ready to move away.

"I wouldn't start worrying, if I were you," Cordy said. "Some big rental truck got stuck trying to turn around on Ranch Road Twelve, although I can't figure what they were thinking when they tried that little maneuver in the first place. The traffic was already a mess, but with that, if she doesn't know some back roads to get around Wimberley, she might just have to park the Rover in a barrow ditch and walk."

"Since it's my Rover, I hope she doesn't. See you."

Twenty-four

There was no one at the gate, which was finally wide open, just like it was supposed to be. I could hardly get Cheech to stop, so after a quick look across the empty parking lot I turned him around. We could lope through the back road of the camp so he could let off a little steam. I bounced too much, but eventually we started working together. It was nice to be out riding with the smell of fresh air, leather, and horse all mixing together.

We rode past the yellow crime scene tape, reminding me it hadn't been a happy retreat.

We ended up at the rock behind the Lazy L. I stopped Cheech and while we both caught our breath, I considered introducing him to Sinatra. Common sense told me that there was no way of knowing how Mr. Blue Eyes might react to some very large competition like Cheech, so I decided not to chance it. Besides, I'd have had to climb down out of the saddle, and I wasn't sure I could get back on.

After a slow lope back, I positioned Cheech at the side of the gate to wait for Shannan. Instead of my Rover, a camp van pulled up, driven by Jeb.

Cheech shied at the vehicle, "It's okay," I told him as I rubbed his neck.

The women came piling out of the van. There were

Sande and Angie, and several others I didn't know, and last was Lynn, our noir beader.

"Hey, Annie Oakley," Angie said, stroking Cheech's nose. "If you stay out here, you're going to miss a great demo on pop-up art cards. I know because I'm giving it in about ten minutes."

"I'm waiting for Shannan," I said. "Be there as soon as I can."

She hurried on, as did the others. All except Lynn. Lynn walked to the side of Cheech so I got a good look at her sneer. "Well now, there you are, in your favorite spot. Katherine Zoe Camden high above the rest of the world."

Cheech didn't like her tone and he started. "Easy, boy." I have never had anyone treat me so abominably in my life, well, except for once or twice in the senate, but I had no comebacks for her.

Lynn said, "What? You don't want to knock me down like you did last time?"

I never remember knocking anyone down, at least not after I got past thirteen and my cousins and I stopped having serious disagreements. I said, "You know, I'm at a disadvantage here, since I have no idea what you're talking about."

"Really?" Lynn raised one eyebrow as she looked up at me. "Well, maybe I should tell you my maiden name. How would that be?"

"Okay. What is it?" I was expecting Godzilla or some such.

"Dornan. Susan Lynn."

Susan Lynn Dornan? Didn't ring a bell—and then it did. I was talking to Susie Lynn Dornan. Susie Lynn who'd come to my sixth birthday party and complained because I was spending too much time on one of the ponies.

Susie Lynn was now Lynn Donaldson, our noir beader. And here she was, still pissed at me after fifty-some years, over something we did at a kid's birthday.

"Susie Lynn Dornan," I said. "I don't believe it. What

a surprise." I started to smile, since it was a homecoming of sorts.

"Oh, please," she said in her snotty voice. "This isn't some happy reunion. You thought you were better than the rest of us back then, and things haven't changed a bit."

I waited until I could speak without spitting, and then I said, "You know, I remember the . . . uh, event you're talking about. It was at my birthday party, and I was up on a pony." And she had said we were rotten rich people and that my grandfather's house, now my house, was ugly. A little flicker of heat rose up in my chest and it occurred to me that I was still holding a grudge, too.

I looked down at her face, so angry and hard; I hoped I hadn't been the sole cause of that. "You know," I said, "I think it's about time that we let bygones be bygones. If I was a brat at my party, and I'll bet my social skills weren't all that good, I would like to apologize. I'm sorry."

A tiny smile started on her face. "You're apologizing?"

This could change her whole life, and who knows, maybe mine, too. "I am. I'm very sorry at the way I acted, and I'm sorry I was unkind to you. So, Susie Lynn, Lynn, would you accept my apology?"

She thought about it, looking up at me. Then she said, "And you still can't get off your high horse to say it."

"Actually, if I get off, I'll never get back on."

She laughed. "I see. Well, I'll take that into consideration when I say, not no, but hell no!"

And with that, she turned around and stomped off.

So much for an epiphany that could change our lives.

Except, seeing her marching down the road all huffy and smug was sad. And while I might still be sitting on a horse, I was smarter than I'd been at six. I was sorry we couldn't at least be nodding acquaintances.

With a tad of regret, I turned back toward the parking area. I had done my best for Susie Lynn, and it hadn't been enough.

Cheech was finally calm and we moved forward, so I

could look up and down the narrow country road. There were no cars that I could see. Nothing but emptiness and some beautiful blue sky.

"Well, Cheech, let's see if we can find a place to get out of the sun," I said. He flicked his tail.

We rode out through the gates and onto the caliche of the public road, just in case I'd missed something. Still no cars, trucks, or Land Rovers. "Okay, how about over there?" I turned Cheech to the right, and we got behind the last row of cars under the shade of a couple of mesquite trees. "Much better," I said.

I still had lots of questions in my mind, and some answers. At least I knew now that it was May who'd talked with someone about her affair with Ron. That someone had told Peterson.

That didn't explain how Peterson knew Shannan and I had lied about our outing on Thursday night. The affair might have been known by everyone in the camp, but where we went was our secret.

Peterson knew I had guns, too. I'd heard him say that. But they were at home, so he had it all wrong, maybe because someone told him wrong. On purpose. And he knew I'd left the camp on Friday morning when I'd picked up Sinatra.

I kept trying to put together who might have known all of those things, and who might have a reason to tell Officer Peterson. Well, the reason was to throw suspicion from them to me. Or maybe one of the Fairfields.

I put my head down on Cheech's neck to think it through. Who knew all those things? Who was there and knew? It was like a hazy picture that wouldn't focus. I closed my eyes. I had all the information, but I couldn't quite get it in place. I kept trying, but one more time I dozed off.

"No clawing me, now."

I heard the voice, which was close at hand, through a haze of sleepiness. I wanted to go back to what I'd been thinking. It wasn't a dream, these were real thoughts; while I was asleep my subconscious must have kept working to figure out who killed May. The answer was right there, on the edge of my mind, if I could just . . .

"That's a good boy," the voice interrupted. "You're such a little sweetheart. And you're going to love it at my house. I know you will. Here we are." A car door opened, and I squinted at the light. "No, no jumping around Sinatra. You have to obey me, remember? It won't be a long ride, but we have to hurry so I can get back before anyone notices I'm gone. They'll just think you got out again. They don't know I kept letting you out."

My eyes popped open, just as the car door closed. I sat up, coming back to life. An engine started, and a little white VW Beetle pulled out of the lot.

Had I heard right? Sinatra was going to live with someone else, or had that been part of the dream? The car was real, it was sliding onto the road.

I knew that if I could just see into the car, it would all make sense. Except the car was leaving.

I looked toward the gates; I needed the keys to a van, but there wasn't time.

I lifted the reins. "Let's go, Cheech," I said. I clicked my tongue and tapped my heels on his flanks. Cheech perked up faster than I did and stepped out carefully, then turned to the road. "I'm out of practice, so don't get too wild."

It wasn't a really good idea, but I needed to be sure, and I didn't have any proof. I guess I thought if I could just see her, and see where she was going with Sinatra, I could get the sheriff to help me.

The VW was moving fairly slowly, but kicking up lots of white caliche dust. Cheech and I got behind the cloud and loped along. I wasn't sure I could go any faster, since I was bouncing like a tenderfoot, my pubic bone hitting the saddle horn.

Come on, Kitz, I told myself, you know how to ride better than this.

I forced myself to settle in, clutching with my knees, holding the reins like I'd been taught. The VW slowed for the big pothole, and I could see the back end of it clearly. I couldn't see inside, but somehow I knew. It just made sense.

"All right, Cheech," I said. "Give it some juice—at the turn just get me close enough to see her. Then we'll go back." I clicked my tongue again, and he took off like a racehorse. Too late I remembered that he'd trained as one, and he really knew how to run. By this time the VW was picking up speed, and so were we. I hung on as Cheech started to gallop. The VW was still pulling away, but we were going faster than I ever remember riding. Dust and wind whipped my face, and my leg muscles were as tight as I could get them.

The white car slowed down far in advance of the turn, and we gained on it. I didn't think the driver had seen us, but suddenly she sped up. I ducked my head behind Cheech's to keep the dust out of my eyes and hoped that one of us was looking where we were going. It would have to be him; I was staring at the car.

"That way," I said, pulling the reins to guide him. He was smarter than I was, he was already veering. "And keep it smooth," I shouted above the noise of his pounding hoofs. "My bottom's not in condition."

The car whipped to the right, not even slowing as it turned onto the bigger road. I lost it in the trail of dust when I heard a squeal of brakes and gravel sliding. "Whoa!" I pulled hard on the reins and Cheech stopped, then whirled and started back the way we'd come. "Whoa."

I reined him in as the sliding sound ended with a crunch of metal against wood. Car against tree. Or fence.

The dust was terrible, and it took a minute for me to see that she hadn't made the turn. The VW had slithered off the road, the passenger side of the car smashed against a gnarly old oak. I slid off Cheech and moved forward to tie him to a bush at the back of the Beetle. My leg muscles were shaking.

"Are you okay?" I shouted at the closed driver's window. When I didn't get an answer, I jerked on the door and it opened. Jennifer practically fell out. "Jennifer, are you all right?"

"I'm fine." There was a slight cut on her forehead. "My head kind of hurts.

"There's a cut."

"Were you following me?"

"I was." Sinatra meowed from the back seat.

"Why?" she asked. "I was just going out for a malt."

"You were?" I was sure she'd said she was keeping Sinatra, but she was so innocent looking. "But you had Sinatra."

"I wanted a little company, that's all."

She climbed out and stood up, shaking her legs as if to work the kinks out. I knew that feeling. I watched her, trying to remember what she'd said in the parking area before the VW took off. I was positive she'd said she was taking him to his new home. Yes, I was sure. She was taking him. Stealing a kitten?

Jennifer was leaning against the side of the car, her arms wrapped around her shoulders as if she were cold. I looked at her sweet face framed with the blonde curls. A tiny trickle of blood was rolling down toward her eye. "Do you have a Kleenex?" I asked. "You have some blood." I reached out to touch her face, but she brushed my hand away roughly.

"I'm fine."

"You're bleeding," I said. I reached around her into the side pocket of the Beetle to pull out a napkin I'd spotted. A blue chandelier earring fell out of it. When I opened the napkin, in the palm of my hand, I was holding an icy blue crystal necklace, another earring, and a matching bracelet. Now I knew for sure.

I looked straight at Jennifer. "I expect you have an explanation," I said.

I don't know what I thought she'd say or do, but I wasn't

prepared for what happened. She reached out her hand, as if to take the jewelry, then pulled it back, and with a small shout, whipped it forward like a striking snake. It hit my wrist and sent a jolt of pain all up my arm.

"No!" I dropped the jewelry to the ground. "What in the world—"

She struck again. This time with a burst of sound and air, then a chop to my neck.

I gasped, and the world went fuzzy. This wasn't going right. I heard Cheech nicker, and the VW rocked. Jennifer spun toward the horse, and it gave me a moment to breathe.

He was snorting and jerking on the reins; she screamed. That upset Cheech more. His ears went back, and he was going to break free if she didn't calm down.

"Be quiet," I said. I moved behind the open door, holding on so I didn't fall. "If he takes to rearing, he can crush you."

"Horses terrify me." She backed up. "I didn't do anything wrong."

That was a lie. "Just be calm, and he'll be fine."

"Nice horsy." She looked frantic. "I hate horses."

Well, it was mutual, but Cheech was calmer than she was. His ears came to a more forward position. "Just talk softly and it will be okay," I said. "They know when people are upset."

"It's your fault. I was just taking Sinatra for a drive. I don't know what you think you were doing."

I rubbed my neck—she'd apparently forgotten about that. I hadn't. I spotted some potato-sized rocks behind the door, and I took a couple of steps to get them. I'd hate to hit her, but if I had to . . .

"You made me wreck my car," she said, her eyes fixed on the skittish horse. "You're going to have to pay for it. I don't have that kind of money."

"Unless you get the Tivolini contract. Didn't you have an appointment? Weren't you and May going in together as Wingfeather?"

She whipped her head around to look at me. "How did you know?"

"Who else could it be? Did she back out at the last minute?"

"We are not having this conversation." She straightened, as if to regain her composure. "Instead, you're going to fall off your horse—it will be a deadly fall."

She took a step closer. I put both hands on the door between us and shoved hard. It shot her back against the door jamb, and her head cracked against the roof.

"Ow. That hurt!" There were tears in her eyes, like she was going back to soft and human again. She whimpered as she wiped away the tears. "You hurt me." She rubbed her hand across her face again, and this time it was as if she was wiping away all emotion. Her face went cold, and she sprang forward. I backed instinctively. She let out a yelp, and I heard a yowl at the same time. Jennifer swung around, and there was Sinatra clinging to the back of her pants. "Get off," she snarled. "Sinatra, damn it!"

She reached to get him, but I came out from behind the door and grabbed him first. "Let go. Don't hurt him," I said. "He didn't do anything."

She lashed out with her leg, and I fell back. Sinatra bolted. I didn't blame him; Jennifer didn't fight fair.

I wasn't going to, either.

I crouched as her fist came toward me, and I veered just in time. I couldn't look down, but my fingers searched the ground and found a rock. A big one. Jennifer had her arm back, ready to punch. I didn't wait, I swung my arm up, and her fist slammed into it.

"Damn!" She doubled over with the pain of hitting the heavy rock.

Now was the time to hit her back—I held up the chunk of granite, but I couldn't do it. Instead, I picked up a second rock. Jennifer rose up and kicked at me. Her foot caught me in the chin, but not full force. I was hearing noises, pounding. I threw the biggest of the rocks, and it smacked her in the shoulder.

Then I heard a horn. There were tires spewing gravel. I turned in time to see the Land Rover coming at us. Jennifer screamed causing Cheech to rear; his rein snapped. He snorted, reared again, and his sharp hooves were just a few feet from Jennifer. She shrieked and scrambled into the car.

The Rover skidded to a halt on the shoulder of the road. There was a cloud of caliche, and through it I heard a door slam. A voice said, "Are you all right?" It was Shannan.

She was safe.

"Shannan?" I shouted.

"Tante Kitzi?"

"Stay back." The dust cleared, and I could see my shining blue Rover, coated in white caliche. Cheech whirled and headed toward camp. "Don't come any closer," I told Shannan.

"Why? Is that Jennifer? Is something wrong?"

I thought fast. "Yes. I'm coming to join you." My eyes stayed on Jennifer. "Shannan, start the Land Rover."

I stepped back from the VW. I couldn't leave, not without Sinatra. "Sinatra?" I let out a soft meow. "Where are you, little bud?"

My eyes were locked on Jennifer as I stepped in front of the VW.

I heard the Rover's engine start up.

I took two more steps and heard a pitiful meow. Sinatra was hiding under the middle of the car. "Come on out, Sinatra. Come on."

"No!" Jennifer tried to get out the passenger's side, but the door was jammed. "He's mine. I love him. Get away from him—I'll hurt you—"

She switched to the driver's side and was out in a second, squatting down to reach under the car for the kitten. More pounding, and I looked up to see two horses galloping toward us. The rider had a hold of Cheech's reins. It was Nate.

"Are you all right?" he called.

"Fine," I said.

"Tell him to get back," Jennifer snapped. She stood up, one arm around Sinatra. "I mean it. I'll hurt him." She came closer and shot out her leg at me. It just missed my knee. "I'll break him in half." She was clutching the kitten.

"You can't—"

"Tell Nate to get back. Now." She almost flung her hand up with the kitten. "You want him dead?"

I threw the rock.

It caught her on the temple, and she went down. A soft moan came from her, but she didn't move.

Warily, I crouched beside her so that I could touch her forehead. She was breathing, but her eyes weren't focused on me. Sinatra mewed softly and crawled onto my lap.

"It will be okay," I said to Jennifer. "It will be okay."

It was a lie, but it was the best I could offer.

Twenty-five

"S'more?" Nate asked, holding out one. The marshmallow was blackened from the fire in front of us.

"Of course," I said. "It can't be camp if we don't do something a little evil."

"I didn't have time for anything evil," Shannan said. She'd had to take more than her share these past few days. It had pulled all of us out of our comfort zone, but her more than the rest of us, maybe because she was young. Or perhaps because she thought that Jennifer was her friend.

Shannan had shared her secret about May and Ron with Jennifer, who had told Peterson. Jennifer had also told him I had guns. Shannan was even Jennifer's alibi in some respects. They'd been drinking when Shannan went to the john and Jennifer slipped off to talk May into making a joint pitch to Tivolini. May turned her down. Jennifer had been furious, and May had died because of it.

At least that was what we'd been able to piece together. Jennifer refused to explain to officials. But I knew.

Beth was sitting beside Shannan. We'd only spent a few minutes talking once she'd gotten back to camp. She'd said she was only here to pick up Shannan, but she didn't seem in a hurry to leave. She looked different tonight, more at peace with herself. I wondered if Ron appreciated that she'd stood by him when he needed someone. I also wondered where their relationship would go from here. Beth said that she was willing to go in any direction, together or apart. She only knew that she would never settle for being second best again. I said, and meant, that I was going to hold her to that.

"Who's next?" Nate asked, holding out another s'more.

"I am," Cordy said.

There was quite a group congregated for a final camp-fire. There were lots of the women from the bead retreat, and almost the entire Wright clan was there. Jeb, however, had left. He'd remembered a pressing appointment that required his immediate attention. He was forced to take a cab back to the airport because Leesa refused to drive him. She, it turned out, was a preacher's kid, Zeke's daughter, but beside that, she worked for her uncle, Nate, as a buyer for Tivolini. I'd had her pretty much pegged from the start.

Angie and Sande were off to the side, still talking rubber stamping, and Beth was eating a s'more—just grateful, she said, that Ron was released. That occurred not because of anything he or his lawyer did, but because when Sheriff Gonzales arrived on the scene of Jennifer's accident, we convinced him that there was good reason to suspect she'd killed May. My bruises were important evidence, so I'd been examined by a doctor and photographed. Luckily, most of the damage she'd inflicted was to my extremities and my neck. I suspected there were bruises on my bottom, too, but those were from Cheech and my poor horsemanship.

A dozen other women were crowded around the fire. Sinatra was asleep in the Lazy L.

Nate, it turned out, owned Tivolini.

"Now," I said. "I'd like to hear the story of how you went from offering a catalog with Mace in it to one with works of art."

It was dark, with just light from the fire, but I'd swear Nate's ears turned red again. He shrugged. "I had the catalog and lots of connections with artisans, so it seemed a natural step."

"I'm the one who convinced him to go upscale," Leesa said.

"Is that true?" I asked.

"If you think I'm going to say no in front of her, you're very wrong. She retaliates."

"And," Leesa said. "He was so grateful, I now own five percent of Tivolini." She winked at Nate. "I'll get more in a few years. And I deserve every share."

"Sweat equity," he explained. "You see, I was remodeling an old home in Dallas, and Ms. Leesa kept dragging me to galleries to get just the right thing. I was surprised at how inexpensive some really beautiful pieces were. When I mentioned I could probably help the artists out by creating a catalog, she was all for it."

"I taught him everything he knows," Leesa said. She didn't look quite as sophisticated as she had the night she'd rolled into the Lazy L, but then she'd been putting in some hard work of late. She had talked with over twelve bead artists and a stained glass artist who worked in Wimberley. I hadn't heard about the final selections, but she seemed pleased.

"Have you decided who's getting the contract?" I asked. "Or is that hush-hush, still?"

She exchanged a glance with Nate, and he nodded. "Basically," she said, "we're going to offer short-term contracts to three different artists. I fell in love with some very different looks, and I think our customers will like the variety." She sounded like a Tivolini buyer.

"Which tells me nothing," Cordy said. "Who are the three?"

Tony Campanelli, sitting beside Leesa, seemed suddenly quite protective. "You don't have to say anything if you don't want to." I wondered how long Leesa would put up with that. I was giving her about fifteen minutes. Knowing Leesa, I suspected she had some investment banker on the line. A nice one, of course.

"Well, I'd like to know," Angie said.

"Me, too," I said.

Leesa frowned, and Nate grinned. "It's your call."

She sighed and reached into her pocket for a piece of paper. One of Beth's chandelier earrings fell out. Leesa picked it up and read off the paper, "Tony Campanelli, Beth Fairfield—"

"Hooray!" I cheered. Several others joined in, and Beth stood to take a tiny bow. Actually, the minute I'd shown Beth's chandelier pieces to Leesa, I knew that contract was settled.

"So, why were you so mysterious yesterday?" I asked Leesa.

"When?"

"Right before dinner. You said you were there to play with Sinatra, but you weren't."

She rolled her eyes. "I was making a cell call!"

"But, wait," Shannan said. "That was only three. Who else is getting a contract?"

"Lynn Donaldson."

Lynn stood up. "Are you serious?"

"Yes," Leesa said. "Why wouldn't I be?"

It was the first time I saw Susie Lynn smile. "And I get to name my own prices?"

"Within reason," Leesa agreed. "But no daggers. The daggers have to go."

Lynn put her hands on her hips, and I thought she was going to talk herself right out of a contract, but she took her time, and finally favored us all with a half-smile, half-sneer. "We'll talk."

"I wouldn't like to be in on that conversation," I said in a whisper to Nate.

"No whispering over there," Cordy said to us.

"Not even a few sweet nothings?" Nate asked.

"No. This is a Green Clover campfire, and they are rated G."

"Kitzi," Beth said, "you're turning red."

I fanned my cheeks. "Personal summer."

Nate grinned. "Miss Camden, would you like to go for a midnight ride?"

"Uh, I don't believe I could ride anywhere after today."

"Fine with me," he said, standing up. "How about if we take a walk." He reached down to take my hand, and I rose, feeling a little like a very graceful phoenix.

"And where are you two going?" Cordy called.

"Just to check on Sinatra," I said. I waved a goodnight to the group, and together Nate and I headed away from the campfire.

Behind us, Beth started singing. Everyone joined her.

"When a Clover Gal goes walking with her one and only man,
Rest assured she'll do the most official thing she can,
She won't let him hold her hand,
For he might not understand,
That a Clover gal's an angel in disguise.
Ha, ha!"

Make Your Own
Paper Beads

SUPPLIES

    Wooden beads, unfinished
    Decorative papers
    White glue
    Acrylic spray sealant

You can use any kind of wooden bead, but if it is painted or varnished, sand it first.

Cut decorative papers into tiny pieces, squares or strips 1/4–1/2" depending on the size of your bead. If the piece of paper is too large, it won't lay flat on the bead without wrinkles.

Put your bead on the end of a skewer to hold while working.

With a small paintbrush, brush a thin coat of glue to a small portion of the bead and place the paper scrap on it. Press it down and brush over it again with the glue. Continue gluing paper to the bead until it is covered.

Let the bead dry completely.

To protect your little work of art, spray lightly; 2–3 thin coats are better than one thick coat, which could cause colors to run.

There are many alternative ways to decorate beads with paper. You can choose a theme, (i.e., Paris—an Eiffel Tower with French words) or a color scheme. You may choose to cut or tear your papers randomly or evenly, like a small quilt. Use paper with foreign writing or letters (ala Kitzi) or color your papers with colored pencils or stamp inks.

Once created, the beads can be used for any project from earrings to tassels.

This project was described by bead artist Mary Newton, who gratefully acknowledges other artists who have done similar projects.

Now Available

A SCRAPBOOKING MYSTERY
SCRAPBOOK TIPS INCLUDED

Keepsake
Crimes

LAURA CHILDS

First in a new
series by the
author of
*The Tea Shop
Mystery* Series

Berkley Prime Crime

0-425-19074-9

First in the
Candlemaking Mystery
series by

Tim Myers

At Wick's End

Includes candlemaking tips!

Harrison Black has to learn the art of
candlemaking fast when he inherits his
Great-Aunt Belle's shop, At Wick's End.
But when someone breaks into the
apartment Belle left him, Harrison begins
to suspect that her death may not have
been an accident.

0-425-19460-4

**Available wherever books are sold or at
www.penguin.com**

pc894

A Berkley Prime Crime Hardcover

A Benni Harper Mystery

EARLENE FOWLER

National Bestselling Author of *Sunshine and Shadow*

Dis Ranch

BROKEN DISHES

Agatha Award-Winning Series

0-425-19597-X